Secrets of the Sanctuary

By Octavia J. Riley

This is a work of fiction. Names, characters, places, and incidents are either the product of the author's imagination or are used fictitiously. Any resemblance to actual persons, living or dead, events, or locales is entirely coincidental.

Copyright © 2019 by Octavia J. Riley

All rights reserved. No part of this book may be reproduced or used in any manner without written permission of the copyright owner except for the use of quotations in a book review.

First edition October 2019

Book design by Poisoned Apple Publishing, L.L.C.
Editing by Poisoned Apple Publishing, L.L.C.

ISBN: 978-1-7348272-1-7

Published by Poisoned Apple Publishing, L.L.C.
www.poisonedapplepublishing.com

Printed in the United States

Nia Rose & Octavia J. Riley
COVEN CHRONICLES
Spellbound & Hellhounds
Secrets of the Sanctuary

Dedicated

To all my friends and family who believed in me. The constant support has not only allowed me to get past a difficult part of my life but motivated me to start the book I've always wanted to write, while also pushing me to better my future by finally going back to school.

Natasha, without you I would have continued spiraling down into depression. You were such a strong pillar of support who really knew the situation I was in more than anyone else could, and you helped me move on. Our 3 A.M. conversations helped me shape the world I'd come to co-create, and I don't think I've ever laughed so hard in my life as I did when we stayed up late playing with hand puppets.

I learned more about myself through my characters than I believe I ever would have had I not written *Secrets of the Sanctuary*. I think all my friends and family wrote this story alongside me, and I just want to say thank you.

DESERT TEMPLE
GAYGHA PESHTPENHVET I ESTVETSYT' AYNNIRUV
THE GOLDEN SEA
BANSHEE BOG
HEAVEN'S HAND
DRAGON'S MOUTH
HELL'S
MOUN
TEM
RED TIPPED MOUNTAINS
SILVER THREAD
TOLVA
LORV
TEMPLE RUIN
JEWELED CA

AND
AIN
E
FOREST TEMPLE
SATVIRIYA
THE CURSED
MIRROR
THE BLACK
FOREST
KEMEESE LAKE
HALF HEART
BAY
DE
O LAKE
THE GENTLE TITAN
THE DEVIL'S PITCHFORK
NOPY
AERISTRIA

Chapter One

She was Like Art; Colorful, Confusing, and Abstract, but Art Nonetheless

The chill in the air clung to her body like a cloak, as her own cape didn't cover much of her arms and chest. The bite of the wintry breeze had her tugging down the soft leather hood to shelter the burning tips of her ears. How she loathed Aeristria's colder seasons, especially during missions.

The crunch from the freshly fallen snow each time she shifted her weight in the quiet early afternoon were the only sounds besides the whistling of the wind through the large trees surrounding the clearing, their branches near barren in the cold. Were she in her normal garb, the nip in the air wouldn't have even fazed her, but, as it was, she was trying to appear as non-threatening as possible. That meant no visible weapons, no face shields masking her identity, and, unfortunately for her, no large wool cloak that made her look twice as big as she was. At 5'9", Thea Bauer didn't need to look any more intimidating than she already was.

Cobalt eyes regarded the quirky, two-story cottage warily. Two wrought-iron staircases on either side of the structure led to jutting balconies under the thatched gambrel roof. The entrance was more or less unnerving with its hulking, thick wooden doors adorned with heavy wrought-iron knockers, presenting themselves in a daunting display to any travelers that should happen upon them. It was even more discouraging when taking in the faint orange, dome-shaped defensive barrier that glowed and pulsed irregularly around the place in distinct warning.

That was not what gave Thea pause, for she could easily pass through the barrier just by being a member of the Coven. Her silver, spelled Coven insignia of a burning phoenix allowed her to pass any and all barriers outside of HQ unless otherwise specified by the higher-ups. No, what stopped her from waltzing up to the massive doors, grabbing the door knockers, and loudly announcing her presence was the far-reaching reputation that caused Spellweavers like herself and other members of the Coven to steer clear of this particular creature sanctuary.

She had chosen this assignment upon being briefed over the dramatic increase in magically inclined refugees taking shelter behind the smooth stone walls of Srbeveara, as well as the correlating disappearances of creatures in the outskirts of the city. She'd always had a soft spot for the magic fauna, even if on more than one occasion they'd tried to kill her. Now though, as she looked up at the warded sanction, she was seriously regretting her decision.

Too late now, she reminded herself grimly.

The High Priest Council had already handed down the task to her, and anything less than her full cooperation would result in her immediate demotion back down to Hunter status, or worse, termination. She squared back her shoulders and exhaled her pent-up apprehension into the cold air, watching the icy cloud disappear and take her unease with it.

The protective dome flared as she passed through it, and the sizzling spell sent tiny shock waves through her body and frizzed out the tips of her springy, ashen brown curls she'd spent nearly all morning trying to tame. Pushing back her grumbling irritation, she flattened her flyaway strands with her palms and stepped up to the door. She made sure her insignia was displayed in plain view because it was the only thing that represented she was a member of the Coven right now.

Just as she was about to lift one of the rusting knockers, the doors were sucked out from under her outstretched hand and went crashing into the inner walls. A whirlwind of bold saffron skirts, thickly lined in a honeycomb pattern, came dashing out in a swirling tornado of gusto. Thea was met with dark eyes that danced wildly, painted in vivid cerulean eye shadow, and a wide, manic grin split the otherwise delicate heart-shaped face in two. Chestnut locks were squarely sectioned and twisted into multiple small buns atop the woman's head. She looked positively strange and the epitome of eccentric.

"*Ú, om estvetsyhon, eats'ily!*" she gushed happily in a fluid, foreign tongue, and slapped her small hands to her freckled, tanned cheeks. Her fingertips were painted in the same rich blue color.

"Uh," Thea cleared her throat around an awkward cough. She hadn't heard another person speak what sounded like the western desert language in this part of Aeristria in years.

"Where are my manners? I am so sorry! Sometimes I get so excited I forget myself." The woman giggled, and despite her heavy, smoky accent, her words came out quite clear.

"That's all right." Thea smiled, trying to regain some semblance of her dignity. She straightened up and stuck out her hand. "My name is Thea Bauer. I'm from—"

"The Coven!" the foreigner finished excitedly, clapping her hands together before she started grabbing at Thea in unbridled enthusiasm and pulled the dumbfounded witch into the cottage. The doors slammed shut with a resounding *boom* that echoed throughout the walls.

Warmth encased her and brought life back to her frozen limbs, and the notes of falling water tumbling over a woman's soft lilt created a strange yet soothing symphony to her numbed ears. She spun around the open entryway while the woman, whom she had yet to even know the name of, babbled incessantly, seemingly happy with talking to anything not inanimate.

She dropped her hood back and fluffed out her now kinked curls from the leather's confines as her gaze fastened onto the cascading waterfall flowing out from the cobbled stone wall supporting a winding, wooden planked staircase. The water crashed onto rocks that had been smoothened over time, forming a perfect circle that surrounded an intricate design in the concrete, where the water seemed to flow into the floor and disappear. The staircase led up to an open second floor where hallways branched out deeper into the building, only partly visible from Thea's position by the entrance. She wasn't able to see clearly over the rustic, tree limb railings.

"Would you like anything to drink, Ms. Bauer? We've got teas, ales, wines…" The woman counted off on her slim fingers while she mentally ticked off the selections in her head before her eyes widened and met her guest's startled gaze. "We've got scones, too!" she whispered fiercely as if it were some amazing secret she was sharing.

Thea waved her hands in polite dismissal. "No, no, that won't be necessary, Ms.….?" She left the subtle question hanging in hopes of earning the woman's name.

"Ú!" The woman's eyes widened again before she burst into a fit of tinkering giggles. "I apologize! I just have not had a real visitor in so long I have forgotten how introductions work! We get so many creatures popping in that really don't want to talk—or can't if you know what I mean—but, I'm Blythe Castel! Please, though, just Blythe is fine." Her dazzling, if not slightly unhinged, smile never wavered.

Thea blinked. "Blythe, then. Pleasure to meet you. I'm just here to ask a few questions, and then I'll be on my way." At Blythe's eager nod, she reached for the thick leather belt clinging to her hips and unfastened a buckle to bring out a small notepad and quill. She grabbed from another pouch and came back with a handful of luminescent dust before blowing it onto the acquired items. The quill's feather twitched before both it and the notepad began levitating.

When Thea flicked her attention back to the ostentatious woman, Blythe was staring at her with the most amazed expression. She couldn't seem to make up her mind on whether she wanted to stare at Thea or the notepad.

"Um…" She found herself clearing her throat for the second time. "What—what is it?"

"It is floating," Blythe whispered in awe. Childlike wonder warmed her dark eyes, and her fingertips flexed like she was deciding if she should touch the feathered pen or not.

Of course, it's floa—

Thea's eyes widened. Oh, she could kick herself right now. Rafe was *so* going to lecture her later on the importance of etiquette.

Blythe was magicless.

She'd heard the rumors about people out west not being blessed by the Goddess, but she'd thought it was just that—rumors. There were many people born without magic in Aeristria, so it wasn't unheard of that someone could be magicless. It was as common as someone with a dominant left hand, but to have an entire race be magicless? History had never been her strongest subject, and now she felt like kicking herself for not trying harder in school too.

She immediately felt a wave of guilt for offhandedly throwing around her magic in the face of someone who would never experience the same mundane conveniences people gifted with magic easily took for granted. Floundering for something to say, a voice glided down from above to alleviate Thea from making an even bigger idiot out of herself.

"So, you've figured it out. You Coven members may not all be as stupid as I thought."

Well, it wasn't exactly a life raft.

Whirling around, Thea's eyes snapped back to the second story, only this time she was met with the hardened scrutiny of a tall, slender woman leaning casually against the railing. She was immaculately dressed in a white, ruffle-neck blouse with puffed shoulder caps and glimmering gold cufflinks. Over the blouse was a leather underbust corset, and a white cravat fit snuggly against her throat. The outfit told Thea two things: she was wealthy and liked putting effort into her appearances.

The woman oozed power and exuded confidence with one hand on the railing, the other holding a hip-length staff. Another clue. She was a sorceress if the choice of amplifier was anything to go by. The staff's head was a buzzing plasma orb with electric blue fingers zapping at the edge of the glass. A shaft of light coming in from a window above ignited the woman's ginger hair aflame, while her eyes held enough ice to freeze anything her celadon gaze landed upon.

At the moment it had landed on Thea. She realized in that moment the less than favorable reputation surrounding Srbeveara did not stem from Blythe's bizarre nature and her unusual taste in fashion, but from the unnerving volume of sheer power that thrummed around the sorceress as if it were alive.

Secrets of the Sanctuary

Thea suddenly felt very small, and not nearly as powerful as she actually was. She had been around many blue cloaks, the High Priests that made up the Coven's Council, and nearly all of them had made her feel underwhelmingly inferior. To be around another magic wielder with this sort of power that was not a part of the Coven was disturbing. Unchecked power such as hers could be devastating to the city of Tolvade, if not Aeristria in its entirety.

"And your name would be?" Thea asked, allowing her voice to carry up to the second floor. She straightened her back, imagining a steel pole as her spine, and that kept her from cowering under the woman's rather unimpressed sniff.

"Cressida. Cressida Katsaros," the woman replied softly, though the words were clear as crystal.

"*Nre enyna T'ee Bauyer e!*" Blythe chirped excitedly from beside Thea, dark eyes dazzling even in the shadows.

"Thea Bauer, hmm? I've heard of your family before."

Who hadn't?

"Are you the one in charge here?" She felt her patience waning, and her insecurity quickly melted away into that of annoyance. She needed someone to start answering her questions. She could be saving lives right now.

A thin ginger brow rose, but, otherwise, the stoic expression remained impassive. "You won't receive any answers to your questions here, Spellweaver. Get out."

Thea sputtered, feeling as if she had just been slapped, but she swallowed back her outrage. Who did this woman think she was? Maybe in the Coven Ms. Katsaros would probably be some big wig Summoner, or, hellfire, she might even be powerful enough to land a seat as a second chosen to a Council member, but the woman was merely a civilian. As an extension of the Coven, Thea's word was law.

"I'm here on an official investigation under the Council's decree concerning the recent influx in refugees. I need to question them—"

Cressida's eyes flared, and suddenly the cinnabar flames of her hair could not hold a candle to the fire brewing in her dark green irises. "You will not, by the Goddess herself, interrogate victims seeking *asylum*. Not while I am here. Now, get out."

Her voice was hard as stone and impossibly unmovable, but, still, Thea persisted. "Wait! Hold the crystal ball, I—I didn't mean—"

"I retract my earlier statement on your stupidity." Cressida waved the hand not holding the staff in a good riddance gesture, and before Thea knew it, she found herself teleported back outside in the freezing cold. She cursed.

Chapter Two

Throw in the Towel, Just Not on the Kelpie

"So, how'd it go?" a casual, raspy voice spoke up from behind her.

Thea spun around, narrowed eyes finding purchase on a lanky noirette standing barefoot in the snow as if the cold was no more than a mere inconvenience to her. She looked like she had just crawled out of a lake by the way water continuously dripped from her tangled, murky black strands. Her thin white robe clung to her seafoam green skin almost unseemly. Actually, that's most likely exactly what she did, as Thea had spotted a watering hole not too far from Srbeveara.

Thea huffed. "I thought I told you to go dry off somewhere, Namara, not make yourself look more bedraggled than you already are."

Namara crossed her arms over her sopping chest, causing rivulets to trickle down her lithe frame and onto the ground. "Don't take this out on me because of your incompetence. I told you to bring me in with you, but *no*," she tossed her arms up in the air dramatically, flinging water droplets everywhere, "Thea knows everything."

Thea knows everything.

A look of sudden contrite passed over the creature's face, and Thea realized she hadn't hidden the grimace as well as she thought she had. She ignored the painful reminder of the past.

"Yeah, just let me drag you along and have you drench everything you touch in bog water," she snapped back, crossing her own arms, though it was mostly in defense from the cold.

"It's a sanctuary for magic-based creatures." Namara pointed to herself. "*Kelpie.*"

"Magic-based creatures born of *this* world. We all know where your kind comes from. Look, I'm not having this discussion with you. I have to report in." She turned around, ignoring the angry gargling noises her Coven-issued pet made behind her. She shoved her hand into one of the large pouches of her belt, digging out a clear orb that fit into her palm like it was made for her. It held a soothing weight to it and lit up with the intention of being used.

She paused.

Mulling over the options in her head, she brought up a different face into the forefront of her mind. The crystal ball buzzed gently before a chiseled face illuminated the surface.

"Good morning, this is—oh, it's you. What do you want, Thea?"

What was this, Pick on Thea Day all of a sudden? "Good Goddess above, could you be a little more professional? You know that thing that comes with being a Summoner? You do remember what that is, don't you?"

A blinding smile flashed across the man's angular features before disappearing, though the amusement lingered in his bright eyes. Bright eyes that blended somewhere on the bridge of blue and green and would sometimes keep her up at night. She would never admit that to anyone, though.

"Someone got a crap mission," his deep voice drawled before those bright eyes of his did a once over. "Or maybe you're just angry you forgot to wear long sleeves. Isn't it a bit chilly for such getup?"

"Banish a banshee, Rafe, will you shut up long enough for me to tell you why I called you?" she hissed, tempted to throw the crystal ball at something. Preferably the sanctuary, though now the defensive barrier would rebound the orb, if not shatter it completely. Gone was the faint orange glow only seen when it pulsed sporadically. The barrier now radiated a threatening vermilion color, flaring like flickering flames and eerily reminding Thea of the woman inside.

"Blasphemy, Thea? Really?"

Thea only glared at the little sphere.

A gusty sigh. "What's going on?"

It was Thea's turn to sigh as she replayed the unsuccessful turn of events in her mind. "I was met with resistance. Kicked me right out after I asked to question the refugees."

Rafe did not appear surprised. "Define your definition of ask."

She balked at the implied accusation. "It wouldn't have mattered if I had gotten on my knees and *begged* her. The sorceress in charge didn't like me from the get-go. She insulted the Coven as a whole and denied me access to the creatures inside. Just look at what I'm dealing with—" she swiveled the orb in her hand and pointed it at the sanctuary.

"That's a rather impressive barrier spell." Rafe's voice took on a more grave tone. Thea blew a quiet sigh of reprieve. As long as she'd known the man, she knew when he took something seriously and when he found sticky situations inappropriately hilarious. "Did you report in?"

She brought the orb back up to meet his musing expression. Her own expression twisted, and she contemplated briefly on saying she did, though she knew if she chose not to report right away, Rafe wouldn't rat her out. She knew he'd done the same thing a time or two.

"No," she finally breathed out. "I don't think I'm going to either—at least not yet." Her gaze wandered back to the angry barrier. She didn't have much to tell them, except for the fact that she'd failed and pretty quickly at that. Her pride alone wasn't going to allow her to notify the Coven of her defeat.

"Well," Rafe's voice brought her back, and she caught the sound of a smile in there, "I haven't been assigned anything yet. Want me to tag along?"

Did Thea really want to spend an entire day dragging around a hulking behemoth with a too charming smile and a horrible sense of humor? The answer was a resounding *no* in her head, but glancing back at Srbeveara, she knew this task was going to be near impossible to do on her own. The last thing she needed was to report her inadequacy and have the Coven send out a couple of inexperienced Hunters for training. She appreciated Rafe's refusal to blatantly ask her if she needed help, instead offering a hand out of boredom. It was times like these she liked the arrogant man.

"You know because you're obviously useless on your own."

Thea scoffed. *Well, there went that thought.* "You know what? Sure, just so I can see the big bad Summoner cower in the presence of the even bigger and badder sorceress."

"You mean like you did?"

Rafe's booming laughter could still be heard even as the connection winked out, and Thea knew without a doubt the rest of the week was going to be just as marvelous as today had been.

She turned and met Namara's black, soulless eyes. Once upon a time, she had been beyond freaked out by the emptiness in the endless pits, but now Thea had come to distinguish the slight differences in emotions.

Secrets of the Sanctuary

Creatures from the underworld, like Namara, were indeed soulless, but that didn't make them expressionless or without feelings. A tether, as well as a mild intelligence spell, kept Thea and her pet together and denied the kelpie's desires from luring innocent souls to their watery deaths. However, Namara had informed her only once that even without the tether, she doubted she could ever go back to the way she once was. That was the day Thea had looked upon the kelpie with new eyes, but she would never let the waterlogged creature know that.

"Come on, let's get you home and dried off," she teased and began trudging through the heavy snow in the direction of the capital. She really wished she had brought along the ingredients for a teleportation spell.

Namara gasped in offense, though it was all for show. "Just for that, I'm not going to offer you a ride."

She barked a laugh. "As if I want to ride into the city on a wet horse with a soaking bottom. I don't think I could withstand the chaffing."

Chapter Three

Note to Self: Beware All Gingers

The sun came out to warm the streets of Aeristria's capital, Tolvade, but the bitter wind remained. Thea did in fact ride into the city on a wet horse, though her bottom was saved after buying a leather saddle blanket. They forwent the actual saddle after a moment of loud whisper yelling in front of the leather goods store, drawing several concerned looks from passersby.

"I don't see what the problem is! You're a horse!" Thea had said incredulously.

Incensed, Namara had exploded with, "I'm a kelpie! Not a horse!" Thus ending their debate.

After purchasing the blanket and leaving alarmed staff behind, they decided on taking the shortest route home through the back allies. Not Thea's most favorite route, but Namara needed to soak in the river that speared through their backyard as soon as possible, and as much as Thea teased the kelpie on drying off, the creature needed to swim as often as she could. It was vital to her wellbeing. At best it was inconvenient. At worst Thea had had to turn down missions on behalf of her demonic pet or go without her.

The sounds of the bustling streets were muffled by the bricked buildings, and there weren't many townsfolk in the alleyways behind and in between the shops and apartment complexes. The few people milling about could only be described as shady, and they disappeared into the shadows at the sight of a Coven member atop her towering, dripping wet, underworldly horse, a sinister luminescent green color that conjured images of sunlight glinting off a swamp. Civilians could pick a Coven member out of the crowd simply by the creature that followed them. Regular people didn't get the kind of pets Coven members did. People could go to any pet store and get the typical run-of-the-mill dog or cat, and some pet stores even offered small magic-based creatures such as owlcats or Will-O'-the-Wisps. However, only members of the Coven were allowed creatures from the nine layers of Hell. The procedure on obtaining one was where second-ranked Summoners, like Rafe, came in.

Pets were more than their name implied, though. They were a Coven member's partner, their protector, and in most cases, became a member's closest companion. They were within the other's reach most, if not all, of the time, so that meant they typically lived together. The stone cottage Thea and Namara lived in was actually a duplex, and the Spellweaver that lived in the other half had a crabby lamia that always hissed obscenities when Namara made too much noise in The Gentle Titan, which was one of the two rivers that weaved through the city. It was essentially the border between the city center and the neighboring district Vemeese, which was the district Srbeveara was in. It was another reason the Spellweaver decided to take on the mission.

Namara didn't bother transforming after Thea dismounted, and the witch had to snag the sliding leather saddle blanket off the kelpie's flanks as the creature picked up her pace and cantered into the river with a shrill neigh.

"Don't strangle the wannabe Medusa," Thea warned as she folded the thick material and left it on the back porch railing before leaving the kelpie outside. Already she heard the second back door being thrown open and hissing ensue before her own door could shut.

She headed straight for her bedroom and didn't take long getting dressed in clothes that would actually keep her warm. She toed out of her black, knee-length, steel-toed leather boots reinforced with buckles and straps, and dropped her leather belt carefully onto the bed. She peeled off the thin cotton pants and replaced them with black leather, lined with thermal material inside. It stretched over her muscular thighs and toned calves like a glove, and she was again reminded how much she differed from other women not enlisted in the Coven.

Women were meant to be soft, Thea. You're going to ruin your image.

She pushed those thoughts to the back of her mind. It was too late to think about them now.

She stripped out of her thin cloak and took off her buckled corset before pulling on a thick white tunic, strapped up the corset once more, and fastened her belt to its many clasps. Her Coven grade winter cloak was thicker, longer, and made of wool, stained a dark slate gray. She pulled on halter-like straps over her shoulders that sheathed her Coven-issued sickle and chain before clipping on the silver phoenix brooch to her cloak. The last piece was a black face mask she slipped over her head. Freeing her curls out from under the material, she pulled the mask over the bridge of her nose to complete her look.

She left through the back door and walked out in time to see Namara splashing a shrieking lamia with her long, equine legs, but she elected to ignore the annoyed glare from its owner. She waved and told the kelpie to play nice as she departed. The walk to the heart of the city from her residence was a short one, and before long the roads became congested.

Secrets of the Sanctuary

The steady *clack, clack, clack* of the cobblestones under her boots was a much more satisfying sound than the soft crunch of snow. The roads had been cleared hours before, and the townsfolk milling about in the streets took advantage of the lack in the slippery substance.

The pungent smells of street food and spices from the makeshift stalls wafted into the cold air, and the smoke from the peat fires roasting the assorted meats and vegetables filled her nose. The dull roar of hagglers shouting prices crested as she maneuvered through the throngs of people crowding around, and she placed a protective hand to her belt slung over her hips. The dagger she also kept strapped around her thigh was a comfortable reaching distance away should the need for it arise. Pickpocketers loved the crowd, especially at peak times such as this.

Humans weren't the only ones offering items up to the market. Imps were the most common among the populace, for they were the silver tongues of the world. They could speak any language and smooth you over with seemingly ideal bargains, only to swindle you when you left. Though, some decent imps slipped through the cracks and went through the process of getting permits and keeping their shops up to code.

Pixies flitted through the air, leaving sparkling dust in their wake, stray dogs sniffed along the ground to pick up scraps, children ran around her legs as they tried catching the falling snowflakes in their mouths before disappearing into the swarm of people, and a group of youths laughed somewhere off to the side. When she glanced over, a young man was trying to right himself after having slipped in a pile of dirty mush leftover from the Cleansers. He didn't appear to be as amused as those who offered him a hand.

Heavy hooves pounded the stone walkway, and she maneuvered to the side as a horse-drawn carriage trotted briskly through the streets with a sign *Mundane Magic* advertising its transportation service. She snorted at the sight. She'd rather walk.

Tasgall's Tavern appeared up ahead. It was the most popular location outside of the Adalith district—the hoity-toity, rich shopping district. It was nestled between smaller shops on either side of its rounded exterior with a conical roof that reached toward the sky, smoke puffing from all of its many chimneys. Behind the long, brick strip of shops, she could distantly hear water cascading over the city's dam into the valley below. Rafe said it made for quite the sight, but Thea never got around to actually going back there to look. She always got distracted by the smell of bar food and bad choices coming out of the tavern.

The place was a hot spot for members, considering the owner discounted drinks for anyone wearing the phoenix insignia. As a daughter of a blue cloak, who was not allowed to join the Coven by said blue cloak, the fiery redhead would often throw herself into conversations that were none of her business while covertly replacing your drink at the same time. She was dangerous in that regard and would run up your bill quicker than you could cut yourself off, but members indulged her and kept coming back. Thea had caught onto her little schemes before long, but not before she herself had been swindled a time or two when she hadn't been paying attention.

She entered the establishment with the loud cowbell banging against the door. The outside world was muffled under the low lull in quiet conversations inside, and the smell of wheat bread and yeast filled her nose while the warmth from the hidden kitchen had her pulling down the face mask. She made her way to the bar just as the owner came around a circular table.

"Whoa, Thea, hadn't seen you in a while," Tasgall said in greeting as she slipped right in front of the Spellweaver with a tray of drinks in her hands. "Must've had one of those days."

"You could say that," she mumbled and slid onto one of the bar stools. The tavern was warmed by the rich wood interior and old antiques nailed onto the walls crudely. It gave off a homey, relaxed vibe, but that could very well have been the mixed magic of the other patrons in the packed pub.

Abruptly, a pixie landed in front of her with an expectant look on her petite face. She was no bigger than a mug of ale, but this particular pixie put many of her kind to shame by way of attitude. She was essentially the bar's bouncer, and one could only laugh at that fact for so long before they found themselves tossed out on their bum in the street.

Her element was nature-based, specifically autumn. The pixie's wild hair curled down to her lower back, covering her bare chest. Her skin was the color of clay, her hair rich soil. Her wings appeared more like changing leaves and unfurled vines, matching the long, ankle-length, leaf skirt she wore. Her eyes were tilted up at the inner corners, morphing with the many colors of the season.

"The usual, Me'Glach."

The pixie was off, leaving Thea to dig out her crystal ball. It whirred against her skin for a couple of seconds before Rafe appeared once more.

"Meet me at Tasgall's."

"Drinking so early in the morning, Thea? I think we may need to have a talk." He grinned, but she could tell he had already started moving.

She rolled her eyes. "It's noon, you big behemoth."

Rafe's thoughtful frown filled the glass. She heard the familiar creak of his door open and saw light suddenly highlight the man's features.

"Huh. Guess so," he mumbled, squinting up at what she assumed was the sun. "Fine. Make sure the seat next to you isn't taken. You buying?"

"We both know Summoners make more money than us lowly Spellweavers."

"Not that much," he winced. "Plus, it's hard feeding Mokana. She requests the souls of small children. They're really expensive on the Dark Market."

Thea fought the grin that threatened to surface. "Your sense of humor is atrocious, and I'm telling her you said that."

He sobered. "Don't you dare." She outright laughed and cut the connection.

Me'Glach appeared again only moments later with a bubbling brew in a frosted glass.

"Thanks. I'm going to need a few of these when you-know-who shows up." Thea's focus flickered to Tasgall laughing at something one of her drunken customers had said as she stealthily placed another drink on the table and took away the empty one. The man didn't seem to notice as he reached for his beverage. Her gaze swung back to the pixie, who watched her with uninterested eyes. "Although you cannot let that little leprechaun serve me anything. I have to afford rent this month."

A slow blink, then a nod. Me'Glach in a nutshell.

The air beside her seemed to sift and twinkle and then—*poof!* Rafe was sitting beside her as if he'd been there from the beginning. The man was a giant among men with skin bronzed by years' worth of work in the sun. Even under his umber winter cloak, there was no concealing the muscles packed in his wide shoulders and back, and when he shifted his arms, the fabric tightened. His hair was what intrigued Thea the most. The shade of midnight and longer than her own, it was silky and perfectly straight without a strand out of place. He often wore it in a tight knot close to his scalp when performing rituals, but during his time off he kept it down—like now. He looked semi-disappointed upon her bland reaction at his sudden arrival and even less happy when she smiled at the screeching rusalka demon throwing her arms around Thea's neck.

"Thea! I haven't seen you in so long—where's Namara?"

"At home, soaking." Thea grinned when the creature stepped back, her pout mirroring Rafe's now.

Mokana was a creature not unlike Namara in that she preferred water to land; however, she could stay out for much longer, and she didn't constantly drip onto every surface. Her instincts were similar to that of kelpies, though. Before Rafe's summoning ceremony when he had been just a Hunter and pulled her out of Hell, she would spend her days escaping the fiery underworld to drag men down into a body of water and watch them drown as they helplessly tried to climb up her slippery body. She would lure them to her not as a lost horse but as a beautiful woman singing into the night.

Shimmering pale hair fell around her lanky frame and tangled around her yellow-clawed toes. Her skin was lifeless, her jaw strong and square, her large nose aquiline. She was dressed in what Thea could only describe as a long beige tunic that reached her pale calves, synched with what looked like the Summoner's belt. The odd outfit was most likely due to Rafe pleading with her to wear something, *anything*. Mokana could never get behind the idea of clothes.

The whisper of wings had Rafe glancing down at the small pixie waiting patiently on the bar counter. He appeared surprised to find her there. "Ah, sorry, Me'Glach. The usual, please."

"Oh! Can I have the Screamin' Banshee?" Mokana's blue-green eyes blew wide at the new drink the tavern was selling for a limited amount of time. Me'Glach merely nodded before disappearing.

"So, besides the fact that you can't go very long without seeing me, what's the real reason for this meetup?" Rafe questioned halfheartedly. His attention was snagged by Tasgall breaking up a drunken brawl on the other side of the bar. He knew better than to intervene on that one. Tasgall was no pixie, but no one got away unscathed when she was angry. Everyone else in the bar, after seeing it was only the short redhead "handling business" as she'd often put it, turned and resumed their conversations.

"You're so full of yourself," Thea said in exasperation. "I wanted to discuss what we were going to do about the sanctuary." She took a sip of her brew. The bubbles had calmed down as it lost its chill.

"We?" His head swiveled back around.

"Yes, *we*, or did you forget you offered to tag along?"

"Tag along where? What sanctuary?" Mokana butted in, glancing between the two, though neither paid her much attention. "You aren't talking about Srbeveara on the outskirts of the city, are you? In Vemeese?"

Both Thea and Rafe dropped their staring contest to turn their attention on the rusalka.

"Oh? Have I managed to catch your attention now? Done ignoring me, are you?" Mokana sniffed, reaching for her milky drink in the tall slender glass the nature pixie had procured. Rafe picked up his crystal glass of warm spiced bourbon, hiding his smirk around the rim.

Thea rolled her eyes. "Cut the crap. What do you know?"

"Not much," she shrugged nonchalantly. "Powerful sorceress in there from what I hear, and that was while I was down under. Mean, too, but she's very protective of anyone that comes into her care."

"I've already discerned that for myself," Thea mumbled quietly, speaking more to herself than to either of the others.

"Oh, what was she like?"

Three heads jerked back to the bar to meet the sparkling gaze of the curious tavern owner, leaning against the counter with a sly smile already forming on her petite, freckled face.

"Frustrating," Thea bit out, glaring into her stagnant drink. "Can you re-chill this, by the way?"

"Sure, granted you give me more details than that." Her smug simper grew into a wide grin at the irked expression the Spellweaver threw her before looking over her shoulder and shouting, "O'Glach!"

Another pixie landed by Thea's drink. She was a stark contrast from her sister and actually looked like a more beautiful, winged version of Mokana. Silver hair pooled around her feet like moonlight reflecting off broken glass. The strands were silky instead of ratted, and her skin matched the snow outside. That was where the similarities ended, but upon first glance, the two could have passed for twins if the scale of their size was the same.

Periwinkle eyes twinkled from the tilted corners, and the ice crystals that modestly covered her minuscule body glinted in the low lights of the bar as she lifted her tiny hand and brought it to Thea's mug. Bubbles once again erupted in the froth. She left as soon as her task was complete.

"Now then, where were we?" Tasgall leaned forward with her chin propped up in her open palms. She was such a gossip monger, and any information one would bestow her she would greedily soak up. She often provided information she had no business knowing in the first place, but the extent of her knowledge on things was still unclear to Thea.

Thea kept her in suspense as she took a long swig of her brew, delighting in the flash of annoyance that crossed the shorter woman's features. She finished off her mug and sighed at the sugary tingle in the back of her throat. Finally, she said, "She keeps this barrier around the entire sanctuary that keeps everyone but us Coven members out. I assume magic creatures can pass by, or maybe they have their own entrance. I'm not sure, but there's another woman that works there, too. Blythe. That one is downright crazy."

Rafe snickered, but Tasgall only seemed more enthralled.

"I'm serious. She's pretty friendly, but there's this glint in her eyes that creeps me out. She's foreign. I think from the west from what I gathered on her accent and apparel. Speaks Ernimoen if I'm right, and I guess the sorceress can at least understand her."

Rafe hummed, swallowing a mouthful of bourbon. The smell was enough to leave Thea crinkling her nose. He watched the action with amusement. "You'll get wrinkles if you keep doing that."

"You'd like that, wouldn't you?"

"*Anyway*," Mokana spoke up, clearly as invested in the conversation as Tasgall was, "as you were saying."

Thea huffed. "She's magicless, which I don't get. Don't magicless people find it hard to—" she shrugged, waving her hand around and around in the air as she found herself at a loss for words. "I don't know, doesn't the glamour that magic-based creatures use make it hard for her to see them?"

"Maybe they don't use glamour when they're in the sanctuary?" Tasgall chimed in, lost in her musings, and Thea could see the cogwheels turning in her head. "Maybe they don't use magic at all while they stay there?"

Rafe butted in, pointing out the obvious. "That would be really hard to do for any magic-based creature, especially if they're under duress."

"Then maybe the sanctuary is spelled to keep magic from being used?"

"No, that's not it either," Thea insisted. "I was able to use Will Powder, and the sorceress, Cressida, put me out in the snow with just a wave of her hand."

"Then are you sure this Blythe woman was actually magicless?"

"I'm positive, Tassie. It's either that or she doesn't know she can use magic, and however old she is, she's old enough to know."

"Fascinating," the alewife said with a grin. "Tell me about the sorceress. I've never seen her, but I've heard the rumors."

Thea thought back to her first impression of the woman, and how power seemed to radiate off of her. "I've never come across someone as powerful as that who was not a member of the Coven." She blinked up from her mug, catching Tasgall's stormy blue eyes. "Honestly, I was a bit frightened by the sheer power she possesses. Imagine a blue cloak, but without the binding agent that keeps them from clogging up the air with their power. Like that, but on a more muted scale."

"What was she like?" Mokana queried in a small, hushed voice.

"Arrogant isn't the right word," she thought, briefly skimming the surface of her brain for the perfect description. "It was like she wasn't at all wary that a Coven member was at her doorstep demanding answers. She didn't even blink, wasn't concerned in the slightest." She snapped her fingers. "Imperturbable."

Mokana sighed beside her, rubbing her temples. "You and your big words."

Rafe turned in his chair to better face Thea, and his lips twitched briefly with mirth. "I think I will take you up on your offer to 'tag along,'" he continued on, ignoring her dramatic eye roll. "I'm curious. I want to see if she's as powerful as you say. I come across the Council members more than the other ranks in my field of work, and though they keep their magic presence under wraps, it does tend to get a bit stifling when you're in their presence for an extended period of time." He shrugged one large shoulder. "I believe I'll be able to accurately gauge her power."

"I've only ever been around my dad," Tasgall added with a faraway look in her eye, "but at night when he takes off the cloak and thus the spell...let's just say if I wasn't directly related to him, I don't think I'd be able to properly function with so much power around. It swarms the air and makes breathing near impossible for lower-level magic users like myself."

"What's it like?" Thea perked up, recalling the similar encounter with Cressida.

Tasgall hummed, and her brows knitted together in thought. "Like...you know when you first walk into a perfume shop? The air's a bit thicker and it's kind of heady, and you can get a wicked headache if you're in there too long? It's like that just...tenfold." She tapped her finger against her lips for a moment before nodding, seemingly satisfied with her comparison.

"Well, the air was definitely thick, but I can't say for sure it was the same. She was a floor above me. I can only imagine what it would be like to be standing right next to her." Thea grimaced and took another swig of her drink, only to remember it was empty.

"When do you plan on approaching her again?" Rafe dug out a small notepad and flicked through a couple of pages before finding the one he wanted. "I'm scheduled for a summoning later tonight, but other than that my work is pretty lax. Actually," he squinted at the page, "I've got a Dark Market raid in three days."

"I was thinking of going back tomorrow." He appeared surprised at that, but she could only shrug. "What's the point in waiting? The Coven expects me to file a report in the next couple of days, and so far, I have nothing to tell them. If she doesn't want a whole squadron of Spellweavers on her property, she'll start talking. Her refusal to answer questions will be deemed suspicious by the Council."

"Oooh," Tasgall wiggled her fingers and giggled, "Thea's got her serious Weaver face on."

"You take all the seriousness out of it when you abbreviate my title like that."

The alewife cackled loudly and waved over another round of drinks.

Chapter Four

A Hoarder Among Us

The next day, Thea was bombarded with the overwhelming feeling of recollection when she stood outside Srbeveara. Only now, it was accompanied by a pounding headache. She had lost count of the number of times she had silently—and not so silently—cursed the short tavern witch that morning. Her limbs were heavy, and her body was incredibly sluggish, and it had taken her a considerable amount of effort on her part to roll out of bed and trudge to the kitchen that morning.

After leaving the tavern earlier yesterday, Rafe and Thea had gone their separate ways, and the Spellweaver had looked forward to a night by the fire with a worn book in her lap. Namara had even promised to cook. Only it hadn't been but a few hours later when the Summoner had called her back up to go get drinks with him and a few buddies after successfully pulling out a powerful agare demon—an exceptionally beautiful, young-looking seductress that was already teaching its master the most vial and horrible curses in every human language on Raen. The blushing young Hunter hadn't known what to do with her.

Namara, the dear, had had a steaming cup of tea already waiting for her when she came stumbling home into the midnight hours. Thea didn't want to even think of the amount of praises she had sung for the kelpie, or about how much she had probably spent on drinks that night.

Secrets of the Sanctuary

Presently, Rafe stood next to her, arms crossed in either contemplation or because it was freezing, and he was just as miserable as she was. His long black hair spilled out from his drawn hood in an attempt to cover his ears from the chill in the air. He appeared to be faring better than her, though she didn't miss the way he winced when he faced the sun or when he looked directly at the bright white snow. Mokana, who was absentmindedly fiddling with Namara's sopping wet locks, was perfectly fine. Thea had learned a long time ago that alcohol did nothing for underworldly creatures that thrived with water.

The barrier around Srbeveara was back to its non-threatening, slow pulsing, orange glow. Thea had stopped herself short of the dome when a series of questions slammed into the forefront of her mind. Would the barrier negatively react to Mokana and Namara? When magic-based creatures sought asylum, it was usually from humans or from creatures born of the underworld. It would make sense if the two pets were unable to cross the threshold. However, they were tethered to Coven members, who legally had access to pass any barrier not erected by another member of higher ranking. So, in theory, Namara and Mokana could pass through, but it could still cause them harm. If it had frizzed out Thea's curls, she was worried it would dry out Namara's skin—and that was something she was not at all comfortable with doing.

Leaving them outside was not an option either, and it had been a risk the first time she had done it. It only happened after the kelpie had sworn she would go hide in the Vemeese Lake not even a stone's throw away from the property. Pets were dangerous and quite capable when it came to combat, but they were still vulnerable to attacks from non-tethered creatures that saw the pet as a threat.

When she voiced these concerns, Mokana volunteered to walk through first and stepped forward. She hesitated for only a moment before she pushed through the dome, and they all breathed a collective sigh of relief when absolutely nothing happened. Namara followed with the same results before Rafe and Thea stepped through after them. The Spellweaver was somewhat surprised Blythe had not already flung open the doors to greet them all like she had done for Thea yesterday. She wondered briefly if stepping through the barrier was the same as ringing a doorbell, but if Blythe really was magicless and Cressida wasn't around, then it was no surprise they hadn't been invited in yet.

Either that or Thea had made herself wholly unwelcome. She pushed those thoughts back and squared her shoulders. Lifting the heavy, wrought-iron knocker, she all but pounded on the wood. The silence that stretched out was filled with awkward shuffling and strained listening, only for no one to come answer the door.

"You must have really made them mad," Namara whispered to the side, eliciting wide grins from the other two. "Why am I not surprised?"

"Shut up," Thea hissed. She grabbed the large handles and shoved the doors open, thrown off momentarily by the weight that almost refused to budge under her touch. She stormed inside and jerked her gaze around to find the focus of her irritability, but no one was present. She ignored the soft feminine gasps as the two demonesses took in their surroundings behind her and considered shouting her arrival, though the attention she would gain would most likely not be the attention she wanted.

She was given a reprieve when a chipper voice rang out, "In here!" It came from the open room off to the side of the entrance. The cheery tone gave Blythe away.

Thea started off in that direction, only to stop short in the doorway. To say that she was overwhelmed would have been the understatement of the era. The room was small, but it was cramped tight even more so as every available space was filled with something.

Small, portly glass jars in every color under the sun hung daintily by the open window, where light reflected off the surface and danced across the wall in rainbow hues, while the vanilla candles within flickered lowly. Braided roped slings decorated with wooden beads held potted plants exotic in nature. Wine bottles from faraway lands graced the floor to ceiling shelves, split up by assorted knickknacks such as globes and glass jars with corked tops. The smell of rose and lavender oils morphed with sandalwood and lightly perfumed the air, brushing one's nose when a breeze wafted in.

Decorative chests were filled with everything from bottled spices and tea bags to bars of scented soaps, packaged incense cones, and pastel-colored salts. Roped baskets in every shape contained soft throws and richly colored scarves. On top of the knotted, distressed white table placed in the center of the room was a green, cast-iron teapot. It was flatter than normal teapots and elegantly scrawled in black patterns influenced by western designs. A piquant scent Thea couldn't pinpoint emanated from the steaming pot.

Blythe was perched with her legs crossed under her vibrant red and gold dress, situated on a wide daybed in front of the table with throw pillows embellished in colorful beads, tassels, and faux furs. On the other side of the table were two gray wicker chairs with cheery yellow cushions. Beside Blythe, which Thea was finding to be the most bizarre thing in the entire eclectically packed room, was Cressida, laid out on her side as she held the woman's hand in her own and stroked a nail polish brush dipped in blood-red paint slowly over Blythe's fingertips.

Cressida did not even acknowledge them, looking up only to glare at the other woman when she began to squirm around too much. Blythe was completely unfazed by the sorceress's aggravation and instead waved Thea further inside. "*Beriv!* Welcome back! So good to see you a—*Ú*, you brought friends with you!" Blythe's eyes went impossibly wide, and Thea was convinced the only reason she wasn't bounding off the daybed was the fact that Cressida was holding her hand in a death grip.

The whole scene was so mundane and almost intimate in its simplicity. She felt she was intruding on a private moment and disturbing their quiet peace—until it dawned on her. She couldn't sense Cressida's magic. That was why it was so peaceful and downright cozy in this cramped little room.

The realization must have shown on her face, for Cressida, who had yet to even look up, remarked crudely, "The bathroom is down the hall if you need to relieve your constipation."

Thea glared at the top of the sorceress's head. "Why can't I sense your magic?" she demanded. "Yesterday I was practically choking on it a floor below you. It should be clogging up the air and making it hard to breathe."

"You mean like this?"

Suddenly, Thea couldn't get air into her lungs. Her knees buckled under the pressure that slammed into her with the force of a speeding ox cart. The only thing that kept her from crumbling onto the floor was Rafe's outstretched arm curling her into his side as he doubled over, retching and heaving in a sad attempt at finding enough air to inhale. She couldn't see Namara folding into herself, nor could she see

Mokana sinking to the ground. She was too caught up in trying to just breathe.

She gasped when the pressure dissolved as quickly as it had appeared, and she sagged against Rafe's trembling side. She clung to him for a few seconds before she realized just who she was hanging off of. Shakily and with effort, she detached herself from him and focused on regulating her breathing.

"What," she gulped down a lungful of air, "was that?"

Cressida finally looked up from Blythe's nails and capped the lid back on the bottle of polish. "You seemed disappointed when you couldn't sense my magic. I was only indulging you." She waved her hand over Blythe's fingertips, muttered something under her breath, and blew over the coats of paint. Immediately afterward, Blythe jumped up from the daybed and leaped over to Namara and Mokana in awe.

"*Vea*, you have really pretty eyes," she whispered to the rusalka, lending her a darkly tanned hand.

"What color are they?" Mokana blinked, a slow smile spreading across her pale face as she fumbled to stand up even with assistance. The presence of strong magic always gave some lower-level creatures a little high.

"Hmm, olive with little gold flecks."

Thea cleared her throat, feeling like she was losing sight of this entire mission. Her fingers curled into the palms of her hands, short nails biting the calloused flesh there. "We came here because we need answers." She was surprised her voice came out so strong.

"I know why you're here," Cressida replied as she picked up the nail decorations from the table and set them back into their collective drawer in the vanity desk pushed up against the wall behind the daybed. "I know you won't give up until I agree, and I also know you've yet to report to your precious Coven." She came back around to the table and poured two cups of tea before handing them off to Thea and Rafe. "Drink this. It will help with the hangover."

Thea cautiously accepted her drink and watched over the rim of the cup as Rafe's large hands engulfed the small thing to the point it was comical. She had to wonder about the sudden hospitality when the sorceress had been nothing but hostile during their first encounter, and just a few moments ago she had nearly suffocated everyone in the room.

She took a small sip before asking, "Why are you being so courteous? How do you know we have hangovers? And you didn't say how you could cloak your magic."

Cressida merely raised an eyebrow and chose to recline in one of the chairs rather than answer. She crossed her legs and relaxed back into the wicker curve before fixing Thea with a sharp glare. "I will only tell you this once, Spellweaver, so listen well. I will allow you to trapeze throughout my home and knock on any door that tickles your fancy, and if anyone on the other side of that door wishes to retell the horrible nightmares they have endured, then I will not hinder your investigation. However," that familiar ice settled in her gaze once again, "if I feel you have intimidated them into answering your questions, or if you so much as lay a finger on them, the agony you felt earlier will not compare to the anguish you will suffer. And you can be sure that the Coven will never be the wiser."

Thea shivered at the deadly promise laid out before her like a sinister spread. Not only would there be some serious pain if she were to step in the wrong direction but there was also the fact that she would never see the Coven again. She'd either be dead, or she would be so mentally damaged she wouldn't even remember who she was. That meant whoever was witnessing these threats would also have to be dealt with. She realized the temperature in the room must have dropped, for she could suddenly see her breath.

And then Blythe was looping her freckled arms around Cressida's neck from behind with a smile so bright it could have rivaled the dawning sun. The air began to warm, and Thea's shivers ceased. The sorceress's gaze shifted from her to the woman behind her, and Thea knew she'd been dismissed. She turned to go, setting down her cup and tugging along Rafe and Namara from the room when the same velvet voice floated back to her.

"Oh, and Spellweaver, you will go about this alone. The Summoner you brought will only intimidate my residents, and the creatures you both possess will only bring forth memories they are trying so desperately to escape."

She opened her mouth to protest, but Rafe stopped her with a reassuring squeeze to the shoulder. For once, he had nothing to say, and that in itself was enough to believe the seriousness of this operation. She nodded wordlessly and watched the three of them move into the room on the other side of the entryway that mirrored Blythe's. She tore her gaze away from their retreating backs to glance at the room she'd just left, but the door had been shut some moments after Cressida's warning.

The thought of being so powerful that one could relax in a closed-off room while a group of strangers waltzed around your house was disconcerting. She knew if she stepped out of line, even without the sorceress watching her, she would be in trouble so quick she wouldn't have enough time to plead mercy.

The staircase was now more daunting than it had been the last time she was here, but she strode up the steps regardless of the dread seeping in the pit of her stomach until she reached the second floor. She had been able to see some details from the ground yesterday, but now she saw the corridors that branched off in five different directions with large informational bulletins posted at the entrance of each hallway. She didn't spend much time looking, but the glances she did spare them told her they were mostly information about the sanctuary's rules, the history, and the magic keeping the property running smoothly.

She dipped down the first hallway, wanting to hurry this investigation along now that she had the go-ahead. The flooring of the hallway was laid with narrow stripped wooden planks stained a deep red. The russet tint complemented the natural tones of the cobblestone walls that arched fluidly around each rounded door that led to a habitat within. She lifted her hand and knocked firmly on each door, but no one opened. Door after door, knock after knock. Nothing.

Thea held in her frustration. She couldn't blame the victims hiding behind the doors. Hellfire, her sudden knocking might have just scared them senseless. Still, something had to have driven all these creatures into Srbeveara, and she needed to know what that was. If that meant knocking on every door until her knuckles bled, she would do it.

The second hallway was worse. While no one had answered her in the first hallway, too many opened the door in the second, only to give the same answer, which was the silent treatment. Thea was beginning to seethe, but, still, she reminded herself that these creatures were not sworn into giving out information. If they didn't want to speak, they didn't have to.

So, after another unsuccessful hallway, she stopped at the first door in the third hallway and noted the ancient character branded into the wood. She frowned. Dead languages had never been her forte back at the academy, but she had studied herself into near sleep deprivation learning them in order to pass. This, if she remembered correctly, had something to do with purity and horns. That didn't exactly narrow it down when she thought of every creature that had horns.

She knocked, and, to her surprise, the door swung open to reveal a meadow. Wildflowers such as poppies, lupine, and daisies bloomed beautifully over the tall grass up to a towering tree line of evergreens. Emerging from the forest was an awkwardly moving, large white entity, shrouded by the shadows of low hanging branches.

Thea treaded in cautiously and marveled at the warmth she felt stepping into the sunlight. When she peered up, there was no sky, no clouds, and no sun to greet her, just an endless void.

"Hello?" She cleared her throat. "I'm from the Coven. My name is—" her throat closed up on her in shock when the creature fully emerged from the forest, revealing a limping unicorn. Its shattered horn glinted in the fake sunlight, and the reason for its limp became apparent. Painfully twisted, its hind leg had healed badly and had become unusable.

It stomped its front hoof and threw back its head, letting loose a rage-filled whinny loud enough to hurt her ears. She stumbled out of the enclosure back into the corridor, which seemed to appease the unicorn, though it wouldn't settle down completely. It continued to stomp the ground and snort, all the while its skinny, puff-tipped tail lashed irately back and forth.

"I'm just..." she lurched forward and grabbed the doorknob, "I'm just going to close this," and promptly shut the door, tripping over herself in her attempt to step away. She took another good look at the symbol on the door, this time memorizing it. She wouldn't be making the same mistake again should she see the same character.

The next room also opened up, this time to a small valley up close to a cliff face. The cool breeze and muted colors made the scene come across as dreary and a moment away from a torrential downpour, yet the sky was the same as it was in the meadow: a white void.

She stepped inside and peered around, awestruck when she turned and noticed the door to the hallway was merely a doorframe situated in the middle of the valley. She could see the hallway on the other side, but peering behind the doorframe revealed nothing but the never-ending landscape.

A low warning hiss came from the cliff face, and Thea spun around to see a gorgon emerge from behind a sharp jut in the rock. Camouflaged by her grayish skin and slithering snake hair, Thea hadn't seen her until the creature began to move. It was then the Spellweaver noticed that the snakes that sprouted from the gorgon's head were half ripped out and merely wriggling as all snakes did after death.

"*Leeeeeavvvveeeee,*" the creature hissed, dragging out the word between her sharp fangs and forked tongue.

"I just want to find out who did this to you," she tried to reason, holding up her hands in a placating gesture.

"*I ssssaid leeeavvveee!*" The gorgon's taloned fingers bit into the protruding stone she'd been hiding behind, and the rock cracked under the force.

Thea jumped back into the hallway and watched as the door slammed in her face as if a strong gust of wind had taken it and thrown it closed. She let out a huff of exasperation and threw a glare at the opening of the hallway as if the root of her problem was caused by Cressida.

The next room that opened for her was an arid desert that stretched out for what seemed like miles. A sun that was not there beat down on her back when she stepped through. Dry, cracking loam went as far as the eye could see, dotted with hardy desert shrubs and barren trees offering slim shadows of shade from their naked branches. Cliffs rose up in the distance, but that was the most exciting thing she could see in the barren environment. She didn't even notice the golden sphinx rise from its prone position behind a huge tumbleweed rocking gently in the low breeze.

It took one long, sorrowful look at her before turning its back and walking away before she could even say anything. Angry red claw marks donned its shoulder blades, surprising her by the length and depth of the wounds. She felt compelled to leave all of a sudden and stepped back, even though her mind kept telling her to press forward. The door swung slowly shut when she finally backed out into the hallway, breaking the spell that been placed over her. She blinked several times in confusion and reached for the doorknob again, only to find it locked.

"Just give me *something*," she whispered in frustration as she moved on. She knocked on the last door of the hallway, already dreading the answer she was going to receive. It opened up to reveal a lagoon, and the emerald water sloshed against the frame yet stayed within the confines of the habitat as if a layer of glass was keeping it from spilling into the hallway.

A mermaid was looking forlorn, resting against a large rock jutting from the surface of the water. Her mauve scales glittered wetly in the illusionary sunlight, and blood freely flowed from the open gashes on her lower half. Her fins lining the sides of her muscular tail had been completely ripped off, and the caudal fins at the tip had chunks missing from them. A large matching slash dominated the side of her face, and dried blood stuck to the yellow limp strands of her hair.

She peered up from under her golden bangs, and the look of absolute misery was enough to freeze Thea in her spot.

The mermaid came undone at the sight of the Coven member, and she let loose a desolate sob and threw her arms up to hide the hideous scars that would never heal. Water exploded from the room, slamming into Thea and sending her crashing into the far wall behind her.

She yelped loudly in pain as she collided with the wall, and instantly her mouth was filled with the water from the lagoon. She slipped on something slimy and crashed down onto the ground. Hacking out the water from her lungs and coughing in a sad attempt to clear her throat, she barely registered the door slamming shut. She ripped down her face mask to spit out the foul taste onto the flooded floor.

Her hair clung to her face and the back of her neck uncomfortably. Her cloak was drenched and now weighed twice as much as it did before, and she could bet her whole month's work sum her leathers were ruined. She pushed herself up using the wall and grumbled about resembling a certain kelpie as she trudged down the hallway, her boots squishing the entire way. She hoped offhandedly there was some sort of spell that would evaporate the water and restore ruined boots. These were her favorite after all.

She stopped just outside the corridor and found the informational bulletins once more. Even as miffed as she was, her interest in how the rooms operated had peaked over the last couple of encounters. She briefly skimmed the first board that documented the sanctuary's history, the owner before Cressida, and when Blythe came into the picture a couple of years ago.

The second board was what she was looking for, as it read:

"The sanctuary is fueled by a collection of magics and Sorceress Katsaros. Upon the arrival of a creature seeking sanctuary, a room is

assigned to them for the duration of their stay, be it temporary or indefinitely. Rooms are separate dimensions carved into the fabric of the natural world. A creature's magic is read, and the result of the reading creates a dimension most similar to that creature's natural habitat."

Just how powerful was this sorceress? The only other separate dimension she knew about was the Dark Market, and the long algorithmic equations and precise calculations it took to create another dimension were vast and way above her head, yet before her was a slew of pocket dimensions that regularly changed and morphed to fit a creature's desired needs.

The third bulletin was merely the sanctuary's rules, such as no negative magic, feuding, or disturbing the other refugees. The list went on, but it was fairly common sense at that point, so Thea moved onto the fourth corridor.

She rapped her knuckles against the first door, hoping against hope she would get something—anything—that she could work with. The large claw marks and wounds she kept seeing were disturbing and concerned her greatly. What worried her most was that there were not many beings out there that could cause such injuries, especially to powerful creatures like sphinxes. Mermaids were also lightning fast in the water, so something had to be faster in order to catch them.

Had the legendary wolves from the Black Forest somehow managed to escape their deadly domain? Nine feet tall and absolutely feral, they were by no means regular wolves. She didn't understand how they weren't bottled up in Hell along with the hellhounds. The more she thought about it, the more she feared it to be true.

She was brought back to the present when a wood nymph answered the door, but she didn't meet Thea's gaze and instead kept her eyes trained on the silver phoenix brooch clipped to her dripping cloak. The nymph didn't seem to question her soaked appearance. She only opened the door wider and stepped aside. Hope flared inside Thea, but she kept her face blank when she stepped slowly into the wooded habitat.

A small pond was off to the side a ways away, and a couple of large, smooth boulders surrounded a gnarled tree stump soaking up the warmth from the sun that wasn't really there. Thea lowered herself onto one cautiously so as not to spook the creature. She didn't dare speak first.

The nymph flicked her gaze over Thea briefly, but their eyes did not meet. "You're here to ask about what's happened to us," she noted quietly. Her voice was thick and low in an accent common among her folk.

It wasn't a question, but Thea confirmed it anyway with a soft, "Yes."

The nymph limped over to another one of the boulders, naked as most of her kind preferred, which allowed Thea to see every scrape and scratch that ranged in length and redness. Bruises littered her body in throbbing purples and healing yellow-greens. Her hair was a tangled mass of unkempt brown locks and frizz. She was in terrible shape, and yet, she was one of the luckier ones.

"Well, my name is Siobhan...for starters," she looked about awkwardly, threading a wild strand behind her ear that refused to stay put and sprang back into place between her two dull eyes. Her name was a quiet whisper—*shi-vawn* was the sound that rolled off her tongue.

"Thea."

Siobhan nodded, looking down at her scraped palms. "You won't believe me," she said quickly. "I don't even believe me."

"I will." This creature had seen something, and by the distant look in her eyes, it haunted her.

Just as her skin took on a stiff, wooden, tree-like appearance, she shook her head and her voice was strong, convinced. The bark growing on her skin receded. "You won't," she shuddered, "but I have to tell someone what happened. I—I need—" She cut herself off as another shudder shook her small frame. Woodgrain flared up the side of her neck in her fear.

"Tell me everything," Thea turned to face the nymph, bending to try and catch Siobhan's gaze. "I'll listen."

For a long time, the creature didn't say anything. An internal struggle warred inside her with every flicker of emotion in her dark brown eyes, blending fear and grief together in a nightmare of flashbacks. Her skin was a constant transformation of human flesh and camouflaged tree. She parted her split lips to speak but closed them again when nothing came out. She repeated this several times, each time giving up when words failed her. She took a large, settling breath, and for the first time met Thea's gaze with eyes the color of a mountain after a heavy rain, and the sorrow flooding them nearly pulled Thea in and drowned her. There was hardness under the sorrow. The walls around her heart were visible from the windows to her soul.

"You want to know what did this to me? What lost me my closest companion?"

Thea nodded slowly.

"A soul eater."

Chapter Five

Two Sides of the Same Coin

Thea thought she'd misheard. There was no way—that wasn't possible. No, Siobhan was mistaken. Soul eaters were creatures from the lowest and most powerful level in Hell. They just didn't walk out of the underworld's prison whenever they wanted. They were too dangerous and possessed too much willpower to even be a Coven member's pet. They, along with other monsters just as powerful as them, were under lockdown even in Hell, guarded around the clock by hellfire-wielding ogres.

She must have looked like a fish the way her mouth bobbed open and closed. Too many thoughts raced through her mind for her to simply pick one, but it didn't matter, because Siobhan was on a roll.

"I barely escaped with my life. Elspeth—she—" a sob tore through her throat, "she distracted it so I could get away. It came out of nowhere. I couldn't even..." She hunched over and wept silently as she pulled her scraped knees to her chest and curled in on herself. Thea watched on in stunned silence, still desperately trying to form any sort of logical sense of her statement. She was too dumbfounded to even offer comfort.

Siobhan's sobs quieted to soft sniffles until, finally, she collected herself enough to lift her head. Her eyes were bloodshot, brimming with emotion that slowly died until the light seemed to fade completely. When she spoke, her voice was distant and cold.

"It was a beautiful day. Cold from the year's first snowfall, but the sky was so bright and clear. Elspeth and I were chasing each other through the trees trying to attract some handsome stray human." She smiled briefly at the memory, but it fell when she continued. "We were playing the human game 'tag,' and I lost sight of her for just a few seconds—she knew her way around the woods better than I did. I..." she paused, on the verge of tears once again, but pushed them back and strengthened her resolve. "I saw movement out of the corner of my eye. I thought it was Elspeth, naturally. I turned around, and *it* was watching me," she whispered the last part with a shudder.

"Hey, it's okay," Thea moved closer to her but dropped the hand that had risen unconsciously to comfort the creature. She didn't know how the nymph would receive her touch and thought better of it. "You don't have to tell me the rest."

"No." Her voice was steel once again. "I have to tell you this. If I say it, I can get over it. I can move forward. Please."

Thea knew firsthand how venting out a horrible experience to someone could help mend the soul. Her voice was soft and full of understanding. "Okay."

Siobhan continued. "It looked like a wraith, but it was worse. Its arms and the lower half of its face looked like rotting flesh. The skin color was this disgusting mixture of green and black. It was just so *wrong*. The smell was horrible. Reminded me of a corpse sitting out in the sun."

Thea remembered once finding that exact same scenario in one of the back alleyways on the shadier side of the city, and the smell had imprinted itself into her brain whenever she thought about it. She fought down the gag that threatened to surface and was glad she had been too hungover to eat anything that morning.

"It wore a really tattered cloak with a hood, but I could still see its eyes and—" her voice dropped down to a frightened whisper and twigs sprouted out from her limbs—"it was like I was staring straight into the flames of Hell."

The news was hard to digest. What she was describing was definitely a soul eater. The Coven was going to have a field day with this. Cressida could possibly face charges for not reporting this to the authorities, whether she knew about it or not.

Siobhan kept on, lost in her train of thought. "I was so stunned I couldn't move. I let it get so close to me before I realized it had even moved. At that moment, Elspeth came running through the bushes. I think she had turned around to look for me. She ran right into its path. She took one look at it and screamed at me to run and I...I ran. I didn't look back, not even when her screaming stopped. I ran and ran and ran. I fell down so many times. I must have been going around in circles for days, but I never stopped running.

"I finally came across this sanctuary. It was the only safe place. I could feel it in the air. I stepped through the barrier and that sorceress—Cressida?—she opened the door, took one look at me, and got me a room without any questions. She just told me I wasn't allowed to use magic to do harm while I'm here or I'd have to leave. I only ever asked her one thing, and that was if another nymph by the name of Elspeth had come to the sanctuary. It was a foolish thing to ask, but I had hope. I didn't see her die. But...I knew what she was going to say before she even answered me."

Thea waited with bated breath. She, too, knew the answer but, like Siobhan, held onto that tiny sliver of hope.

"She said no."

Thea plodded down each step that led her back to ground level. Though the artificial sun had warmed her clothes, the ice remained in her veins, and a shadow clouded her heart. If soul eaters were on the loose, were other demons of the same caliber out there as well? Had there been a prison break down in Hell? Hell didn't have prison breaks ever, but what Siobhan had described was the very definition of a soul eater. What unnerved her most was that soul eaters didn't leave giant claw marks or take chunks out of their prey. No, when they took a soul out of a person, that person fell in a heap of flesh, devoid of all color. When they killed magic-based creatures, they stole the magic, their "soul," and the same thing happened. How long had this one roamed? How many had it taken before it targeted the wood nymphs? How many more souls had it taken since then?

Her foot touched the gray concrete floor, bringing her out of her brooding. She could hear bubbly laughter in the room Rafe, Namara, and Mokana had gone in. It sounded like they hadn't been left to themselves for long.

She stepped into the room silently. If the room really did mirror Blythe's, then her room was actually bigger than it looked. This room was spacious and much tamer in its decoration. It also boasted floor-to-ceiling shelves, but leather-bound books filled them instead of trinkets. A writing desk claimed one end of the room where Cressida sat ignoring everyone and filing paperwork. Two couches placed around a circular tea table were occupied by the other four. Rafe and Mokana took up one, Blythe and Namara the other. Namara's section of the couch was soaked, which the insane, colorful woman next to her seemed to find fascinating.

Rafe noticed her first, and he must have sensed her turmoil when a look of worry flashed across his face. This caused Mokana to take notice, then Namara and Blythe. The room quieted, and for once, Blythe looked serious. The expression was as foreign as her native tongue. If she was looking at Thea with such an expression, she had to have known what happened. It was only plausible. Why else would she appear so somber after laughing giddily only moments before?

Involuntary shivers of adrenalin began to possess her the more she stared down at Blythe. Anger was an easy emotion to latch onto, and she wasn't afraid to admit it was the first one she expressed when faced with difficult situations. "Did you know?" she whispered angrily, fists curling at her sides.

A flash of light overtook the room in the amount of time it took her to blink, and suddenly Cressida was in front of her so fast she hadn't had time to stumble back before she was jerked forward by the harsh grip on her damp cloak. Power surged through the air, clotting the room and forcing Thea to her knees as she choked on the magic. Cressida's voice was low, malevolent. Her eyes were hard as the peridot gems they resembled. "She knows nothing. Magic-based creatures do not approach the magicless—you know that, Spellweaver."

Thea weakly smacked the sorceress's hands away. Just like that, the power in the air vanished. She gasped and stood back up on shaky legs as she glared with everything she had. "That doesn't mean she didn't know. You two sure seem close. She could know everything like I'm sure you do. I know you know what they went through, and you failed to report it to the Coven. I could have you locked up for this!"

"What we seem like is none of your business, and I do not disclose the happenings of my residents. Not to her, and not to the Coven. How many of your kind would try to come through here if they knew victims of demon attacks resided here?"

"Try?" Thea countered, her eyes narrowing.

"You heard me, Spellweaver."

"Hold up, you two." Rafe shoved a large arm between them both, having walked up to them while they'd been in the midst of baring their teeth at one another. Cressida leaned back so as not to touch him with a disgruntled look on her face. "What do you mean 'demon' attacks?" He searched Thea's gaze, but she dropped it to the floor. His gruff voice deepened. "What did you find out, Thea?"

She glared at Cressida again before turning to her colleague. "A soul eater is on the loose."

Those words caused an immediate uproar.

"What in hellfire are you talking about?" Rafe demanded.

"How is that possible?" Namara jumped up from the couch to race to Thea's side.

"Are you sure it was a soul eater?" Mokana was at her other side just as quickly.

"What haven't you told us?" Rafe to Cressida.

"A lot."

"Thea, this is serious! We have to tell the Coven!" Namara cried, too close to her ear.

"If a soul eater is on the loose, so are the other demons from Hell's prison!" Mokana fretted.

"You better start talking, Sorceress." Thea heard Rafe command.

"I have nothing to say to you."

"How can you say that?" Namara angrily spat. "Lives are at stake!"

"I'm placing you under arrest for further questioning —
"

"The hell you are, Summoner."

A heavy *slam!* silenced the room. No one had noticed Blythe, quiet in the midst of chaos, slip from her seat over to one of the bookshelves and pluck a thick tomb. It was opened to a page marked *Soul Eaters*.

"'Soul eaters, while they do not work together to corner prey, do travel in skulks — or groups — to cover more ground like a plague that scours the world in search of their next victims. The last sighting was recorded in the Elvan Era. It is said that if one has been sighted, its skulk is nearby. They have never been recorded to target magicless people, but that does not mean they will not devour a magicless being's soul if left with no other option.'" She peered up from the page she read from, meeting the eyes of every individual in the room.

Thea had never seen the woman outside of her normally bubbly self. This person before her was alien. Her dark eyes were as sharp as the jagged crags that crashed ships in the night. The personality switch was enough to keep everyone quiet as she continued. Cressida was the only one that did not look surprised. Thea could have been imagining it, but it looked like a proud glint entered the sorceress's gaze.

"Soul eaters travel close together. If there has been a prison break, many more would be out there, and we would have been alerted. Likewise, the High Priests of the Council would have made this known to the rest of your Coven. It is possible only a few demons have managed to slip through the gates of Hell, unnoticed until now."

The voice of reason it seemed. Thea thought back to Siobhan upstairs, the many creatures that barely escaped with their lives and had seen their companions killed. She spoke first as the silence continued.

"I'm going out to eradicate it."

Rafe whirled on her. "No, you're not."

No, you're not.

She gritted her teeth together and spat, "You hold no authority over me, Rafe, second rank or not." She knew he had not shot her down purely because she was failing to go about this the way she was trained. He thought she couldn't do it.

"Doesn't matter. You haven't been authorized to act on this."

"I hardly ever need authorization to do anything, or have you forgotten I'm a Spellweaver now? It's been two years since I've graduated from Hunter status."

"You know this is different," he growled, the blue in his aqua eyes shining over the green the more incensed he became. "We're talking about demons, Thea. Third-tier demons that haven't been sighted in over two hundred years, for Goddess' sake!"

"Blasphemy, Rafe? Really?" She queried, throwing his words from before back at him.

"Thea."

Don't expect any support from us!

"Look, this is what I've been trained for!" She finally shouted. It had been a mistake to bring him along with her. He couldn't see her for the elite soldier she was, too stuck in the past. All he saw in her was the fresh-faced academy student on her first day, fumbling for directions and too nervous to speak up. That wasn't her anymore. She had wrangled black magic users crazed from the poison that clung to their bones, shut down businesses tied to the Dark Market, and captured and released a herd of wild unicorns stampeding through the streets of Tolvade single-handedly. She had often come home with broken bones, cuts that ran deep and horrific images that ran deeper. She wasn't a rookie to risking her life, and she'd rather die saving someone than to live and let others be sacrificed.

His shoulders sagged, but he looked far from saying his piece. "None of us have been trained for something like this. There's a reason no one's ever been able to summon third-tier demons, especially ones from the last level. They possess too much strength and willpower to be a Coven member's pet. They would kill you in your sleep, if not before. There has only been one occasion—one—where someone has been able to pull a creature from the ninth level of Hell, but it had been a dumb, drooling, guardian ogre that I had to blast with an intelligence spell. Actually," he paused with a thoughtful expression, "it was blasted with two, and I was surprised it didn't implode on the spot."

"Two?" Mokana and Namara marveled in unison. Cressida looked so done with the conversation at that point and slipped out from what had become the huddle puddle of ignorance. Thea could sympathize with the sorceress for once, but she could also understand the creatures' incredulousness.

One intelligence spell had taken Namara from a water flinging, wild-eyed, bucking, nightmare of a horse to what she was now, and had taken Mokana from a hissing, spitting creature that lunged at anything in range with the intent to maim to her present condition.

Thea scrubbed her face when the three continued conversing about that blasted ogre. "We're getting off subject," she barked, "and if you hadn't realized, there is a soul eater—with the possibility of more demons—out there as we speak." She massaged her temples in frustration, swearing that the onset of another headache was fast approaching. Where was that tea Cressida had poured them earlier? She never even got around to drinking it.

Her words seemed to snap Rafe out of whatever nostalgia he was experiencing. His eyes, having calmed back down to that marbled, in-between color, flashed back to ice. "You're not going out there to deal with this on your own, Thea, end of story."

You're going to shame all of us! For what? So, you can go play pretend hero? You're not going!

She was not prepared for the outright indignation and fury that surged through her in that moment. She yelled, "I don't care what you want!" and marched forward until she stood toe to toe with him. He glared back at her, unperturbed by her anger. "Either you have my back, or you don't. Run off and tell the Coven for all I care. The only thing they're going to do is send out a bunch of Spellweavers who also haven't trained for something like this — or worse, Hunters, because why not? We don't know the magnitude of demons when we haven't seen one in over two hundred years, so let's just send out a bunch of inexperienced graduates. *I'm sure they'll be fine.* I don't think so. This is my mission, Rafe, I'm going to be the one to handle it."

All her frustrations were bubbling up into this manifesto of emotions that she didn't even know from where it was all coming from. Was it betrayal? Wounded pride? Did it come from Siobhan and the need to avenge her and the other nymph? All she knew for certain was that she was useless standing around arguing a moot point.

She didn't linger long enough to contemplate the wounded looked that crossed his features like she had physically struck him, and instead fled the room. She didn't dare look to see if he followed, didn't need to, because the only sounds that followed her out were Namara's wet foot slaps on the concrete floor.

She flung the doors open, though not as easily as Blythe made it seem and met the chilly bite of the winter wind that gusted into the sanctuary. She made it just outside the barrier, about to order her pet to transform—wet pants the furthest thing from her mind—when a heavy, meaty hand clapped onto her shoulder and spun her around. She opened her mouth to spout off, but a scathing glare from Rafe silenced her for the moment. She prepared for the inevitable *if you're so stuck on being suicidal, then leave! Have fun dying!*

"If you're so stuck on being suicidal, then I'm coming with you."

She faltered.

"What?" She tried to jerk out from his hold on her, but his grip only tightened. "Why? Trying to prove something?"

"The only one trying to prove anything is you."

She did not have time for this. Again, she tried shoving his hand from her shoulder, and again it refused to budge, only tightening in subtle warning. Thea didn't do subtle warnings. Once more, she came toe to toe, nose to sternum, but she refused to think about their dramatic height differences now.

"Fine. If you're coming along, make yourself useful. Can you teleport us?" Right before Thea left Siobhan, she'd gotten an estimated location the wood nymph had last seen the soul eater.

"'Can you teleport us?' she asks the senior wizard," Rafe grumbled to himself as he stepped away from her, dropping his hand and beginning to bind his hair up in a clasp. Any other time, Thea would have cracked a smile, but she was still angry with the second-ranked member.

"You know the drill." He jerked his thumb over his shoulder in the direction of Srbeveara. "I need something from the forest we're teleporting to and the location's coordinates."

"We bringing the nymph with us now?" she asked dryly.

Rafe growled in frustration and dragged his hands down his face. "Weren't you the one that wanted this to be quick?"

"Right. Namara." She tossed her head in the direction of the sanctuary and watched as, for once, the creature didn't give her any lip. The kelpie gazed warily at the two Coven members before heading back inside to collect the ingredients.

Rafe got to work pulling out the other necessities for the spell: a coin-sized stone that glittered in the sun in flecks of white and gray called zircon, and when he closed his fist around it, it shone brightly through the cracks between his fingers before disintegrating into dust. He sprinkled the powder in a small circle, then took out a small vial of milky, mother-of-pearl colored liquid—the blood of a Celestial being, to which Rafe muttered something about it being expensive, and poured a small amount into the center of the circle. He turned to find Namara, wearing a funny expression, holding out the proffered items.

"What is it?" Thea questioned quietly, so as not to disturb the Summoner's concentration. "That was quick." She watched Rafe dump a few leaves from Siobhan's habitat and one curl from the creature's tresses into the circle.

"Cressida already had it ready. Told us to get out and not come back."

"Gladly."

Rafe took to position. Arms outstretched beside him, hands raised to the Goddess, head bowed, eyes closed. His hands flexed in a signal for them all to grab onto him. Thea grabbed his left hand, next to her Namara grabbed her free hand, Mokana grabbed the kelpie's other hand and completed the circle when she held Rafe's right hand. Everyone closed their eyes, but it was the Summoner's duty to envision them all in the center of the forest. If he did not envision everyone in attendance, they would be left behind.

The world shifted out from under Thea's feet, and the wind picked up, blowing through her curls and racing up the gaps in her clothing, eliciting shivers that danced along her spine. She could feel when the world righted itself around her, and she knew before she opened her eyes that something was wrong.

Chapter Six

No One's Home

Thea's vision was blurry for only a moment before it cleared, and the nymph's home stretched out before her. It was deathly quiet. Nothing moved. Nothing but the swaying branches of the large evergreens that towered ominously overhead. The wind crept through the trees in hushed whispers, alerting the still forest of its visitors. The forest did not whisper back with idle chirps of birds, or with the chitter of energetic squirrels. It did not respond with heavy snorts from crossing deer or the rare passing unicorn. The forest remained quiet in the presence of guests, and in that moment, Thea felt truly and utterly alone.

"Something's not right." Namara's usually soft-spoken voice resonated around them. The wind stopped, and the sound of silence that followed was deafening. Thea never realized before how loud white noise was until it was gone. Goosebumps skittered down her arms, and the hairs on the back of her neck rose to attention.

"Come on," she encouraged in a mere whisper, but even that seemed to echo throughout the woods. She didn't remember the crunch of snow ever being quite so loud, but the abrasive sound grated on her nerves and made her want to turn around and shush everyone. Instead, she studied the ground she walked on.

The snow looked completely untouched, and even if it had flurried recently and covered the ground, there should have been some signs of life. There wasn't. No hoof tracks, no thin, womanly footprints from the wood nymphs, no shoveled snow pits from squirrels hiding their findings, no rabbit pellets, and no carcasses left from the wolves. Entirely empty and equally as unnerving.

"Mokana," she breathed out slowly, aware her voice carried in the air, "aren't you familiar with these woods?"

If she remembered correctly, before the days of the creature's pethood, news of a rusalka trying to drown the village boys spread around the Vemeese district and made its way to the capital. Thea had been in her last year at the secondary academy, but she remembered as soon as Rafe graduated and joined the Coven, when he summoned Mokana, the rusalka tormenting the town disappeared. She'd always found it coincidental but had never confirmed it. She was going out on a limb even now.

Mokana side-eyed her, nodding slowly. "I'm surprised you put two and two together. Yes, I used to know these woods, but it's been a long time, and my past life is a blur anyway."

Thea blinked, stunned in the knowledge that really had been Mokana. "It just came to me, honestly. Maybe we can find a landmark to jog your memory?"

"Hold on a minute," Rafe intercepted, looking bewildered and borderline offended. "That rusalka was you? Why didn't you tell me?"

"I'm sorry," she barked suddenly, shattering the stillness. "Forgive me for not telling you everything about the darkest part of my life that, to this day, still haunts me. When we get home—if we get home and don't die out here chasing feral demons—we'll share every dark, horrible, embarrassing secret and mistake we've ever made. You can go first." She flung her long platinum hair over her alabaster shoulder and stomped off in the direction they had been going.

"Goddess help me, you step on one female's toes you step on them all," Rafe grumbled before taking off after the creature.

"Goddess wouldn't help you much either, her being a woman and all," Thea muttered as he walked away and rolled her eyes skyward, about to join them when her gaze landed on Namara who had been unusually quiet throughout the routine spat.

Rather than stand around listening to the squabble, the kelpie had slunk away and stood before a giant, gnarled tree with thick limbs swooping down low to the ground from the weight they carried. Thea shuffled up to her pet's side, who she noted for the first time was looking less waterlogged than usual. She snatched up a strand of hair and realized it was a lot browner than the black, murky color she always believed it to be. A single drop of water clung to the damp curl before gravity gave way and it fell to the ground.

"Namara—"

"Don't worry," her pet quickly assured her. "I have until the end of the day before it gets bad. I just haven't been soaking as much as I should be. I've been trying to condition myself to need less time in the water, but I guess it's not working."

"But why?" She tried to meet Namara's eyes, but the kelpie stubbornly refused to look at her. "If this is because I sometimes have to turn down missions then—"

"It doesn't matter, it's obviously not working. I've been trying this for months. The results are always the same."

Months? Her kelpie had been putting her life at risk for months, and she had been completely unaware of it? Thea felt like kicking herself. She could usually pick up on things like this. Why didn't she notice? More importantly, "Why didn't you tell me?"

"We'll discuss it later."

The dual crunches of snow behind her informed Thea the other half of their group had turned around after noticing their absences. Thea closed her mouth upon their arrival, though she wanted to argue the point. Namara was a private creature, though, and she had to respect that. So, Namara didn't give Rafe and Mokana a chance to read the situation before she was asking, "Would this be enough to jog your memory, Moka?"

Mokana narrowed her aqua gaze but wisely said nothing. Instead, she faced the century-old tree. Her pale lips twisted into dissatisfaction, and a glimmer of recognition surfaced.

"Well?" Thea prompted.

"Yeah, I remember climbing up this big boy maybe a decade ago, real late at night. The villagers had sent their dogs after me." She studied the tree for a long time, letting out a heavy sigh. Before the rest of them could ask what was wrong, she was sinking her sharp claws into the darkened bark and clamoring up the tree. She perched herself on a high branch, straddling the limb as she twisted around.

Rafe looked up at her in total perplexity. "What are you doing?"

"This helps me remember what direction the hounds came from." She swiveled around the branch again, legs crossing and moonlit-colored hair billowing in the breeze. She frowned and leaped from the tree to land gracefully in front of Thea. She flung an arm out in the direction past the tree to the right, one taloned finger pointing the way. "That's the way to the village."

Secrets of the Sanctuary

The rusalka turned on her heel and led the way, not bothering to see if the others trailed after her. Thea kept pace with her pet, but if Namara noticed the worried glances that were thrown her way, she ignored them.

When Thea couldn't get anything out of the kelpie, she met Rafe's curious gaze. He'd been watching the exchange but had known better than to say anything. She knew he saw the worry she was trying to hide. He was too astute, and he knew her too well. She sidled up to his side and wordlessly he lent her his strength, and she said nothing as she drew from its endless supply. All she had to do was be near him to feel grounded. Most times she hated it, refused it, but not this time. She shoved her pride to the back of her mind for now.

The odious feeling of the forest returned the closer they neared the village. It was growing in suffocating levels. It even affected Mokana and Namara—creatures that had been raised in the depths of Hell, surrounded by monsters one could only imagine in their darkest nightmares. They kept pausing and glancing over their shoulders, eyes sweeping the underbrush, ears strained for strange noises. Thea could feel sweat building across the skin of her forehead even as the tips of her fingers burned from the cold inside her gloves.

When the creatures suddenly stopped, the hair on the back of her neck rose once again. She shoved past the two of them into the forest's clearing, and the breath caught in her throat. Not a single soul milled about in the little town. Absolute silence greeted her.

It was just like the rest of the forest—quiet, empty, abandoned. There should have been smoke puffing out from the bricked chimneys, children wreaking havoc in their yards bundled in heavy cloaks, men shoveling the snow out from the pathways, carts stationed outside shops with impatient horses clomping at the cobblestones. There was none of that. The cottages were devoid of all light and warmth, the shops' doors blown open from the wind, and a cart was tipped over with hay spilled out in the street.

Thea's voice sounded hollow to her own ears. "Split up. We'll meet up at the street clock when we've cleared the rows. The sun is going to set in the next few hours, and we don't have the ingredients to teleport back. I am not going to be here in the dark with a soul eater on the loose."

"I have rubble from the stones of the sanctuary just in case," Namara piped up, glancing at the sewn-on pocket on her robes.

"That's the last place I want to be, but we'll use it in an emergency."

Rafe nodded curtly and reached behind him to pull out a thick wooden staff that elongated the more he pulled from the end. It stood as tall as him when it reached its full length with a large golden hoop at the top. The hoop was sharpened to a razor's edge, doubling as a close-range weapon, but it could also repel enemies at a distance with an orb of sickly yellow plasma that shot from inside the circle. It could neutralize or, if needed, kill upon impact.

He set off on the edge of town, Mokana trailing after him a few steps before branching out to sweep a different section. Namara chose the center of the village, leaving the other edge of town to the Spellweaver. Thea unstrapped her sickle and chain and ventured out into the clearing. To call the place small was generous, and Thea knew by splitting up that the entire hamlet could be checked in a short period of time. That was if they didn't run into trouble.

Peaked cottage roofs blanketed in snow and decorated in icicles would have made for a cozy, inviting place to stop for the night had they not been empty of the life that had given them purpose, standing frozen against the harsh elements.

Thea kicked down the door to the first boutique, Phoebe Spells'
Crafts and Creations, but was met with silent, stale air. She
peered inside briefly, calling out to anyone or anything that
lurked inside. The untouched shelves with jars, candles, scrolls,
and bottled herbs looked untouched, layered in dust. A broom
was leaning against the wall with its pile left unattended, and
the register drawer was popped open. The money lay inside,
forgotten. Thea moved on.

She wasn't exactly discreet as she searched the other
buildings, kicking down each door and poised to fight. The
sight in each one, however, was much the same. Mundane
scenes captured in time, only without the people present.
Plates set at the table with no one to eat from them, dishes
soaking in stagnant water, laundry half folded. Dust and ash
from the fireplaces had been blown everywhere and onto
everything. It was as if the people of the village had
disappeared instantly as they went about their daily lives.

The more she saw the same thing over and over, the
more she expected the next cottage to be the same. It was in
those moments she feared that she would grow complacent
and leave herself open for an attack. She gripped her sickle in
her hands with zealous determination. It was the only weapon
that had called to her from the Coven's massive armory.
Carved from the bones of gargoyles, her sickle and chain could
fly through the air faster and farther than any normal weapon.
Her dagger was great in a pinch since wands were overrated
and just as fickle as the fairies that crafted them.

She was nearing the end of her short search with only
one cottage left. She braced herself, knowing it always had to
be the last one the monster wanted to hide in. She steeled her
nerves with a large, steadying breath, leaned back, brought her
leg up, and kicked the door so hard it snapped clean off its
hinges. It clattered to the floor with a hollow sound that echoed

throughout the house. She rushed inside, sickle raised, eyes gleaming.

Nothing. Everything was the same as the other houses with nothing out of place until—she froze. A mother lay toppled over a chair, clutching a stiff bundled blanket to her chest. Mouth stretched open in a silent scream, eyes unseeing, filled with terror. Frozen tear tracks glinted in the low light against snow-white skin.

When the reality of it all collided with her, she grabbed for a handle that wasn't there to slam shut a door that was on the floor, and in her haste to get away she tripped over her own feet out of the home. She toppled backward and crashed into the ground. Bile rose in the back of her throat, and she clamped both hands over her mouth, but the images of the dead mother and what she could only assume was a—

—she ripped down her face mask and retched into the snow beside her, dry heaving and drooling as her stomach cramped harshly on itself. She sobbed in wet, choked breaths and could feel her nose running and stray hairs clinging to the corners of her teary eyes and spit-slicked lips. She spat the foul taste from her mouth miserably before she collapsed back in the snow and gasped for air. She swiped wet gloves over her face and hissed as the wind sliced at the dampness of her exposed cheeks.

Then Rafe was there, chasing away the cold and drawing her into him. She fastened her arms around his neck and clung to him while the tears fell. The images repeated themselves over and over and over again in a vicious loop in her head. She was barely aware that their pets had taken up beside the two in protective stances.

"They—I..." The words felt awkward as they rolled off her tongue, her lips too numb to shape sounds into words. It was hard to swallow, harder to think. She hadn't been prepared for this. She thought she had been ready for any surprise, but the sight before her hadn't crossed her mind in the heat of the moment. She had been too stupid to think, and so she hadn't. She'd just blindly charged out into the middle of the woods with one of the evilest and dangerous creatures to ever exist, and she thought she could handle it. She couldn't even handle the death of the innocent, and that was all she was going to find if she kept searching for the soul eater. She was so selfish. The woman in the cottage could have been any one of her friends because she had rushed them into this on a stupid whim to avenge a wood nymph with a sad story.

If you're so stuck on being suicidal, then leave! Have fun dying!

Rafe said nothing as she continued to internally berate herself. He only stood her up and dusted the snow off her. It seemed to draw her out of her self-hatred, because she flinched and jerked out of his hold, releasing his shoulders she had so desperately been clinging to.

She cleared her throat and swept her gaze over the rest of the village, looking anywhere but at the Summoner while she dried her eyes. "What did you guys find?" She pulled her face mask back up over the bridge of her nose and reveled in its slight reprieve from the chill.

"Aside from mostly empty buildings, the same thing," was his quiet reply.

"Most of the shops I searched were empty, too," Mokana added. Namara nodded in solemn agreement.

"There weren't nearly enough corpses for a village this size, and the Coven wasn't made aware of any influx in people seeking refuge in the city. Could they have escaped to another village?" Rafe asked with eyes trained on the Spellweaver. She knew what he was trying to do. Ask her questions with simple answers, to get her talking, to get her into thinking about things other than what was inside that cottage. She latched onto his lifeline.

"Not possible. Reports would have come flying in had they escaped with their lives." She shook her head once as a negative. "If not by those that escaped then by the beings that sanctioned them."

"Unless the next town over is worse," Namara voiced a concern they hadn't thought about. Thea shuddered at the thought.

"Well..." Mokana began, but the grimace that surfaced cut off her next words, and Thea knew she wasn't going to like whatever the rusalka had to say. "Well...maybe we haven't thought of all the possibilities."

"What are you talking about?" she hedged with bated breath.

"Well—this is just a hunch—but, um, what if all the disappearances were caused by hellfire?"

Chapter Seven

One Hell of a Fight

"Hellfire?" Thea repeated.

"It would make sense," Rafe concurred in grim reluctance.

Thea rubbed at her eyes with the heels of her palms. Her face mask didn't cover her eyes, and she could feel them drying out in the icy wind. "Okay," she sighed and ran her frozen, gloved fingers through her curls. "Okay, what creatures can use hellfire again?"

Mokana gawked at her. "You don't know?"

"Do I look like a Demonologist to you?"

"Okay, calm down," Rafe interrupted with his hands raised in a placating gesture, not looking at either female directly lest he incur their wrath. "Underworld creatures aren't exactly a Spellweaver's forte, especially those that use hellfire. Creatures that use hellfire are mostly found in the third tier and therefore don't usually concern Spellweavers or Hunters. As a Summoner, it's my job to know in case one gets summoned."

"So, which creatures can use hellfire?" Thea crossed her arms, prompting Rafe to get back to the subject.

"Hellcats, the ogres that guard Hell's prison—"

"They're doing a fabulous job, by the way," Namara muttered disdainfully.

"—demon princes and fallen demon princes—or throneless ones—devils, and hellhounds."

"It couldn't be hellcats," Mokana stated matter-of-factually.

Thea's brows scrunched in confusion. "Why not?"

"For one, hellcats are not tier-three demons. It wouldn't be hanging around a soul eater. It would be running in fear of its own life. Secondly," she waved her arm in a sweeping gesture of the village, "do you not notice that none of these buildings have been touched by hellfire? Hellcats are messy and chaotic. If it were them, the whole town would be nothing more than ash."

"Same goes for the ogres," Namara explained, glancing at Rafe. "Besides the one you double blasted with intelligent spells, they really are dumb, aggressive, and possess a one thought processing mind. If they were even aware of a prison breach and came above ground looking for those that escaped, they would have flattened this area and maybe even destroyed the forest as well. They're not careful creatures."

"Okay, that leaves the princes, devils, and hellhounds." Thea wanted to add a sarcastic *yay* to the ominous mix but decided against it.

"Demon princes won't leave Hell on the off chance they could be overthrown," said Namara.

"And fallen princes are waiting for every opportunity to do just that," finished Mokana.

Thea sighed and pinched the bridge of her nose. "Down to two, then, detectives."

Namara ignored the jab and replied seriously, her voice low, and her eyes glassy as she remembered something. "It's not a devil."

Thea recognized the change in her behavior and waited for the kelpie to continue. It was rare for Namara to share anything on her past life, and she had a feeling that was exactly what she was about to do.

"I only ever came across one once, and though I don't remember much on my time spent as a mindless creature spawned by Hell, I do remember that particular event in crystal clarity." She rubbed her arms, leaving wet trails along her seafoam-colored skin. "It was about three hundred years ago, and I had just drowned my first victim. He was just a boy, but back then I didn't care, only driven by instincts. Instincts that screamed at me to run away because there was something watching me. I looked up into the blackest eyes I'd ever seen peering out from behind the reeds of the riverbank—they were bottomless. Hell's final layer curled up inside those eyes. I was quite far from the riverbank, so I couldn't see much past the horrifying expression, but it was what I'd felt that stayed with me for years after that. That riverbed held a sinister aura around it for a long time." She shivered and, if possible, her pale skin lightened even further. "It's not a devil."

Thea blew out a breath and moved to embrace the wet creature, though she came away less soaked than she normally would have. It reminded her that they needed to leave soon, and the first thing she was doing when they got back was grounding her kelpie to the river outside for the next week. "Hellhounds it is. We need to go. I'll report to the Coven officially after I take Namara home."

"I'll fill out a report as well," Rafe offered before he turned and marched off in the direction they'd come from, calling over his shoulder, "And I'll go raid the shops for some teleportation ingredients. I'd rather walk from the sanctuary than—" he cursed viciously. Thea jerked her attention from her kelpie and froze.

Standing at the edge of the forest, shrouded in the shadows of the surrounding trees, was a creature that had, until recently, only been described in legends. Its wraith-like body was covered by a black, tattered cloak that clung to its back like the plague, just as the wood nymph described. It hovered just above the ground, floating there as silent as death while strips of its ripped cloak whipped in the icy breeze; the breeze that brought with it the smell of rotting corpses. Nausea churned her stomach. She clutched her midriff, willing the rolling waves to cease. She couldn't see the being's eyes from where she stood frozen in place, but she'd heard the stories, listened to Siobhan's encounter to know what lay beneath.

One thin, bony arm lifted from the folds of its cloak, pointing at them, and shivers raced up her spine. Instinctively, she moved to cover Rafe's blind spot, but a snarl ripped through the air, faltering her steps and stopping her heart. She heard Rafe curse again. Mokana hissed, and her claws fully unsheathed into lethal daggers as she took a crouched position. Namara immediately collapsed to the ground on her hands and knees. Her bones buckled, muscles stretched, and her limbs contorted. Her body doubled in size as she thrashed, her skin rippling and graying out, becoming slippery, while her black irises bled into the whites of her eyes. When an echoing scream erupted from her throat, which resounded with the pained wails from every victim she'd ever drowned, her transformation was complete. Between her hind legs was not a regular horse tail, but more similar to that of a scaleless mermaid's. Thea had seen this third form of Namara's only once before and looking at it now brought her a sense of dread.

The cause of the snarl slipped from the shadows of the soul eater's cloak, and Thea watched in horror as a hellhound emerged from the forest. As large as an ox, with bare, leathery skin the color of coal; coal that seemed to burn with the flames of Hell around the creature's chest where a fiery glow emanated. Smoke followed the creature as it crept closer, and a large flame danced from the tip of its hairless tail, slashing the air angrily. A mane of matted, singed hair gave way to two spiraling horns. When it growled again, a rattle echoed around the sound, and the glow in its chest spread to its throat.

Everything blurred when the hellhound lunged.

Shrieks, snarls, and harrowing bellows erupted around her. Rafe swung his staff, energy razing. Namara reared back with an enraged wail, and Mokana jumped onto the hound's back and let out a bloodcurdling scream.

"Thea, get out of the way!" someone roared.

Thea scrambled back, tripping over the rocks under the snow, and landed sharply on her tailbone with a pained cry. Her sickle she had just reached for was knocked out of her grasp on impact, and she clamored back hastily on scraped hands before stumbling to her feet and shoved herself into the nearest shop, the door flying open and crashing into the wall.

"Crap, crap, crap!" She scoured the racks for the ingredients she needed with her heart in her throat, her mouth dry, her head pounding as she knocked over potted plants, toppled over shelves, and pushed over irrelevant items that weren't what she was looking for.

"We have to get out of here. We have to get out of here," she repeated in her desperation as she ripped open cabinet doors. The wood splintered under the strain, loud pops dulled by the roars of her comrades as they came off their hinges. Something crashed outside. The spike of copper in the air hit the back of her tongue.

She cursed and spun around, smacking open the shop's door with a bruised hand and narrowly dodging a yellow plasma ball just as she crashed into the door of the next shop. She smashed jars onto the floor, yanked open drawers—nothing. High pitched shrieks exploded from outside, the snarls closer. The smell of rotten flesh struck her. She nearly tripped over an uneven floorboard, coughing roughly into her arm as she tossed objects off the shelves before —*found it!*—

plucking the zircon off the shelf and barreling out into the fray right as the wall inside collapsed. She screamed from the ear-splitting blast, the reverberations in the ground tripping her up and causing her ankle to buckle. Pain shot up her leg, and her vision flashed white.

Someone was bellowing for her, but the words were lost to the howls of the wind and monstrous beasts. Something large, black, and smoking darted in front of her, causing her to flounder, almost dropping the zircon clutched to her chest. Hellhound. She stumbled to a halt just as the creature sprung into her path. Her mouth felt like sand, her heart thumping so wildly it hurt. Where was her sickle! Black eyes, razor-sharp teeth snapped too close to her face and she reacted, dodging the clamp of jaws and kicking out her leg to connect with the creature's jowl. She cried out and crumpled to the ground ungracefully. Pain flared up her leg again. Her ankle was sprained now.

Get up! Get up! GET UP!

She struggled to her feet, biting her lip so hard it bled when the pain seared her to the bone. She heard the panting, felt its hot breath around her neck, knew it was closing in—

—a hellish whinny replaced the vicious snarls, and the hot breath was gone. She threw her body's weight into the door of the next shop with her shoulder, throwing it into the wall where the wood cracked down the middle, and she immediately spotted the bottled white blood she needed. She grabbed three.

She hobbled out of the building, the tears leaking from her eyes blinding her. She felt more than saw something headed straight for her, and ducked a leaping Mokana, feeling the wisp of hair *whoosh* over her body. She gasped for air, her side was burning, her ankle stung, her shoulder ached. She ignored it, moving as quickly as she could into the clearing not affected by the battle. More snarls, more screams. Rafe was yelling.

She dumped the contents onto the snow, dropping to the ground as she shakily spread out the items before her. Something was missing—what was missing? She gasped.

"Namara!" she screamed, whipping around to find the kelpie. Namara collided her thick tail with the hellhound's side, sending the creature hurdling into a stone cottage, damaging the structure, and causing the boulders mortared together to collapse onto its back. Sickening crunches echoed throughout the hamlet.

Namara raced over to shake the sanctuary's stone rubble from the confines of her dripping wet mane. She grappled for the items, abruptly distracted by the sounds of the demon dog's bones cracking and popping back into place. Her mouth fell in absolute horror. How was the creature not dead?

Rafe bellowed her name.

She lurched back around, focusing her attention on the spell. She swallowed a lungful of air and blanked out her mind, reciting the spell's instructions in her head.

First, crush the zircon in your palms then sprinkle the remains in a circle. Not a perfect circle resultant from the tremors in her hands, but she moved on. Next, pour the blood into the center of the circle—done. Dump the rocks into the pile. Okay, take the position, close your eyes and raise yourself to the goddess—*please, Goddess, guide us on our way*—okay.

"Guys!" she shouted, but only the clash of bodies and the screeches of dueling creatures met her ears. She couldn't open her eyes, or she'd have to start all over again. "Guys!" she tried again, louder, her voice wavering from the strain.

A hand slapped her palm, causing her to yelp. It was the only warning she got before clawed fingers gripped her other hand. Two down—

"Namara?"

"Here!" Rafe's rough voice was close to her ear.

She pictured Srbeveara just as she had seen it that morning. She pictured her, standing with her arms crossed, Rafe beside her, Mokana playing idly with Namara's drying hair. She envisioned the sounds of the forest around the clearing, the hum of the barrier's orange glow.

The last thing she heard was the enraged snapping from the hellhound's jaws as the putrid smell of the soul eater closed in around them before the world fell away.

When Thea came to, the first thing that registered was the cold seeping into her body. Her backside wet from the snow, she pushed herself up and let out a ragged groan. Pain was the second thing, shooting up her leg with every tiny movement, flaring in her side and throbbing in both shoulders. The third thing, and by far the most unfamiliar, was the faintness of the tether that held Namara and her together. Like a cord pulled taut, one could thrum it to summon each other. It was difficult to lose one another, but sometimes, if the pair clashed over and over again, the cord could slacken—but this, what she was feeling now, was as if the cord was vanishing.

She pried her eyes open against the blinding white snow and flinched. Rafe was coming to beside her, Mokana huffed and hissed in what could only be pain, but Namara was not moving.

"Namara!" She scrambled on blistered hands and worn knees, biting back the pain stabbing her through the ankle. She shoved damp fawn tresses out of the way and gasped at the pale face devoid of the light green color she normally wore. She rounded on Rafe, who was blinking the sensitivity from his eyes.

"Go get help! Now!" She turned back around and hauled Namara up, cursing viciously as the weight from the limp kelpie rendered her useless with a bum leg. She screamed her frustration, shaking her pet with all her remaining strength.

"Wake up, Namara! I can't carry you! *Get up!*"

"Help me carry her!" someone yelled from behind her, and red and gold skirts plopped down beside them. Blythe shoved Thea's hands aside, her eyes steel, her hands steady. They skittered over the creature, searching.

"She's alive, but she won't be if we don't get her inside. Can you carry her?" she directed the question at Thea.

She shook her head quickly, the words not making it past the lump in her throat.

Blythe locked eyes with someone over her head. "Grab her upper body."

Rafe pushed by, hauling the unconscious kelpie up from under her arms while Blythe picked up her feet. Thea watched from her prone position on the ground as they rushed her pet inside. Her attention was drawn away by the sharp hiss from the rusalka panting a little ways off. She crawled over, shoved her arm under Mokana's, and they both awkwardly climbed to their feet, wheezing and groaning the entire time.

They stumbled when they passed through the barrier, the little wisps of energy sending shockwaves through their battered bodies. Thea leaned against the doorframe with Mokana losing consciousness, limp and bearing almost all her weight on the Spellweaver. By the time they had hobbled inside and collapsed on the couches in the room Thea could only call a parlor, Cressida was strolling in with an impassive air about her.

Secrets of the Sanctuary

The rather bland expression she wore contradicted the shimmering champagne evening gown that clung to her every curve. Sitting atop her head was a matching, matte top hat that completed the look with cursive scrawling written on it in a language Thea couldn't decipher. Cressida was deceptively calm for an emergency situation—or maybe it wasn't deceptive at all. She had made it clear she didn't exactly welcome the party from the get-go.

"Well?" Thea tried for demanding, but her voice came out breathy. She couldn't get enough air in her starved lungs.

"She'll live," was all the sorceress said at first, then, with a thoughtful purse of her rose-tinted lips, wondered, "I assume you found what you were looking for?"

The question was rhetorical, but Thea found herself croaking hoarsely, "Worse." The news that Namara would live had her slumping back into the couch cushions in relief. Mokana was snoring quietly beside her, lying haphazardly in a huddled heap.

Cressida hummed noncommittally, sweeping past the Spellweaver with her gown elegantly trailing behind her. She glided down into her high-backed chair as if the world wasn't falling apart and picked up her fountain pen and continued on with her paperwork like that was the number one priority at the moment. Watching her calmly write and sign pieces of paper in the most unhurried fashion had Thea finally snapping.

"How can you be so calm about this? You know for a fact feral demons are on the loose!"

The faintest of smirks quirked the sorceress's lips before she looked up with wide, innocent eyes. "What is there to worry about? Won't the Coven protect me?" Her feigned innocence dried up instantly. "I, and whomever I choose to protect, will be fine should the world burn down in flames. Of that, I have no doubt."

Thea went to remark something about overconfidence, but the sound of heavy, scuffed footfalls tore her attention away. She watched Rafe enter the room and land gracelessly on the couch opposite her, his heavy weight sending the small sofa back a few inches. Cressida huffed her annoyance.

"How is she?" Thea asked quickly. She knew Namara would live, but at what cost? Would she be forever confined to a pool? She didn't know how underworldly creatures worked, and it wasn't like Cressida was a fountain of information.

Rafe flashed her a small, reassuring smile before it morphed into a wince. His breathing was still uneven. "Blythe said she'll make a full recovery, but in order for her to do that she'll need to spend a week here soaking in the healing waters."

Thea took a moment to let the information sink in. Namara would be okay. She sent a silent thank you to the goddess for small miracles. "Did she get a room here?" How much were rooms here anyways?

"No, she's in the hidden spring behind the waterfall," he pointed in the general direction of the entryway. Thea's brows crinkled, and she looked off in the direction he was pointing as if she could actually see the waterfall from her spot on the couch. She hadn't thought there was anything behind the waterfall, but she guessed that was why it was called a 'hidden' spring.

"A week, though?" She sighed when all he did was nod. "And she'll be completely healed?" Another nod. He eyed his sleeping pet, and upon noticing her wince, started to dig around in his pouches. He muttered something about being low on gold dust before he kneeled beside the rusalka. A spearmint green glowed through his large palms while he hovered them over her body. Mokana seemed to calm, and her breathing regulated. He pivoted and brought his healing spell onto Thea's body next. The pain in her ankle disappeared, and she sighed in relief. Every ache and twinge vanished, and she felt better than she had in a long time.

She dug around in her own pouches, and the healing spell illuminated her fingertips while she ran them a few inches over the Summoner's body.

"I'm sorry," she whispered when she finished, and she knew he understood she meant about everything. About rushing headlong into danger. For risking all of their lives because she had believed she could save the day.

"We learned a lot today," he replied in the same soft tone. "No loss, no gain, right?" He cracked a smile with winter-bit lips, though it fell too fast to relieve her. "But in all seriousness, we should report to the Coven soon." He stood from his kneeling position and righted the other couch before lounging back in its soft cushions, stretching out his long legs with a hearty groan.

She felt like groaning too, only for a different reason entirely. Goddess, she had nearly forgotten about the Coven. What was she going to tell them? Would they lecture her, commend her, demote her, or praise her? She could never tell with the Council. Every meeting with them was a less-than-desired experience. Worry gnawed at her as the grim reality set in, and it was not just from her upcoming meeting. She knew the Coven's knee-jerk reaction after many years in their service.

"How many members are going to die when the Coven sends them out to dispel the soul eater and hellhound?" she directed at Rafe, and she did not like the expression that came across his face. It was likely the High Priest Council was going to send everyone in the Coven out after these creatures. Was this going to spiral out into a war? Were her co-workers and all the people she went to the academy with going to die fighting a pointless battle? If a Summoner, Spellweaver, and two creatures from Hell itself weren't enough to take out even one third-tier demon, let alone two, then what good was a Hunter fresh out of school?

She could tell whatever Rafe was thinking mirrored her own thoughts, but, nevertheless, he continued, "It doesn't matter what we think. We swore an oath to the Coven when we joined that we would not withhold our findings and that we would come forward with the truth."

Thea rolled her eyes at the mention of the 'oath.' Basically, it was Rafe grasping at straws when he was left without a decent argument. A stickler for staying in the blue cloaks' good graces, which, if she thought about it, was always the best course of action. The Council's word was law, and by extension her word was law, but that didn't make her impervious to their decree. Still, this was too serious a situation to be mindlessly following orders.

Rafe pressed on. "The High Priests will know what to do. This is not the first time the world has had to deal with feral demons of this caliber. We can push them back again."

Thea scoffed at such a ridiculous, dreamy-eyed sentiment. "Newsflash, Rafe, anyone that ever knew how to dispel demons is long dead because the last time they had to deal with them was over two hundred years ago, and all the records the Coven kept with those spells were burned to a crisp at the turn of the century." She held up a hand to stop him from arguing with her. "We're sitting ducks right now. How many Coven members are going to die before the blue cloaks get off their podiums and help out? You tell me that and I'll go skip over to HQ right now and tell them everything that happened. This is bigger than upholding an oath."

Cressida snorted.

"*What* is so amusing?" she barked, whirling on the sorceress.

"Just the thought of those Priests doing any actual work. I've never seen the elusive 'blue cloaks' that you seem to think so fondly of." She never stopped her cursive as she eloquently stated her blunt opinion.

"I don't see how you can be so calm about this. This affects you just as much as it does everyone else. Your sanctuary is pretty full. How much longer before you have more creatures than rooms? If you know anything, you better start talking, sorceress."

A quiet sigh hushed the room. Cressida set down her fountain pen, poised expression in place, and steepled her fingers in a diamond against her lips. She looked at the witch as if for the first time, and Thea held her gaze stubbornly.

The chair scraped against the concrete as Cressida stood, idly brushing the invisible wrinkles from her sparkling gown and righting her top hat before she plucked her staff from its leaning position on the desk and strolled out of the room, calling behind her with a soft, "Follow me, then."

Chapter Eight

Medusa's Dark Magic Kiss

Thea threw a glance at Rafe, who merely shrugged one large shoulder before the two hurried out of the room. Cressida had not waited for them and was already at the waterfall, brushing the water aside, and it peeled back as if it were a fabric curtain. Thea didn't question the magic involved in that action and slipped past the stream quickly so she wouldn't end up catching the water when it came back down. Rafe's healing spell had helped assuage her tenderness from the already wet clothing scraping against her skin, but she didn't feel like getting drenched all over again.

Behind the waterfall was a large, spacious, manmade cave. The walls were rough, and the low hanging roof resembled an actual cave's ceiling with jutting and arching dips that forced Thea, and especially Rafe, to duck at certain intervals. They followed the sorceress around a bend, and Thea immediately spotted Namara and Blythe—who had somehow changed into something so...normal. Dulled breeches and a gray button-up rolled to her elbows. So used to seeing the woman in bright colors and obnoxious patterns, Thea found herself thinking the outfit was as strange on Blythe as Blythe's regular attire would be on...anyone else. She was kneeling on the ground beside a large, deep blue pool where Namara floated unconsciously. The kelpie's natural color was already returning.

Cressida stopped beside the woman, peering over Blythe's shoulder as if concerned with the creature's wellbeing. "Blythe, the demon isn't going anywhere. Why don't you go get ready for tonight? These two will watch over the kelpie."

Blythe perked up at the suggestion, burnt sienna eyes sparkling in delight. "Can I pick out your outfit for tonight too?" She jumped to her feet, practically buzzing with excitement. "Can I? Can I? *Khndrym aink'!*"

Cressida dropped her gaze down to her outfit then back up to the bouncing woman. "What's wrong with what I'm wearing now? This *is* what I was planning on wearing for later."

Blythe stopped hopping from foot to foot, a pout forming on her bright pink lips. "Cressi, you have been wearing that all day."

"I have *not* worn this all day, but even if I had been, I fail to see the problem, peacock."

"It is custom. You promised, *om keresela.*"

"All right, all right." The sorceress tossed her hands in the air in defeat, eliciting a happy squeal from the other woman. "But," she emphasized with a pointed look, "nothing too extravagant."

"*Eau, oherki!*" Blythe bounded out of the cave, and her girlish laughter echoed off the walls as she splashed through the waterfall.

"How long did it take you to understand her?" Thea questioned to the side.

The softness on the sorceress's face dried up so quickly Thea wondered if it had ever been there at all.

"It took years of tutoring, and even then, I cannot grasp the accent, which is essential because it throws entire words off. Ernimoen I feel is as equally frustrating as trying to learn Gremlic." Cressida huffed. She abruptly spun on her heel and continued down the path that wound around the pool until they reached the farthest wall. She turned her head just enough to regard the other two over her shoulder as she said, "Blythe does not know about what I am about to show you. Should she find out, you will find yourself back down here in the company of your worst nightmare. That very nightmare is down there now, contained. Depending on your behavior, that can change."

She faced the wall and lifted her staff, jabbing the stones in a series of quick taps. The rocks gave way to an open cavern where a large spiraling staircase led down into pitch blackness. It was only illuminated by flickering torch sconces attached to the rough stone walls, but they could hardly hold back the darkness threatening to swallow them up.

Cressida immediately entered, and Thea rushed to follow her. The last thing she wished for was to lose sight of the sorceress in the dark. As soon as she and Rafe crossed the threshold, the wall closed back up behind them, startling the Spellweaver. Claustrophobia was a new sensation she was not thrilled to experience.

Water droplets echoed somewhere off to the side, but she couldn't see anything more than a couple of steps in front of her. The smell of musk and pungent herbs burned her nose, and she tried unsuccessfully to snort the scent out of her nostrils. The air was thick and humid, a stark contrast from outside. Her breathing grew labored, and she held a hand to her chest to alleviate the sudden pressure. Fear prickled sharply along her arms, and the overwhelming feeling that something was going to reach a pale arm out of the darkness and snatch her up was threatening to overtake her rational mind. Her throat swallowed convulsively around a dry lump. Her nerves were still too on edge to properly —

A heavy hand rested on her shoulder. It was not enough pressure to throw off her descent, but it was enough to center her focus. She sucked in a lungful of air, and the nerves receded into the back of the bleaker parts of her mind, where they would hopefully stay a little while longer. The hand removed itself, but she could still feel the warmth from where it had been.

Thea knew when they had reached the end of their downward spiral. Eerie green light escaped the room it bloomed from, licking against the stone walls of the stairwell as if welcoming their arrival. Cressida swept inside without hesitation, but Thea was slower to follow her in.

"Do hurry up," the sorceress called, "it is the end of the world, you know."

With Rafe acting as her shadow, she slipped inside the chamber, and the first thing she noticed was the sinister lime flames casting the small dungeon in a sickening glow. However, it was what was inside those flames that caused her to pause.

Lounging against the wall like it was the most comfortable place to be was a scantily clad, blue-eyed, blonde-haired seductress eyeing Cressida as if the woman were a veritable goddess. Those eyes flicked briefly over them, and an amused smirk graced blood-red lips that practically oozed sensuality. Thea swallowed dryly. She had never been attracted to the fairer sex, but that didn't mean she couldn't appreciate someone as beautiful and alluring as the person—thing—held captive on the damp cobbled floor.

She glanced at Rafe to gauge his reaction. His eyes were intensely focused on the female, though not in the way she might have guessed. Suspicion, mistrust, and even a little disgust rolled off the Summoner. Thea was impressed, though she would have to tease him later. It was hardly the time.

Cressida couldn't have looked less impressed. "Put away the toys, Asmo, I'm here to have an adult conversation."

The seductress pouted dramatically, though there was amusement in her icy blue eyes that twinkled like the hardest of diamonds. "You're no fun, Cressi."

"Don't call me that."

"Why? You abbreviate *my* name."

The sorceress rolled her eyes skyward, though she'd get no help there. "I give power to you otherwise, you know this."

A put-out sigh from its plump lips, then a sharp gasp, "I could change into that little magicless kaleidoscope? Bet you'd let me call you Cressi then?"

"You wouldn't be able to pull off the crazed gleam in her eye. Now," she waved her hand at the creature, "show them your true form. I don't have all night."

"You're no fun," the creature repeated with a teasing smile, but in the next moment, its feminine features started to melt into sharper angles and more prominent muscles. Golden waves that swept along the damp stones receded into shoulder-length, platinum strands. Its eyes swirled into twin dark abysses, and honeyed skin that showed off luscious curves grayed out and stretched tight over a corded frame. The dress, if one could call such a thing a dress, shifted into ebony plated armor that protected the stomach, outer thighs, and shins. Skulls—which Thea noted were decidedly not human— adorned the creature's shoulders, and a leather belt slung over the exposed, now very male, hip bones. A long thin breechcloth clung from under the stomach armor and lay between his sinewy legs. It was the only thing keeping the creature modestly decent.

She felt heat rise in her cheeks as she viewed the cracks in the ceiling with sudden interest.

Then it clicked.

She gasped, snapping her attention back to the sorceress, who was now regarding her with a single raised brow. "That's a demon prince."

"Always the observant one, Spellweaver." Cressida nodded, and Thea wondered if she was imagining the hint of pride in the sorceress's tone at her realization. "However, that's not entirely correct. Actually, Asmo is a," she eyed the demon with a hair's breadth hesitation, "a *fallen* demon prince."

The demon dubbed Asmo scoffed. "First, you summon me in the dreariest of dungeons, butcher my beautiful name and whittle it down into something utterly stupid, ignore all my advances with cold disinterest, and then have the audacity to insult me." Black eyes blinked up at Thea and Rafe, and he shrugged. "Honestly, I don't know what I've done to deserve this."

Cressida smiled tightly. "Blondes aren't my type."

"Now you tell me."

"Blast it all with hellfire," Rafe griped suddenly, glaring hotly at the bickering duo. His large hands settled on his hips in exasperation. "Did I just hear you say you summoned it—" he jabbed a finger in Asmo's direction—"by yourself? And what is it even doing down here in the first place?"

The prince clucked his tongue. "Rude."

Cressida merely shrugged, her glittery dress catching the light of the jade flames. "As of right now he's being a thorn in my side."

"I didn't even ask for this!" Asmo exclaimed, though his cries went ignored.

"You did not summon a throneless one," Rafe said in finality, slicing his hand through the air.

A menacing hush fell upon the room, and the flames holding the prince in question flickered. Cressida clutched her staff in a white-knuckled grip, and the wisps of energy inside the plasma orb buzzed loudly. Thea found it hard to breathe, as if all the air was replaced with something thicker. Her fingers itched behind her to grab at her sickle but froze when she felt nothing was strapped to her back. She threw her gaze to Rafe who held the woman's intimidating stare. Thea needed to diffuse the situation before they found themselves in another battle.

"Why couldn't she summon the prince by herself?" They both knew Cressida was strong. She was strong enough to rival the power of a horde of Summoners.

Rafe never dropped his glower, though he sounded much more resigned when he answered her. "It takes a group of Summoners to perform even a basic summoning. Not only do you have to be in control of your own power, but you have to control everyone else's powers at the same time. It's why the same Summoners are not used in the next ceremony: it drains them mentally, physically, and magically."

Okay, not helping her understand any better.

"What's a basic summoning?"

He sighed, and his body relaxed its confrontational pose. Cressida also seemed to reign herself in. The heaviness in the air lightened, and the pressure on Thea's chest lifted. "A Hunter's power is gauged, and from there we are able to detect if the summoning will be basic or more complex. We have to control the creature the Hunter pulls from Hell, and a basic summoning is when a first-tier creature is pulled—which is often the case. To pull something from the second tier is obviously much more dangerous and requires total concentration. To pull something from the third tier is unheard of, and to pull something with more will power than the tether can control is, simply put, not possible."

"I did have help in summoning this demon," Cressida assured, "though make no mistake, Summoner, I did summon him alone."

"I'm not following."

"I'm not surprised. You have not witnessed a tenth of the power I wield, and yet even I needed assistance in bringing him here."

"Is it the same help that enables you to fluctuate your power?" Thea wondered curiously, but her question obviously wasn't going to get a response by the way Cressida's lips thinned. Trying another route, she found herself demanding, "If you're so powerful, why don't you eradicate the hellhound and soul eater yourself? Why leave them out there and let them continue killing and hurting other beings?"

If Cressida would join forces with the Coven, if she could control a demon prince, then Thea's brethren wouldn't have to die. Hundreds of lives could be saved. Thousands more if she counted all the creatures and animals that would be spared.

Hope swelled in her chest—a hope that died when the sorceress arched one perfect eyebrow and cast a dubious glance at her captive. "What say you, Asmo? Should I help aid in their little predicament?"

Asmo shrugged, a wolfish grin accompanying the amusement that could somehow be found in his soulless eyes. "I don't know," he hummed while a manic grin unfurled, showing off dangerous canines. "They do seem a bit ungrateful for all the trouble you went through in gifting them with my stunning presence."

Cressida made a sound of agreement. "You're right, they are a bit crass."

Thea huffed. "Cressida—"

"Tell you what," the sorceress interrupted, "you help me, and I will help you in return."

Rafe latched onto her proposal. "What do you need help with? And how will you help us?"

"Before I can help you, I must have your assistance first, otherwise even I will not be able to control Asmo from doing whatever he pleases once this barrier is down. We have an agreement, but..." She left the statement to hang with another shrug.

"What do we need to do?" Thea questioned quietly. She was almost afraid to know the answer. What could the most powerful woman outside of the Council possibly need help with? If she could summon a demon prince, what was there left that she couldn't do?

"I need you to tether me to him."

Thea felt her jaw drop. Tether her, an incredibly powerful sorceress, with an incredibly powerful demon prince? Was she mad? The chaos that could ensue! The whole world could burn down at their fingertips! Demon princes, even fallen ones, possessed too much willpower to control fully. One would have to channel their entire focus on manipulating the creature to their will, but once that person lost focus or fell asleep there was nothing stopping the demon from slitting their owner's throat in the middle of the night, thus severing the bond and freeing themselves to do whatever they pleased. The world would be in flames by nightfall!

Thankfully, Rafe beat her to the punch with his unbending refusal. "Absolutely not. Do you know how many laws we would be breaking? We cannot tether a non-Coven member with a demon prince. You are asking the impossible of us. We would have to procure a tethering stone—something that hasn't been seen in years, except for on the Dark Market, considering a summoning stone summons *and* tethers, rendering tethering stones useless. The only people that would need a tethering stone would be those outside the Coven who want to bind themselves to a powerful creature. It's why the law was passed banning them in the first place.

"Then, there's the actual tethering spell I would have to perform, also not common and extremely difficult to find. I should also add that I've never performed the spell before, but let's ignore that fact because what you're asking me to do would be considered black magic. I couldn't do it, and furthermore, it would show up in HQ's viewing room, and Coven members would come flooding your doorstep. You would have to perform the spell, and I would have to neutralize the magic as best I could. Even then it would still ping on the Coven's map. If we managed to pull this off and break every law we've sworn never to break, we would still be unleashing Hell, literally, on Raen." He sliced his hand through the air once again, and his voice boomed throughout the small chamber. "*No.*"

The silence that followed was deafening. Asmo whistled loudly, and a chuckle escaped him. Both of Cressida's brows were raised so high Thea thought they would disappear into her bangs.

"Wow. I never expected the big bad Summoner to throw such a hissy fit." She and the demon prince shared a look of understanding. Then, "It's almost like he thinks...I was giving him a choice."

A snap echoed off the chamber walls, and the room plunged into darkness.

Thea realized all too soon what had happened. She gasped and jumped back but couldn't grab the amulet around her neck fast enough before something was slamming into her and sending her flying into the wall behind her. Her head smacked off the cobblestones, pain blossomed along the back of her skull, and her head began to swim.

Green flames erupted an inch away from her, and she found herself staring up into the blackest, oldest eyes she'd ever seen. In that moment, she remembered Namara's words. The demon prince's eyes were chasms—so deep they lured you in unwillingly, pulling you into your death even as you screamed at yourself to run. Hell was truly captured in the bottomless pits.

Then they were gone. Something pulled away from her, and she realized belatedly that something was Rafe. He had been the one who shoved her into the wall and shielded her with his body. She'd have to thank him for that later, even though that move would have both gotten them killed. She was also going to need another healing spell to fix the knot she could already feel growing on the back of her head.

She watched the demon prince slink away to the wall he'd originally been lounging against, the green flames following him. Her blood ran cold as she realized he'd been able to move throughout the chamber the entire time. Rafe seemed to realize this too, she noticed, and he was looking much paler than he had before.

"Now listen and listen well, Spellweaver, since you seem to be the only one here with any sort of sense. I'm not asking you to tether me, I'm telling you to. In exchange for this, Asmo will eviscerate any escapee you should wish to have annihilated until I feel I've upheld my end of the bargain. But," her voice dropped into a soft lull, and with the change came the feelings of unease creeping into Thea's soul, "if you should continue to refuse my offer, well then, I have no use for Asmo anymore. I'll have to set him free—for there is, after all, no one who knows how to de-summon a demon once it's here." She ended her speech with a simple shrug as if she wasn't just contemplating the initiation of the end of the world.

All the hopelessness and gravity of the situation finally caught up to Thea, and she ended up asking the age-old question everyone eventually asked the villain. "Why are you doing this?" She took a step toward the sorceress with the unspoken plea to stop this madness. "Don't you care about the damage he'll inflict upon the world?" She had to know the demon wouldn't stop at mere trickery. He wasn't an imp. He was one of the vilest, most cunning, monstrous creatures of them all, and he wrapped up his evil in charming smiles and quaint conversations. There was no telling how many souls he'd tortured, how many creatures below him he'd sent out to wage war on humans, how many families he'd torn apart by possessing a daughter or son, or how many civilizations he had a hand in collapsing. He'd had thousands of years to manipulate, force, threaten, break, and ravage. Unleashing him onto the world would be catastrophic, and yet what she was asking for to prevent all of that from happening could very well be worse.

The sorceress didn't seem surprised by the question. In fact, she smiled, and it was an actual smile. Not a maniacal grin, not an arrogant smirk, but a smile that told the tale of sorrow so deep Thea would never be able to fully understand. Cressida wasn't even looking at her anymore. Her eyes were cast away, glassy and far off, and for a long moment she didn't speak, and Thea was beginning to wonder if she'd get an answer out of her. The quiet pause in the dungeon continued, but it was not the type of silence that came with bated breath and anticipation, nor was it awkward or painfully unbearable. It complimented the sad smile and wrapped around the sorceress in a blanket of desolation.

"I never did care for this world. Only one thing has ever shown me any sort of kindness," she finally whispered. Her eyes softened, matching the colors of the tender flames that now fluttered delicately low on the floor. For a moment, she looked years younger. Then she shook herself and straightened her spine, and the image shattered. "As for the why of this all, it's very simple. I'm dying."

"What?" Dying? Where had that come from? She looked as healthy as a habrok.

"I'm sure you've heard of it before. It's quite rare, but everyone born with magic in their veins knows of Medusa's Kiss."

Thea inhaled sharply. Yes, she did know about Medusa's Kiss. Alchemists, researchers, and magic wielders had come together for decades to find a cure for the disease, but every treatment option failed, and every experiment yielded inconclusive results. The disease slowly, over the course of years depending on how much power one had, ate away at a person's magic while their body internally shut down. Rigor mortis would set in hours before their death, turning them to "stone" until they passed away. It is said to be a very painful and excruciating death.

"I don't need your pity. I don't actually plan on dying."

That certainly caught both Coven members' attention. "Medusa's Kiss in incurable," Thea stated flatly. That was what made the disease so widely known.

"Yes, yes, I'm well aware that there is no cure for it." Cressida waved those concerns away as if she'd heard them all too many times before.

"Then...?" Thea was lost, and she did not enjoy the feeling. The sorceress was throwing too many new experiences her way, and she hadn't liked one yet. She prompted the sorceress silently with her gaze alone.

"Tell me this, Spellweaver, if you were suddenly told you had a fixed amount of time left to live, would you resign yourself to your fate, or would you find any method there was to survive?"

The answer was obvious enough, but Thea still wasn't following where the sorceress was going. Cressida must have read her confusion, for she continued.

She motioned with her hand to help the witch along. "Would you search only in the white pages of the book for the answers, or would you venture into the...darker chapters?"

It was easy enough to connect the dots from there, and Thea gaped at the woman as if she'd suddenly sprouted a second head. "You used black magic." She couldn't believe she'd never realized it before. "That's why you can just wave your hand around without an incantation—you cut out the middleman. You can create something basically from nothing, but...you're still sane?" How was that possible? Sure, Cressida was incredibly powerful, but how much of that power was actually hers? Had she always been powerful, and how much more powerful was she before Medusa's Kiss had caught her in its deathly web?

Cressida nodded, but something else flickered in her gem-like irises. Before Thea could discern what it was, it was gone. "Some wouldn't think so, but, for the most part, I am still of sound mind. Every day is a battle, I can assure you of that. It is why time is so very important, but until you showed up on my doorstep, I hadn't had much hope in the outcome. Yesterday, when I sent you away, was the day I summoned Asmo. And I had my own deflectors in place." She glanced at Rafe before continuing. "I used dark objects for that, and they sent the black magic to another location. Like I said before, you Coven members are not as smart as you'd like to think you are. Anyway, I knew you would be back, but then you had to run off and try and prove yourself. I figured if you ended up killing yourself, you weren't as promising as I'd hoped you'd be."

It was strange hearing Cressida, the sorceress who seemed to hate everyone that wasn't Blythe, give her praise, especially considering she'd just gotten done threatening the two, but aside from the backhanded compliment, something she'd said had Thea wondering.

"Summoning him wasn't the first time you used black magic."

Cressida chuckled, and the sound was husky and warm, and it seemed to surprise everyone in the room, including the sorceress. She cleared her throat. "No, I've dipped my hands in the forbidden jar too many times to count. They're stained black at this point. I've always been able to suppress the cravings after I dabbled. I never once experienced the urges to go back to practicing in the dark arts, not until that disease started sucking the life out of my magic."

At that moment, Thea acquired new-found respect for the woman. She didn't like the sorceress, and she absolutely despised being backed into a corner, but to live every day with less strength than you had the day before, while simultaneously fighting back the addiction of a drug that promised the world—she was speechless.

"We're getting off subject," Cressida coughed, earning a grunt from Rafe and snicker from the prince. "I learned while researching through black magic that, while there is no cure for Medusa's Kiss, there is a way to get rid of it."

"A way that involves a fallen demon prince?" Rafe sneered, casting a venomous glare at the creature. It childishly stuck its tongue out.

"In order to explain the reasoning for summoning the prince, I must first explain the properties of Medusa's Kiss. The disease is not actually attached to its victim's magic, but rather the victim itself. If it were simply attached to the magic, the host wouldn't die when the magic was depleted. However, if the magic was suddenly no longer there, the disease would have nothing to feed itself, and would thus go about finding another host."

Rafe, the ever-suspicious, demanded, "What if it jumps onto one of us?"

To which Cressida scoffed so hard Thea wondered how she didn't choke. "Preposterous. Diseases like this don't *jump*. Honestly, how have you obtained second-ranking within the Coven when you're so incredibly ignorant? It concerns me if the rest of you are like this, it really does."

The Summoner growled, but before he could spit out another nasty rebuttal, Thea was shoving him aside with a dozen questions. "How do you know it doesn't jump? Does it say so in that textbook you were reading? Where does it go if it doesn't attach itself to someone close by?"

Cressida clamped her fingers and thumb together in a shushing gesture. "Enough, enough, Spellweaver, I will tell you everything to your heart's content later, but for now trust my word that you or your Summoner friend will not catch the disease."

"Like we trust your word," Rafe quipped, earning a glare from both women in the room. Surprise and then betrayal flashed across his face upon registering the annoyed glower coming from Thea.

"Anyway," she rolled her eyes at his theatrics, "you said something about the magic no longer being there. How would that happen? Are you talking about disguising your magic?"

The sorceress's lips twisted into a frown. "I'm afraid it's much more severe than that." She sighed, her rigid shoulders drooped, and as if all her strength left her, she slumped against the wall.

Alarm flooded Thea, and she stepped forward to aid the woman, but Cressida waved her away. "The only way to be rid of the curse is to transfer my magic, but the problem with that is that magic was never meant to be transferred in the first place. Magic is living, breathing, just as you and I. It carries intellectual properties. When magic is transferred once, it adapts, changes, so that it cannot be transferred again. Medusa's Kiss, because it is not attached to the magic, does not follow it when transferred." She wiped the sweat from her forehead and licked her lips, and Thea wondered if this was the effects of the disease, or if the black magic urges were growing stronger.

"How do you transfer your magic?" she hedged. Worry began to gnaw at her. What would a sorceress as powerful as Cressida be like if she were drunk on black magic? She nearly shuddered at the thought.

"With a black magic spell, and because it is a black magic spell, I will have to be the one to perform it. It requires an immense amount of power."

"Hence why you need to be tethered to the demon prince," Thea concluded. All the pieces of the puzzle were starting to fit together. However, one final piece had yet to reveal itself. "How are you going to get him to comply? He has too much willpower to bend for you, tethered or not."

"Asmo has agreed to be tethered to me, which will boost my power enough to perform the spell, and when the magic is transferred, so too will the tether be transferred. In exchange for this, he will be allowed to return to Hell, where he will regain his throne with the surge in power he gains from tethering himself to my magic."

If Thea mulled over everything, the entire plan was extremely well thought out. Medusa's Kiss would have nothing to devour, which would cause it to move on, leaving Cressida alive, and because she would then be magicless, she wouldn't eventually fall victim to black magic. She got what she wanted, and the throneless one got what he wanted.

"Where would you transfer your magic?" Surely, someplace where no one could aimlessly come across it.

A smile, just like the one before, surfaced. Sad, with an obscure gaze, that transformed the strict, cold sorceress into an exhausted young woman who just wanted to live. "You cannot transfer magic where magic is already present." Her throat constricted her words, turning them hoarse. She again swiped at the sweat beading on her temple. "Magic is like a fingerprint. Everyone's is basically the same, yet completely different and unique. Magic won't bind to other magic. I would have to transfer it to something that didn't already have magic. Something…or someone."

Thea gasped. Everything clicked. "Blythe…"

Cressida gave a tiny, imperceptible nod. "When she showed up at my doorstep all those years ago, I immediately wanted to turn her away. What could I, someone who ran a shelter for magic-based creatures, do with someone who couldn't even practice? I did turn her away, in fact, but she kept coming back. Every. Day. It wasn't until one time she showed up with a black eye that I invited her in." Anger radiated off Cressida as she recalled the incident. Her voice came out deceptively soft, dangerous as she said, "People like to pretend the magicless are treated fairly and just like everyone else. Not always. It's frowned upon to discriminate against them for being simply what they are, but it still happens. So, I agreed to hire her, and the little chit actually refused *me*. She said she didn't need to be pitied and then promptly left. Gone like a brightly colored storm. The next day she was back, as if nothing ever happened, and proceeded to go about explaining all the ways she could actually help my sanctuary. I listened for once. She knew more about magic than most people who possess it."

Her eyes regained their strength, and Thea could see the stubborn resolve from across the dungeon. "If I could make her life better—if I could make her happy just by doing this one thing, then I will feel like my life has amounted to something. So," she took a large, shuddering breath, and straightened her shoulders. When she met Thea and Rafe's gaze, her eyes were sharp, and the sorceress that fiercely protected the sanctuary was back. "Will you help me?"

Thea opened her mouth to accept, "We—"

"We'll accept your proposal."

"What?" She whirled on the Summoner. She hadn't expected him to jump on board with the idea of going behind the Coven's back so easily.

He didn't bother meeting her bewildered gaze, too focused on the other woman. "Don't make us regret our decision."

Cressida's gaze hardened. "I never planned on it. In the meantime, you best report to your precious Coven. I don't care what you tell them, but do not, by any means, mention this conversation to anyone outside these walls. Is that clear?"

"As a crystal ball." He nodded. As Thea glanced back and forth between the two, she realized she and him had just sealed a deal with someone that could potentially be worse than the devil himself, and that the exchange might just be worse than giving up a soul or two.

Chapter Nine

Crispy Bats, Coffee Shops, and Cracked Crystal Balls

A blizzard was coming down from the northern mountains, and already the shop owners were closing up in preparation for the oncoming storm. Tents were packed away, fresh produce was getting boxed up, and trinkets and knickknacks from the neighboring districts were carted back to where they came from. The only businesses rich enough to afford buildings to house their merchandise were open, and business was definitely booming. Thea witnessed it all in bland disinterest.

It happened every year—winter would come, snow would be on and off throughout the months, but at the end of the season a huge blizzard would blow down from the north and blanket the entire city in varying inches of snow. Cleansers would be called out almost more so than the Hunters, but the Hunters would have their fair share of work cut out for them, too. As part of the lowest rank in the Coven, they got handed all the dirty jobs. Thea didn't miss it.

She watched the citizens of Tolvade dip off the ice-slicked sidewalks and into their cottages and townhomes, burlap sacks full of groceries weighing down their arms. The wind had picked up that morning and now howled through the quickly deserting streets. It caught the cloak hanging from her shoulders and tossed it around, flapping loudly in the air.

She pushed her black face mask higher onto the bridge of her nose with thick gloved fingers. Donned in extra layers and equipped with a warming spell, the chill didn't bother her. Rather, it helped to clear her head after the morning she'd somehow survived.

She had reported to the High Priest Council bright and early. Rafe had accompanied her to file his own report, and low and behold, the Council already knew about the mysterious release of demons. Their calm demeanors had only caused anxiety to spring forward and look at the Council in a whole new light. Why hadn't they told anybody? They went on to inform her of the passing law, temporary until the "situation is resolved" that each Coven member be assigned an extra partner. A buddy system, in layman's terms, as if a creature from Hell wasn't enough.

Though, remembering the carnage from the abandoned village had her stomach souring and chills racing down her spine. She blamed it on the cold despite the thicker layers she'd bundled up in that morning. She was spared the flashbacks when her crystal ball had begun buzzing in her pocket on the walk back to her duplex. Rafe had tagged along with her and paused by her side while she answered the call. He provided magnificent shelter from the wind.

Blythe filled the glass's surface, extremely close up and already making Thea severely uncomfortable. Her eyes were painted in a vibrant burnt orange, lined with ruby red, and her lips were glossed over with a gold tint. Her skin practically glowed roan in the light, and her freckles faintly dusted over her high cheekbones. It was obvious she wasn't the one placing the call—being magicless and all—but she went on to inform Thea that Namara had woken during the night.

"I'm going to head to the sanctuary and see her," Thea announced after the call had ended. Rafe and Mokana both stopped in their tracks and turned back to face the Spellweaver, causing Thea to nearly run into them.

"What?" They both said in unison, surprise evident in their expressions.

Thea shrugged, not seeing the big deal in her statement. "I have to see her. Imagine if it was Mokana." She eyed Rafe knowingly before pushing past the two and continued on her way with her new destination in mind.

"What about the Dark Market run?" Rafe caught up to her easily with his longer legs, striding beside her on the sidewalk.

Thea chewed her lip. Giving up one of their opportunities to procure a tethering stone to see Namara was not a choice to be made lightly. "You have your regular squad, right?" Rafe had told her stories about the squad that he went with to the Dark Market, and she knew that it was the same group of people every time. He explained only once before that it was set up like that to build trust with the other Summoners, and trust was severely needed when treading into dangerous waters such as the Dark Market.

"Of course. The only thing that's changed is the day of the raid, which is supposed to start in the next two hours." He quickly glanced at the sun to note its placement in the sky and frowned. "Maybe less than that."

"I think it would be too suspicious if I tagged along with you, especially since I've never been to the Dark Market before. Besides, what happens if we find a tethering stone? We can't just take it in the presence of your squad members."

"Let me worry about that, and it won't be suspicious with the new law in place," Rafe stated, but Thea was already shaking her head.

Mokana piped up behind them. "If Thea's not going can I come with her to see Namara?"

The Summoner sighed and glanced over his shoulder with an apologetic look. "I know you want to see her, Moka, but you know you have to be guarding the safe-house while I'm on the other side of the portal. Besides," he added quickly when the rusalka began to pout, "you don't want to be there when Namara starts lecturing her."

Thea cringed. "Yeah, well, I have a few choice words I'd like to say to—" she bit her tongue. Rafe and Mokana still didn't know about what caused Namara to nearly die in the first place. "Never mind," she said in response to their questioning stares.

She and Rafe parted ways after that, against the Summoner's wishes, but only with the promise that they would meet up later that night. She took off as quickly as her cold limbs could carry her, though when she arrived at Srbeveara, she'd almost wished she'd taken her time.

Blythe was waiting with both sanctuary doors open. She was dressed in a burnt orange frock that came up just under her chin with an attached cape that fell to the ground and brushed against the stone flooring. The color on the inside of the cape was a shimmering turquoise with gold, circular patterns. Her hair was sectioned down the middle and styled into the shape of ram's horns, bejeweled in unpolished ruby and turquoise stones. She seemed mesmerized by something and kept sticking her bare foot, decked out in gold bangles and a ruby anklet, in and out of the doorway.

When she didn't notice Thea's arrival right away, the Spellweaver cleared her throat loudly. Blythe's head jerked up, bestowing her sparkling chestnut gaze on her visitor.

"Look at this!" she chirped excitedly and grabbed onto Thea's arm and jerked her forward. Immediately, Thea was engulfed in Srbeveara's warmth. Just as abruptly, she was pushed back out into the cold. This repeated several times before Thea regained control of her arm with an exasperated huff.

"Do you mind telling me what you're doing?"

"You don't notice?" Blythe queried innocently, unperturbed by her unrefined behavior. She stuck her gold-tipped fingers in and out of the doorway quickly.

Oh. "You mean the containment spell?" Containment spells were used for many things, though they were popular in keeping heat within a certain area. They tended to be pricey but were common enough in businesses and well-off homes. Srbeveara appeared to be no different.

"*Zermeneio i.* Amazing." She continued to dip her hand in and out of the spell's limits a few more times before it registered why a Coven member was even on her doorstep. She jolted back and clapped her hands to her bronzed cheeks. "*Ú,* my apologies! You must be here to see your friend! Come, come!"

Once again, Thea was grabbed by the wrist and yanked inside where the doors slammed shut behind her and echoed off the walls. Without a moment's hesitation, Blythe plunged through the waterfall with the Spellweaver in tow. The eccentric woman gave an elated cheer while Thea was left sputtering and blinking water out of her eyes.

"It's about time you got here," Namara griped somewhere off to the side, though Thea was too busy wiping her face dry to see exactly where.

"First of all," she snapped angrily when she could finally see clearly, and leveled the kelpie with a scathing glare, "do *not* cut an attitude with me when you're the one who put yourself in danger."

The caves hadn't changed since yesterday, not that she expected them to, but one never knew what to expect at the sanctuary. The manmade pool took up a large section of the main cavern, and there were branching pathways that twisted and disappeared around jutting cave walls. She wondered where they led and how far they went, and if they were currently underground or if this was the creation of the sorceress manipulating the fabric of the natural world.

Her eyes drifted back to Namara, who was submerged in the water up to her shoulders. The kelpie's twinkling black eyes narrowed from her spot in the large pool.

"Says the one who went charging headfirst into a brawl with not one, but *two*, demons from Hell! When have you *ever* rushed into something without a plan?"

Blythe, who had been standing idly by the whole time, shrunk in on herself in the charged atmosphere. "I'll just go…make everyone some tea," and promptly fled the caves. Namara stared after her retreating back in confusion.

"The kitchen is around that bend," she commented, pointing a dripping finger in the direction of the opposite way Cressida had led Thea and Rafe the day before.

The Spellweaver pivoted in her spot and saw the bend in the roughly textured cave walls. Curiosity nagging her, she ventured closer until she could peer around into a massive enclosed kitchen.

"Wait, wait, wait, are you telling me she has to walk through the waterfall every time she needs to eat or cook something?" Thea wrinkled her nose at the massive design flaw, regardless if it was a gorgeous, rustic kitchen.

A massive hearth took up the entire wall, and inside a blazing fire was steadily crackling under a cast-iron cauldron with some type of meaty stew Thea could smell from where she stood. Beside it was a large, elegantly designed, wood-burning stove, though it was cold at the moment. The sink bowed out from the wall, big enough for a person to sit in. Shelves that had been carved into the wall held everything from plantains and jarred seasonings to slabs of dried meat and unsliced loaves of bread. Barrels lined the wall under the shelves full of wheat stocks and a variety of dehydrated beans and rice.

Namara snorted behind her. "No, that waterfall is spelled to open up whenever she asks it to. She just chooses to run through it. Now, if you're done admiring the kitchen, I'd like us to get back to our conversation."

Thea sucked her teeth in annoyance and eyed her soaking clothes in disdain before she faced her moody pet. Namara had propped her elbows up on the edge of the pool and rested her chin in her palms, eyes flashing her irritation. Thea was happy to see that the kelpie's color had started to darken into its natural green shade, though it hadn't fully returned yet. She had obviously recovered enough to voice her displeasure in her master so vehemently though.

She sighed and stated reluctantly, "I'm sorry. I shouldn't have done what I did. I'm not just saying that either," she added when her pet went to open her mouth. Namara clicked her jaw shut and her tense shoulders relaxed as the anger faded. The kelpie always forgave easily, regardless of the transgression, but only if the other party was sincere in their apologies. She was no pushover.

Thea continued with a cheeky smirk, "I even apologized to Rafe without any prompting." She watched her pet's eyes light up with mischievousness.

"Oh, really?" Namara raised an eyebrow in mock disbelief.

Thea rolled her eyes. "Yes, really. I can admit when I mess up." She toed off her boots and peeled off her drying socks before she sat down on the ledge and dipped her feet into the warmth of the healing waters.

Her pet smiled and swirled a finger around the ripples created by Thea swishing her feet back and forth. "That *was* a really big mess up."

Thea scowled and kicked water at the demoness. "Like you're one to talk. Do you have any idea how scared..." she heard her voice rising, bouncing off the cavern walls loudly, so she took a large breath to calm herself before another fight could start between them. She blew it out slowly, and caught Namara's gaze and held it as she stated softly, "I was so afraid I was going to lose you. Our bond was so faint. You weren't even green anymore—you were drying up right in front of me," she paused, watching the ripples she made spread out over the surface of the water, then, "Did you know your hair color is actually really close to mine when dry?"

"How horrible," Namara scrunched up her nose, earning another wave splashed her way. Silence descended upon them with only the sound of water dripping somewhere off in the distance.

"Just don't do it again," Thea said quietly after a short while.

Namara hummed a resigned sound. She watched the ever-constant stream of the waterfall and nodded slowly. "I won't if you don't go running off without a proper plan next time. My sole purpose—my entire existence now revolves around protecting you, and the fear you felt when I was dying was the same fear I felt when we were in the midst of battle."

Thea felt her heart squeeze in her chest. She'd never forget that feeling of almost losing Namara. Words couldn't describe it—the sheer hopelessness, the fear, the panic, the anger, and frustration. So, she, too, nodded and agreed to the kelpie's request. "Deal."

"So," her pet perked up suddenly, startling the Spellweaver. "What'd I miss?" Namara settled her crossed arms on the pool's ledge and got comfy.

Thea looked over her quizzically, a brow raised in confusion. "What are you talking about?"

"Drop the act, Thea. You were tense when you came in here, and it wasn't from our impending confrontation."

The second eyebrow joined the first, disappearing into Thea's bangs in her surprise. "I've been rubbing off on you if you're using two big words in a single sentence."

Namara refused to take the bait and instead stared at her master unblinkingly.

Banish a banshee, she didn't want to have to tell her so soon. She felt her shoulders slumping and sighed aloud. "I was going to tell you," she assured. *I just wanted a little more time.*

"This doesn't sound good."

"That's probably because I may or may not have made a deal with a fallen demon prince that Cressida has locked away in a dungeon." She pointed down the pathway that led to the hidden doorway for emphasis.

Silence filled the cave, heavy and thick. Thea waited with her breath held, watching her pet struggle with the thoughts that must be a tangled mess in her head. The kelpie's jaw slackened before snapping shut, only to hang loose a moment later.

Thea took the silence as her chance and began telling her from the beginning what had transpired while Namara had been comatose. She'd barely gotten done with her retelling before the demoness exploded.

"YOU WHAT?"

Thea flinched at the shrill trilling noise that bounced around the cavern and caused her ears to ring. She opened her mouth to explain, but the kelpie was not having any of it.

"I'm out cold for one day, *one*, and you not only lie to the Council, but you go off and make deals with a shady sorceress and a demon prince, telling them you'll go running off *without a proper plan* to the Dark Market, all so you can find a tethering stone for a black magic spell that will unleash a power on the world that it has never seen before! You don't go tethering black magic sorceresses to *double-dipping candle-sticking* demon princes unless you're trying to bring about the end of the world! You signed up to save it! Now you're leading it to its demise!"

Thea surged to her feet, hurling expletives left and right. "Is that what you think?" she exclaimed. "That I'm willingly doing this? That I wasn't backed into a corner by a demon from Hell's most dangerous level? She's dying, Namara! You think that woman cares about what happens to the world after she dies? I *am* trying to save this world, but if that means going behind the Coven's back to do so, then I'll gladly do it! Because if I refuse, what's stopping Cressida from saying "screw everything" and releasing the throneless one on the city? He may have lost his throne but fallen princes don't lose all their followers. He'll have droves of demons destroying the city by nightfall, and if I can prevent that then I will do anything to make sure it doesn't happen!"

"How can you be so sure he won't do that anyway?"

"I don't!" Thea screamed, and the silence that followed after her statement was more resounding than the screaming had been. "I don't," she repeated, quieter this time, and the gravity of the day prior was taking its toll on her all over again. "But I do know the world has a better chance of surviving if he draws power from Cressida's magic and reclaims his throne and never comes up to the surface because he'll be too busy running his portion of Hell."

"And I'm just supposed to sit here and wait while you go off risking your life again and again?" Namara growled lowly, but the focus of her frustration had shifted onto the situation itself rather than her wayward owner. She spun away from Thea and smacked the surface of the water angrily.

Thea felt that familiar squeezing in her chest again and quietly sat back down over the ledge. "I can't wait around for you to heal. But that doesn't mean I'm going in on this alone." She was quick to assure her tense pet and snagged a thick lock of wet hair when Namara still refused to look at her. She yanked the creature backward and locked her legs over Namara's chest in a vice-like hug from behind.

"This isn't the first time we've been separated because you couldn't come with me on a mission," she reminded.

Namara exhaled through her nose in annoyance. "It doesn't make me feel any better considering you're going up against feral demons," she uttered, though the muscles in her shoulders and back relaxed slightly.

"Well, it should, because like I said I'm not going in on this alone. Rafe and Mokana will be with me—Coven ordered a buddy system in place until all the demons are either eradicated or confined."

At that, the kelpie relaxed completely. "As long as he'll be there watching over you. I trust him."

"Thanks," Thea snorted and rolled her eyes playfully, even though Namara couldn't see her. "You should trust me more, you know."

"Shut it. I could drown you right now and not feel guilty right away."

Thea hid her smile in the kelpie's hair and let her have the last word.

She left Srbeveara before either of them could become more emotional, but not before she was corralled into a bone-crushing, wet hug that left her soggy all over again and freezing when she stepped outside. The stinging winds had stolen her breath, and she hadn't managed to get it back the entire trek into the city—on foot, because Namara was still sanctuary bound, and teleportation spells were too expensive to perform on a daily basis.

As Thea continued aimlessly walking down the sidewalk in order to kill time before she met up with Rafe, she remembered the pointed look Cressida had cast her before she'd left the sanctuary. It was subtle, and anyone on the outside would have seen it as no more than a passing glance, but Cressida didn't do "passing glances." She had turned her back on the Spellweaver to catch the tail end of Blythe's incessant blatherings of sand wyverns in the deserts she once lived in, dismissing Thea altogether.

Right. Find a tethering stone before a fallen demon prince descends upon the city. No pressure. Where was she supposed to start looking, anyway? There weren't any more Dark Market assignments to be handed out, and if there were they were months in advance. Her only hope was to use the new buddy system to her advantage and come with Rafe on his next prescheduled raid. How else was she going to get—

"Aye, you."

Thea jerked to a stop and swung around where the nasally, heavily accented voice had come from, hand clutching one of the small daggers in her belt.

Oh, banish a banshee, no.

The most infamous imp with a reputation that preceded his short, hip-high stature stood merely steps away from her. Leslie Templeton. Everyone in the Coven knew Leslie, the imp with the most arrests, most citations, and who held the record for the highest volume of call-in complaints within the entire imp community.

"You wanna buy a sundial?" He tilted his head to the side in invitation and pulled back one side of his rugged, black trench coat that dragged the ground as he walked, revealing several rows of pockets lined with merchandise. Inside, sundials that looked like they were made of the cheapest material stuck awkwardly out of the pockets, along with cloudy and chipped crystal balls, and powders that appeared to be sawdust or crushed seasonings. She wrinkled her nose. He smelled verily of brimstone and cumin.

Thea narrowed her eyes in suspicion. The imp narrowed its own in return. She could only guess Leslie had spotted her silver insignia and realized who she was, though, with eyes that were inked entirely in blackness, there was no telling exactly what he was focusing on. A frown twisted his gnarled features.

"You wit tha Coven?"

"Maybe."

This was wrong. She should just arrest the imp for whatever he's done and move on. However, she refrained from questioning him when a dangerous thought nagged at her conscious.

"Then maybe I ain't got business wit you." Leslie's large pointed ears twitched, and he turned away, his tail peeking out from under his coat to swish angrily behind him.

Now or never. "Not even if I'm trying to find something?"

The imp was in her personal space so fast Thea had to steel herself from stumbling back a couple of steps.

"Well, in that case, you've come to the right imp. Whatcha lookin' for? I gotcha wands, need a wand? No? You don't need 'em? You don't need 'em. You know what you need? A new crystal ball." He dove a stubby, weathered hand into his trench coat and rooted around until he apparently found what he was looking for. He whipped out an older model crystal ball, chipped and bubbled in some spots. "Oh yeah, gotta make those calls. Need a Grade A crystal ball from ole Leslie — Leslie'll take care o' ya. A Grade A crystal ball for a Grade A Coven member, eh? Eh?" He winked.

"It's cracked."

Leslie blinked. "That's a hair."

Thea crossed her arms. "Pick it off."

The imp eyed the crystal ball, slid his gaze back to her, then back to the orb again, before chucking it over his shoulder. It clattered behind him, rolling into the mouth of the alleyway. "You don't need that. Who needs a crystal ball? Not you. You know what you need —"

"Do you have a tethering stone?"

Leslie threw his hands up in the air and stepped back. "Wow, really? You think just 'cause I look like some shady merchant, I gotta be connected to the Dark Market like that? Really? I am offended."

Thea's hard expression faltered. "Oh, come on, I didn't mean —"

"Nah, nah, s'cool. You think I ain't used to the stereotypes? Is it because I'm an imp? It's because I'm an imp, ain't it?" The imp sniffed, looking away with the most dejected expression he could muster. He peeked up at her before shifting his gaze back down to the dirty snow at his large feet.

Thea sighed loudly up at the sky. One of these days she was going to stop putting her foot in her mouth. "Look, I'm sorry, Leslie. It was wrong of me to assume you knew anything. I did not mean to...stereotype you." She cleared her throat and looked away, never having been good at damage control.

Leslie's chipper attitude was back with a broad smile, sharp teeth gleaming in the street light's faint glow under the darkening gray sky. "Eh, fogetta 'bout it. Do I look like the type o' guy to let somethin' like that get unda my skin? Thick as nails, baby, thick as nails. 'Sides, I like you. You seem like you got it goin' on, so I'mma let you in on a little secret. I know this guy who might be able ta help ya. I'm all about connections, baby. I run this street."

The sound of a window opening up from above snagged Thea's attention. She turned to the alley between the two run-down townhomes and watched as another imp, affectionately referred to as Ma in the community, poked her head out. Her white, neatly braided pigtails stuck straight up into the air, tied with ruby red ribbons and surrounding her smaller, less pronounced horns. She grinned widely and waved. The large, golden hoop earrings jangled in her pronounced ears while the gaudy rings on her fingers glinted and sparkled in the artificial light spilling from her kitchen. Thea also noticed the well-put-together look the female imp wore: a black, high-waisted dress with white polka dots, lined in white fringe with capped shoulders. Beads adorned her neck, a small row of red above a larger row of white.

"I thought I heard someone out here that wasn't my Leslie!" she called in the same heavily accented voice as her son, though hers was much higher in pitch. "My, my, if it isn't my Thea baby! How you been, darlin'? You should come up for dinner! I made Leslie's favorite! Spaghetti with extra crispy bat wings!"

Thea schooled her features from showing her sudden urge to vomit. Only once had she decided to be polite and come up for dinner, and it had decidedly been the last time. Nearly gagging at the memory, she hid her grimace with a practiced grin and waved. The female imp had an incredible memory. Leslie hadn't remembered her, and she doubted he would. As many times as he had been in and out of jail, it was no wonder he couldn't recognize individual Coven members, even if she had arrested him personally three times before. Ma, though, Ma never forgot a face.

"Hey, Ma," she smiled weakly.

"You look a little green, eh?" Leslie snickered beside her. "You want me to tell her you don't like her cookin' for ya?"

"I swear to the goddess herself I will cuff you where you stand," she hissed back, never dropping the smile from her face and praying she didn't look as sick as Leslie implied.

Leslie dropped the smirk. "You know, Ma, she really gotta be gettin' back to work!" he yelled up to his mother.

"Oh, that's too bad! You're such a hard worker! You know, Leslie, you should really find a job like Thea! How you gonna get a girlfriend with no job?" It was Thea's turn to snicker.

"Ma, I gotta job! I'm makin' money, ain't I?"

"You need a good payin' job!" Ma shook her triple-ringed finger at the imp. "No self respectin' young lady is gonna marry a panderer! I expect grandchildren before I turn a century older!"

Leslie pointed back. "I know where this is goin', Ma! I already know! We ain't doin' this today! C'mon, we're goin'." Leslie tugged on Thea's cloak, not at all amused by her stifled chuckles.

"Don't you use that tone with me, Leslie Templeton! Where you goin'? Leslie!" She frowned, but it didn't last long as she waved with a, "Bye, Thea, baby!"

Thea grinned back at the imp and waved in parting. No one actually knew what Ma's real name was, which was a bit concerning if she really thought about it, but seeing as the female imp never so much as stole a wallet, the Coven had no reason to investigate her.

"All right, all right." Thea ripped her cloak from Leslie's grubby fingers when they relocated to another alleyway. This one wasn't as sheltered from the winds, and she wanted to make this quick. "You said you know a guy."

Leslie popped the collar on his trench coat and smoothed out the deep-set wrinkles in the fabric, taking his time before answering her. "Oh, yeah, sweetheart, don't getcha panties in a bunch."

Thea glowered and stepped threateningly closer toward the imp. He flinched, bravado gone, and he hastily stepped back. "All right, all right, all right!" He held his hands up in defense. "So, I know a guy. What's in it for me?" Always the opportunist.

"I won't arrest you for selling counterfeit goods or solicitation."

Leslie looked offended, and it was a common expression by now. "Whoa, whoa! These ain't counterfeit, toots—"

"Let's say I believe you," Thea interrupted, crossing her arms over her chest and settling the imp with a hard glare. "I know you don't have a permit to sell. It hasn't been updated in the Coven's database for three years."

Leslie was silent for a moment, his black eyes shifting in their sockets as he weighed his options. Then, quietly, "And you'd be willin' to overlook all...this? Fo' me? If I do this...fo' you?"

She nodded solemnly. Rafe would kill her for this because, whoever Leslie knew, she knew she'd be dragging the big Summoner along for questioning. She trampled down the feelings of guilt. She felt so corrupt in that moment, agreeing with an imp to let crimes slide for information that would lead her to a tethering stone that, in her possession, would raise all kinds of flags, which would only lead to the discovery she was working on the side with a powerful sorceress, who just so happened to have a demon prince held captive in a dungeon below a magic sanctuary. All for the greater good, of course, but the Council wouldn't concern themselves with the details.

Leslie stuck out his leathery hand in agreement. "Okay, okay, you gotta deal, but—" he whipped his hand back when Thea made to shake, "I wantcha to ovalook all futcha encountas when we cross paths."

Thea bit back a curse and gave an imperceptible nod as she clasped the imp's hand. The moment their shake ended, Leslie pulled out a card and handed it to her, which she turned over and read.

The Grim Bean?

She glanced up, hoping this was some kind of joke the imp was pulling on her. "Did you seriously just hand me a business card for a coffee shop?"

Leslie somehow managed to roll his all-black eyes. "Do I look like the kinda imp to be pullin' ears? You think I'm pullin' your ear?"

Thea's brows pinched in confusion. "Are you—what?"

"Nothin', nevamind. Look, the guy that runs the shop, he's the guy you wanna talk to. Just don't tell him I sent ya."

"Then how am I going to talk to him if he doesn't know I'm coming?"

Leslie blinked. "You're right. I'll tell 'em you're comin', but don't be involvin' me afta that, got that, Blondie?"

"Fine," she scowled, "and I'm not blonde. My hair is light brown." To her, it was, anyway.

The imp shrugged. "Blonde, brown—it's a honey brown. I'mma start callin' you Honey Badger, 'cause you kinda mean too."

Thea sighed.

Chapter Ten

I Can Explain. No, Really.

"You didn't."

Thea felt herself sighing once again in exasperation. How many times was that in a single day? Why did the universe feel like conspiring against her? The only upside to this was that she knew her colleague so well she was able to gauge his reactions before he acted on them. She knew the inevitable conversation with the Summoner would lead her to this point, thus the reason she had chosen Tasgall's to meet up. Rafe was always easier to handle after a couple of drinks.

"I didn't have a choice," she heard herself repeating and wondered if the patrons surrounding them thought she sounded as much of a parrot as she felt. Then she remembered she'd paid Tassie for a privacy spell. "You don't have any more Dark Market raids lined up for some reason."

"I told you it was because Runerite has been shut down until further notice. For whatever reason, all Summoners are on standby." Rafe massaged his temples with one of his massive hands. He'd been stressed since he came back from the raid and had gladly accepted Thea's invitation for drinks. He sipped his amber concoction and sighed at the slow burn that slid down his throat.

"Because that's not suspicious at all," Thea mumbled into her own drink. Never one to tolerate the strong stuff, she often opted for the smoother beverages that snuck up on you. Mokana had ordered the same cucumber cocktail she had but hadn't quite taken to it, so she sat on the other side of Rafe quietly blowing bubbles in it through her straw.

The rusalka had been so demure as of late and being denied of seeing Namara earlier hadn't helped any, but she would no doubt brighten when she went to see the kelpie later that night. Rafe had resigned himself to taking her, but only on the promise that they wouldn't stay for very long. He was too mentally drained to deal with a snarky sorceress and a bouncing, bubbling, bizarre foreigner for an overly long period of time.

"This is too good an opportunity to miss," Thea insisted, unperturbed by the Summoner's reluctance. She stuck out her bottom lip, and her expression morphed into that of a pitiful pout. It wasn't above her to use unconventional means to sometimes get what she wanted. If she was willing to go behind the Coven's back to potentially save them all, she was willing to sacrifice a smidgen of her pride to convince Rafe through pouting. She was just buzzed enough to do it without much thought, and Rafe was three ales down and that was enough to consider it.

She wasn't so buzzed that she didn't notice the way his gaze lingered on her bottom lip right before he scowled at her and turned back to face the bar. "I should have never offered to help you with Mr. Dawkin's potion properties notes. It's all been downhill from there," he muttered around the rim of his mug.

Thea snorted, dropping the pout and picking up her own glass to hide her triumphant smirk, though the mirth in her eyes was obvious. "Oh, please. You couldn't turn a blind eye to a damsel in distress back then any more than you can now."

Rafe cast her a sideways glance. "Apparently not."

It was on the tip of her tongue to reply with a witty comeback, but she swallowed it and instead queried, "So, does this mean you're coming with me to the Grim Bean tomorrow?" She took his long-suffering sigh as a yes. "Also, I'll need to start crashing at your place."

Rafe sputtered and choked on the remains of his ale. A laugh burst forth from her when Mokana started thudding heavily on the Summoner's back. "Ow," he finally growled, swatting the rusalka's hand away. "I forget how strong you are sometimes." Mokana bit back a grin. He turned his half glare on Thea, his eyes a bit watery and red-rimmed, and his voice came out hoarse. "Why do you need to crash at my place?" He waved Me'Glach away when the pixie flew by, silently asking if he wanted another drink.

Thea lifted one shoulder in a leisurely shrug. "Your duplex is bigger than mine, and it'd be easier to move a few of my things over than trying to relocate both you and Mokana to my place. Plus, my neighbor's pet is rude."

Mokana perked up from her seat. "That makes sense, and, yeah, that lamia is *lame*." She grinned at her own pun, pleased with herself.

"That was terrible," Thea snickered.

Rafe frowned at both of them and cut off any further conversation with a wave of his hand. "Stop right there, you two. What are you talking about? Why do you need to crash at my place?"

Thea kept her features schooled. "I just told you, because—"

"Thea."

She cracked a grin that spread from ear to ear. "I take it you didn't hear the Council this morning when they said all Coven members are to be paired up at all times?"

"Yes, but you didn't feel the need to be paired up today when you decided to bargain with an imp." The man's confused expression turned stern, which she waved off without a second thought.

"Namara had just woken up. You couldn't have expected me to go with you on a raid when all I would have been able to think about was her. Besides," she sniffed haughtily, then caught herself and frowned at the action. She was not her mother. "It worked out all right, I think. Anyway, back to the subject at hand. The Council decided we all start pairing up, and, by the end of the night, everyone in the Coven will have gotten the memo. I mean, if you have someone you'd rather pair up with, that's fine, though it will make our life a little difficult when it comes to enacting out our plan with Cressida."

She was mostly teasing, but it was true she needed to start living with Rafe for the time being. She detested admitting it, but without the protection of Namara, she was a sitting duck. She didn't doubt her abilities against a human intruder, but without her kelpie, she wouldn't even get out alive against a feral demon. She was going to need someone watching her back, and Rafe was the only one she could trust as much as she trusted Namara. If she had to choose anyone to do a suicidal, maybe pre-apocalyptic mission with, it would be him.

That and the nightmares had returned. Without the distracting clanging of pots and pans in the kitchen, as her pet tried cooking something with the strange ingredients in her personal cabinet, or the idle chatter and soft splashes from Namara in the large soaking tub to pull her mind from the self-deprecating prison it often sought, she had been helpless in the quiet stillness of her home. Not even the wind had aided her, having died down at some point last night. She had tossed and turned until the early morning. When she did get some sleep, nightmares plagued her. Thea hadn't realized just how ingrained the creature was in her life until she was suddenly not there. Knowing someone was under the same roof as she calmed her sanity and allowed her thoughts to clear.

She blinked when Rafe exhaled heavily and kept her small smile to herself. He leveled her with a look as he said, "You know as well as I do, I wouldn't have anyone else. You come over enough the way it is anyway."

"Only because you're a better cook than Namara." They both purposely ignored the rusalka idly swirling the milky green liquid in her glass with her claw and smirking knowingly at them.

Thea polished off her mug with a quick gulp. "Then it's settled. Hope you don't snore."

"He doesn't, but I do," Mokana stated with a giggle. Thea's startled expression garnered a louder laugh from the rusalka and a hearty chuckle from Rafe. She opened her mouth for some sort of reply, but it was cut off with a girlish, high-pitched *eep* when her chair rattled, and a loud slam blasted throughout the tavern.

All three of them swerved in their stools and peered over the bar to find a blitzed ogre sprawled out on the floor. Its frazzled, raven-haired owner managed to appear worried and exasperated all at once as she checked up on the beast.

"I believe it's time for us to go," Thea piped up and stood from her seat. "The bar's already getting rowdy." She reached over and grabbed Mokana's drink and downed the glass. No point in wasting drinks.

"Is that the ogre Dean and I double-blasted with the intelligence spells?" Rafe wondered aloud, sipping his ale and not looking ready to leave in the slightest. He grimaced at the beast on the floor and looked away.

Mokana hopped down from her chair, more than eager to go see the kelpie. She watched the ogre give his owner a goofy, drunk smile and laughed at the scene. "It doesn't appear to have worked."

That night, Thea curled up with one of her soft throws on Rafe's couch and watched the flames in the hearth lick lazily at the burning logs within. The sound of the wind howling outside picked up and whipped against the side of the duplex. She had her own spare bedroom, though she wasn't tired enough to retire for the night. There were enough bedrooms for all four of them, but the smallest was currently being used as Rafe's office. He'd said he'd have it cleared out before Namara fully recovered, and then he'd left her to her own devices to do just that.

Mokana had indeed brightened up after visiting the kelpie. By the time she and Rafe had gotten back to the duplex, Thea was unpacking everything she might need over the next couple of weeks. She didn't know how long the Coven would keep the buddy system in place, but she anticipated it wouldn't reverse until all the unchecked creatures from Hell were sent right back to where they came from. That thought opened open a whole new can of worms, and Thea wished she knew how to fix it.

Thea knows everything. She sighed and snuggled deeper into the blanket. She didn't know everything. She wished she knew everything, so she could fix the mess they were in, but the things she now knew terrified her.

Let them fend for themselves, was the next cruel thought that crashed into the forefront of her mind. She slammed it down as fast as it came. She had always fought against that harsh sentiment. Let others fend for themselves? What kind of being saw another in need of help and walked right by without a care? Not her. She'd rather stretch herself thin than refuse aid. It was the reason she joined the Coven, and yet, when it mattered, what she had always refused to do was exactly what she was doing now.

She felt the familiar tingling in her lips and in the tips of her fingers. Her chest was also beginning to tighten.

You're going to get yourself killed, and for what? You'll disgrace your whole family, and for what? For what? Did she even know anymore? A painful ache throbbed in her chest as her heart began to pound heavy against her ribcage.

Fine then! Join the stupid Coven and kill yourself! Have fun! Her lip trembled as it quirked into a smile that fell quickly. Have fun. She'd had a lot of fun before this mission. She'd enjoyed the thrill her work had brought her every day. It was always new, exciting. The rush of adrenaline every time she took down the bad guy, or helped someone in need, or saved someone's life was what drove her. She'd had the Council in her back pocket when she needed them, and she had been able to trust and rely on their judgment. Harder days ended with laughs at Tasgall's Tavern, even if the next day the bill made her regret it.

Don't expect your father and me to support you. She hadn't. When she ran away from that dysfunctional family of hers, she never expected them to aid her in any way. She was paying the academy's tuition back with years of service in the Coven.

She never planned on relying on her parents from the start, when she'd been bumbling around lost in the seemingly gigantic hallways of Runerite, clinging to her acceptance letter like a lifeline while struggling to hold onto the mountain of textbooks clutched to her chest. Suddenly thrust into the world with newfound independence, she'd been too poor to afford even a satchel. She'd wanted to find her classroom before her locker but had immediately regretted that decision.

"Do you need help with that?" someone had asked behind her. She'd heard the snickers and the whispers—she was from *that* family. All that money and she wanted to join the *Coven*. She'd been prepared to turn around and bark out some harsh insult but reeled back at the sincere gaze directed at her. The gaze that had belonged to—

"You're doing the thing again," a deep voice halted her reverie. She relaxed the breath she didn't realize she'd been holding, and her shoulders slumped at the release of tension.

A mug of steaming hot chocolate was shoved into her field of vision, interrupting her view of the fireplace. She took the cup gratefully and let the warmth seep into her palms before taking a careful sip. Little marshmallows tickled her nose. She regarded the Summoner out of the corner of her eye as he lounged back in the cushions of his old sofa. It groaned under his weight, and Thea latched onto the excuse of a change in topic.

"Your couch is going to break one of these days."

He stared at her with a look that told her he knew exactly what she was doing, and that he knew she knew that he knew, but he went along with it anyway. He raised one thick shoulder in a shrug. "I've had it for years."

Thea felt a smile tug the corners of her lips, remembering so many years ago when he'd asked her for help moving it into his first apartment. His whole gaggle of a family had shown up to help. All seven brothers and six sisters, plus mom and dad had cleared two oxen carts by the time she'd gotten there after filing her latest report at HQ.

The introductions had been long and grueling with three sets of boy twins, a set of girl twins, a set of girl triplets, and two siblings born singularly—like Rafe had been—to go through. That hadn't even been the biggest kicker that day. The girls all sported L names, and the boys all had R names after their mother and father, Larissa and Robert MacBain. Thea's head had practically spun that day, and she wasn't even ashamed to say she couldn't remember everyone.

What she did remember was the price sticker that had still been stuck to the side of the couch, and how she had come up with the brilliant idea of slapping it onto his back under the disguise of a job well-done pat. He had walked around with it on for a whole afternoon before she and the rest of the family couldn't hold in their laughter any longer.

She shifted in her seat and heard the creak from the worn springs and chuckled. "I could always move my set in here." She bit her lip immediately. Why did she say that? She hadn't meant to say that.

Rafe grunted, a light-hearted look in his blue-green gaze. "Just how long do you plan on staying here?"

It had meant to be a joke, a jest, but it brought along the thoughts and questions she had been trying to avoid all night. How long *was* she going to have to stay there? How long would it take for them to get rid of all the demons? Could the Council even pull off such a feat? Would Cressida pull through, or was Thea unleashing Hell on the world for nothing? Was she unleashing Hell on the world regardless if Cressida did uphold her end of the bargain anyway? How many people were going to die if they screwed this up? What if they had to battle another hellhound or a soul eater? What if she froze up like she did last time? What if someone died because of her? What if what happened to Namara happened again, but this time they couldn't get her to the sanctuary? What if was Mokana, instead? What if it was Rafe?

"Thea."

She blinked back the wetness threatening to spill down her cheeks and flashed him her best smile. "Please, give it a few weeks and you'll be begging me to stay. I bet Mokana is tired of doing all your dirty laundry anyways."

He didn't take the bait this time. He didn't laugh her off, didn't roll those aqua eyes at her, or mockingly tell her she was too buzzed to follow a conversation without spacing out. He set down his empty mug on the end table by the couch and, without hesitation, opened his arms.

You're never going to find a man who'll love you.

She was moving before her brain could catch up to what she was doing. She wormed up against his side and leaned her head against his chest. He reached over her and snagged her abandoned blanket and tossed it over her head, smiling when he heard a chuckle come from under the throw. She kept it over her head, encasing her in warmth and calming the panic clawing at her throat. The tears could fall freely without the weight of his gaze on her. His heavy arm held her secure and quelled her racing heart, and they settled into the calm of the night. The only sounds that could reach her now were the pops and crackles of the fire and his steady breathing.

Chapter Eleven

A Whole New World…Dimension, Whatever

The smell of coffee roast was heady and thick in the air, and it was so pleasantly warm in the cafe that Thea wanted to do nothing more than curl up in a booth by the window with a steaming cup and forget about the world's problems. She steeled herself against the temptation. She was not here for coffee and had to remind Rafe as much when she caught him eyeing the menu.

Both of them had agreed earlier that morning to go completely undercover. They exchanged their Coven grade cloaks for older, cheaper garments to fight the cold wind blowing through Tolvade, along with ditching their insignias. Thea kept her black face mask, and while it was her signature look, it was almost always accompanied by her mass of tawny curls, which were now pulled back into a severe bun. Mokana stood on one side of her, and on the other side was Rafe who looked nothing like himself.

He wore glamour that changed his massive body into something leaner, and now he stood shoulder to shoulder with her instead of towering above her. His long black locks that often reached his lower back when down, were now choppy, short, and curled around his ears. Blond to boot. His eyes disturbed her most, now a flat brown.

"I have the oddest crick in my neck, Thea," he said in reply to her earlier statement. "The least I can do is buy myself a macchiato." He said it so nonchalantly like there wasn't any hidden meaning behind that comment. Thea refused to flush at his words and quietly acquiesced to his coffee request.

With the Summoner appeased they took their place in line. The sun was barely peeking out over the horizon and yet the line was nearly to the door. Thea resisted tapping her foot in impatience. She'd already gone over the possible scenarios in her head on how she would corner the creature she was looking for—Sheldon, apparently was the imp's name—and conferred with Rafe on the option of simply asking to speak with the manager. The point of this mission was to not get distracted with coffee, but it seemed Rafe was going to derail that minor detail.

A furious ringing of a bell signaled they were next. When they reached the counter, Thea jerked to a stop. She had been expecting the gremlin waiting patiently for her order— after all, the Grim Bean was known for being run by the creatures—but it still struck her with surprise when she came face to face with one.

By the Goddess, has it been a long time since I've been here.

Large, exaggerated, floppy ears nearly the same size as its small body sat perched atop a squished, round head. Circular eyes of white and gold blinked owlishly up at her, though she suspected it was less a look of surprised innocence and more so its natural expression. It was almost cute with its black tiger stripes over olive skin, giant feet, and short, stumpy tail.

I really want one, she refrained from saying. Instead, she waved a hand in the general area of the menu and recalled her favorite drink from the past. "Um, give me the medium caffè aeristriano. Make it a double shot." She felt like she'd need the caffeine for the oncoming day. She went on to spell out her name when the gremlin gave a sharp, guttural bark and gestured to the marker and cup in its claw-tipped hands. She then stepped aside for Rafe and fiddled with the string on her coin pouch, ready to pay when they were done.

"Macchiato. Large. Cow milk is fine. I don't feel like pissing off Bernard today."

Thea glanced up and caught the relieved look that flashed across the gremlin's face before also barking at Rafe for his name, which he had to repeat twice. "Who is Bernard?" she asked low enough that only he could hear her.

Before he could answer, Mokana was shoving past both of them. "Well, that ornery unicorn is just going to have to get over it. Some of us don't get to choose our jobs," she tossed a look over her shoulder at Rafe to drive the point home. "So, I don't want to hear anything from him. I would like a large cappuccino with two shots of espresso, and I want unicorn milk with that. Mokana. M-O-K-A-N-A." The relieved expression on the gremlin vanished, and the creature grumbled and chittered its complaints in its odd little language as it wrote down the rusalka's name.

"Sounds like you're the ornery one," Rafe reprimanded gently once they had paid and herded themselves over to the other counter to wait. She huffed in agitation but had the good grace to look remorseful.

"I'm not very sociable without my morning cup."

Thea nodded her agreement, but she wasn't looking at either of them as she did so. She watched the gremlin that had rung up their order yap loudly at another of its kind to, what she assumed, take over the register as it hopped down onto the ground. Another gremlin, more portly and shorter in stature, crawled gracelessly up onto the counter while the first padded over to a door marked with what she could only guess were various hazard and "employee only" signs in a multitude of different languages. It hesitated a foot away from the door and sent a pleading look over its shoulder with its large, golden eyes.

"Rada rada-ka?" It croaked questioningly.

Mokana, having been chastised already, simply nodded with her arms crossed tightly over her chest.

The gremlin faced the door again but peeked another glance over its shoulder when it moved only a foot closer. "Rada ra?"

Annoyance flashed across the rusalka's pale face, but she kept the small, polite smile in place while biting out the words, "Yes, I'm sure."

The gremlin shuffled closer to the door and dared to look back once more. Thea automatically knew to move a step away.

"Rada—"

"For all that is blessed by the goddess, *yes!* I want unicorn milk!" she finally snapped, earning a harsh hiss from Rafe. The creature jerked back and threw open the door, apparently more afraid of Mokana than whatever it was that lurked inside.

Immediately, a tidal wave of coffee beans lurched into the open space and crashed onto the floor. Thea wrinkled her nose in disgust but noticed no one in the cafe even blinked at the chaos. Another crash echoed from somewhere within, causing more beans to spill out onto the floor, and an angry whinny belted from the inside of the room. The sound alone caused her to wince, but again, no one else seemed bothered by the kerfuffle.

"That's Bernard," Rafe said close to her ear, chuckling when she flinched in response. Her glare lacked any heat, and when another sharp neigh pierced the air, she turned her attention back to the door and tried peeking over the counter to see if she could see what the "ornery unicorn" named Bernard looked like. It was too dark to see anything—that or a privacy spell was placed around the door to keep prying eyes from seeing what they probably shouldn't be seeing if the heated nickers inside were anything to go by.

"Cha-rada ra rada-ka baka baka!" The gremlin babbled angrily, kicking beans out of its way and waving their empty cups in the air before chucking them inside and slamming the door closed. It turned around, saw the beans still littering the ground, and groaned gutturally before reopening the door to begin scooping up the mess.

"Not that I don't love you being here," Thea started after turning her attention away from the grumbling gremlin to Mokana, "but why are you here?" They couldn't exactly bring the rusalka with them on an undercover mission. Very few Coven members had rusalkas, and the others didn't look anything like Mokana. Rafe wouldn't be able to concentrate on two glamour spells, and Thea knew that she wouldn't be able to either for the simple fact she was going to be too enthralled by her first sighting of the Dark Market. A simple slip-up was all it would take.

Mokana didn't even look offended. "Yesterday's raid was sort of a last-minute adjustment, so we didn't get enough time to stop by and get a cup of coffee beforehand. It's tradition to come here before a raid, and since we don't know when Rafe's next official assignment will happen, he said I could come along today."

Thea glanced at the Summoner, but upon meeting those flat brown eyes glanced away. "I didn't know you guys went to the Dark Market that often," she lowered her voice, though it wasn't enough to hide the underlying excitement she felt. She'd been utterly fascinated by the Dark Market since she was a child.

"Outside summonings, there's not too much else for us to do." Rafe shrugged. "It takes a lot of concentration to uphold glamour, especially in dangerous situations. Before now, there weren't a whole lot of perilous missions only Summoners could handle besides the blood mages in Borlimane and the Dark Market. Spellweavers have enough on their plates, and Hunters are too inexperienced to go. However, I've never gone this much in the past couple weeks before."

Thea raised a brow at that. "Interesting," was all she said, to which he leveled her with a hard stare.

"I put my faith and trust in the Council, but even I will admit there might be some shady business going on in the inner workings of the Coven."

"Such as what we're doing now," she helpfully supplied with a teasing smile.

Rafe turned away from her with a petulant frown. "Please don't remind me."

It was the *slap, slap, slap* of eager footfalls that alerted them all that the gremlin was back with their orders, two cups in his hands and trying to balance the third on top of his head, which had an odd sparkle to it. Mokana grinned and plucked the cup off the gremlin's head and waved the two farewell before slipping out of the cafe.

Rafe and Thea collected their respective drinks, but before the gremlin could retreat back to the counter she asked, "May I speak to your manager?" It spun around with a questioning trill. It eyed Rafe—who was absolutely not helping the situation with his blissed-out expression upon taking his first sip—before returning her gaze. It shrugged its knobby shoulders and wandered back to the door it had been so nervous entering the first time. She watched it raise its claws to the door and clicked them against the polished wood in a sort of practiced rhythm.

There were no jittery nerves when it opened the door, but what surprised Thea more than that was when the door swung open, the tidal wave of coffee beans didn't come flooding out onto the floor. The gremlin stuck his head in, seemingly found who it was looking for, and babbled out a series of short, sharp sounds.

A voice floated out from within the room in Gremlic, and the gremlin looked completely offended by what was said.

"Rada ka-ka cha-da!" it cried indignantly. Thea wondered if the creature inside, who she hoped was this Sheldon imp, was implying the imp had done something wrong. The same voice returned with pacifying chirps.

The gremlin turned and strode back to the counter without a backward glance. Thea could hear movement, the squeak of a chair, and papers ruffling before a figure popped out into view.

Though a bit taller than Leslie, the imp still bore the same bumpy, toady skin with large skinny ears and all-black eyes. He wore a black vest over a white, hand-sewn, drawstring shirt. His black trousers were synched at the ankle just above thick, black combat boots.

"What can I do fo' ya, Ms…?" The imp possessed the same heavy accent Leslie did too, and she wondered if that was just an imp thing.

"Don't worry about it." She leaned up against the counter to put herself more on the imp's level. "I was wondering if we could speak to you in your office?"

Sheldon regarded her with a single raised, hairless eye ridge, and his black gaze swept over her in assessment. "Who sent ya?"

"A very nice imp with a very nice mother."

The imp scoffed, and it was a rough sound. "That Leslie's neva been nice a day in his life. Now his motha, on the otha hand, now that's an imp." He grinned, mouth full of sharp teeth.

He turned and barked at one of the gremlins, who startled at the sharp noise and ended up jerking its marker in a haywire squiggle against the cup it was holding. Glaring at the imp all the while, it tossed the cup over its shoulder, snatched up another one, and began rewriting the order anew.

"Like they don' make noise in this establishment," Sheldon grumbled to himself. He flung open the gate to let them behind the counter. "Gotta do everything myself 'round here."

Thea left her cup of coffee sitting on the counter, no longer interested in the drink. They slipped inside, and Thea had to fight down the disgust when her boots kept sticking to the floor. If she'd been here as a member of the Coven, she would have ordered a health inspection on the place. As it stood, she wasn't on the dial right now, and even though there was a high probability she wouldn't see Sheldon again, she had to remind herself she wasn't here to interrogate anybody. Doing so could blow their cover and thus the whole operation. Leslie might be okay with making deals with Coven members, but this imp probably had too much responsibility on his shoulders to take the risk.

When they stepped inside the office and shut the door behind them, Thea once again had to quell the disgust rising in the pit of her stomach. Papers were strewn everywhere. All over the stained carpeted floor, falling out of stuffed filing cabinets, haphazardly placed in giant, unorganized piles on top of an awkwardly leaning desk. Food had been left over, spilling out of an overflowing trash can in the corner of the room, and the execrable scent of rotting fish permeated the air.

Secrets of the Sanctuary

Oh, I'm definitely filing for an inspection if we get out of this alive, she thought to herself as she eyed the dingy walls where permits and licenses hung in crooked frames and looked decades old.

"Sorry 'bout the mess." Something about Sheldon's tone of voice said he wasn't sorry at all. She glanced over at Rafe who no longer looked cheery and was regarding his drink warily.

She cleared her throat to gain the imp's attention when it was snagged by the teetering mountain of paperwork on his desk. "What exactly did Leslie tell you?"

Sheldon shrugged, giving nothing away with his schooled expression. "First things first, what's in it fo' me if I help you?"

"I know Leslie's mother quite well."

"Who don't?"

"I'll mention the next time I drop by a certain someone doesn't like her cooking." She'd heard such things were close to blasphemy in the imp community.

Sheldon gasped, dropping his nonchalant façade. "You wouldn't."

"And that he was only trying to get closer to her to steal her secret recipes and sell them on the Dark—"

"All right, all right, all right." The imp threw up his hands in defeat. "I can see why Leslie said ta be wary of honey badgers. Didn't make sense at first."

Rafe snorted his amusement into his hand and received a sharp elbow to the side.

"He only said you was lookin' fo' a tetherin' stone. Told 'im I didn't have one, but he said the way you was actin' was like you'd do anythin' to get one." He squirmed under her gaze, clearly uncomfortable with where the topic was broaching.

137

"He would be right."

The imp let out a gust of air, one large ear twitching. He settled his inky gaze on the both of them. "I don' wanna see you back here afta this. I ain't no personal pocket portal transportation service. We're done after this, you got me?"

Thea nodded. If they made it out of this alive, this was the last place she'd be coming back to, and Sheldon was getting shut down. "Fine with me."

Sheldon swung his focus onto Rafe. "You, quiet mousey, you got me?"

Rafe blanched. That was probably the only time the Summoner had ever been compared to a mouse in his life. He didn't voice his complaint, though, and merely nodded.

"All right, you two," the imp stood up and dug around in the deep pockets of his trousers. "I'mma bout to show you somethin' the likes a which you ain't neva seen befo'e."

Well, he was right about one of them.

Thea stood back and watched in silent amazement as Sheldon flung his hand from his pocket, and a large, swirling vortex was thrown up. The center was obsidian and bled into amethyst outer edges, and the circumference of the portal was as big as Thea.

"I'll only tell ya one thing, and that is only 'cause portals be finicky things. This'll take you to the outamost edge of the dimension. The only way to get back to this world is through the portal at tha otha side. There was somethin' else…" he tapped one weathered finger to his sharp chin but merely shrugged. "Eh, can't be too important. Now get outa here, befo'e the thing closes."

Rafe handed over his cup of coffee to the imp, who tossed it over his shoulder in the general direction of the trash bin. The Summoner enclosed one of his hands around her wrist to keep them together. They shared a look for only a second before she stepped one leg through, and then the rest of her body followed. Ice traveled up her body as she was slowly pulled through the portal, and a dull roar filled her ears. She was cold all over, and she felt like she couldn't breathe, but at the same time, it felt like breathing was unnecessary. Then she was being spat out onto the hard, compact ground. The only thing that had kept her from face-planting the dirt was Rafe's grip on her arm. After years of crossing through portals, he knew how to make it out standing.

The sounds of the market greeted her before her eyes adjusted. Above her, an endless white void, just like in the sanctuary's mini dimensions. Below her feet, a dirt road that, if she were to keep walking in one direction, she'd end up right back where she started. She'd lose her mind thinking about it too hard, so she turned her attention to the Summoner beside her.

"Time to put your permanent scowl to work," he said to her in a low voice, and she would have bitten his head off had he not started slinking off into the crowd. She trailed behind him silently, avoiding eye contact with every hooded figure she passed.

The smell of iron reeked in the air, and she tasted it on the back of her tongue. Pitched tents, roughly sewn together from scraps of dirty cloth, and makeshift huts that had been slap-dashed and hastily assembled lured customers in with shiny trinkets, black magic spells, illegal potions, and poisonous brews. Weapons gleamed in the light of the fires that had helped forge them, while sharp clangs reverberated over the dulled noise of the market from the blacksmith as he worked to bend glowing red metal.

"Never let your eyes linger," Rafe murmured into her ear. "Never stare, even if it's something horrific. You show an ounce of emotion here and the operation is compromised."

Secrets of the Sanctuary

Thea swung her gaze to meet her fellow Coven member's, but he was already blending into the current, leaving her to blindly follow after him.

Chapter Twelve

Eternal Rest for the Wicked

"What if we find what we're looking for?" She kept her voice low and stuck close to the Summoner's side. How she missed his hulking frame right about now, with how it had always been able to part through the city's packed streets with ease.

"Keep moving. Don't look interested. I heard whispers yesterday that an auction was happening today. We have a higher chance of finding it there."

"Do you think that's why you-know-who moved the raid up from today?" she whispered, clinging to the loose fabric of his cloak when he began slipping farther ahead of her.

Rafe didn't answer her, though she didn't need to speculate too hard. It was obvious. The Council rarely, if ever, bumped up the date of a Dark Market raid. Raids took weeks, sometimes months of careful planning to formulate. One detail changed, and the entire thing could be ruined. What she didn't understand was why they would feel the need to. Was there something on the auction stage they wanted? She couldn't trust the Council any more than she could trust Cressida, and that was saying something.

They passed by stacked steel cages where a vile individual was shoving a stick in between the bars and jabbing at the trapped Cyan Spider Monkeys inside, eliciting sharp cries and pained yowls from the creatures. Their natural bright blue faces and pristine white furs were washed out and dulled, and their ribs jutted out from their skinny, malnourished bodies. Rage like she'd never felt before washed over her and had her stopping in the middle of the street, gripping her hidden dagger. A harsh yank on her arm kept her moving before she could mutilate the man and blow their cover.

"What did I *just* tell you?" he snarled under his breath.

"I'm sorry," she griped, throwing a glance back at the poor creatures. "Did you even see—?"

"Of course, I did," was his soft reply.

She finally looked at him, *really* looked at him. Even through the flat brown of his glamoured eyes, she could see the steel traps protecting a tender heart. She said nothing, just gave him a weak nod of understanding. He seemed content with that and turned around to continue forward.

She now understood why Rafe always came back from raid missions emotionally and mentally drained. To have to walk away from creatures in need in order to save them later had to be one of the most heartbreaking decisions one could make. No wonder Summoners were chosen for their complete control. They had to keep not just their magic in check but their emotions, too.

"The auction starts soon. It's just up ahead in that big dome building." He nodded to the huge structure just past the tents and huts. It dominated the market grounds with its enormous structure. Everything but the domed roof was made entirely of light gray brick, and it was far more detailed and ornate than the huts and shops surrounding it. The copper roof, oxidized until it was now jade in color, gleamed brilliantly under a sun that wasn't there, and green-tinted copper finishings touched up the other unique details of the building. Stuffed ox carts were stationed by the side entrance. Their merchandise was concealed under tarps to keep prying eyes from seeing what was soon to be entering the stage.

"Keep your eyes peeled just in case," he spoke into her ear, and Thea had to repress the sudden shivers his voice caused. It was cold, devoid of all emotion, and when she had caught a glimpse of those flat brown eyes again, they had been much the same. Her feet felt like they'd been filled with lead as she followed him. She didn't want to be here anymore.

The tents they passed on the way caused bile to rise in the back of her throat. Rabbit heads with a single, curling horn glued between their ears were lined up on one table, along with wolf pelts still bloody and dripping from being recently shorn off, valkyrie feathers bundled together for black magic spells, and ripped off hydra fins that had been flattened with a mallet lay dried out before the crowd.

Another table had a jar of large, scooped-out eyeballs stuffed inside with a single label slapped on the glass reading "cyclops eyeballs" right next to a bioluminescent jar labeled "poison from gorgon snakes." Beside that were containers of what Thea thought were embryos of various magic-based creatures.

"Can all these things really be used for black magic spells?" she quietly questioned.

Rafe nodded solemnly. "You'd be surprised. This is all relatively tame to what you will find on the auction stage."

She swallowed around the dry lump in her throat while sidestepping two hulking men testing out the sharpness of a battle-ax on a tree stump. "What if we don't find the…thing today?" The one man swung the ax faster than anyone she'd ever see swing before, and the ax split the stump under it as if the wood was made of butter.

"Then we come back tomorrow, and if Sheldon refuses, we threaten to shut down his business." Rafe hadn't even glanced at the display from the men, but Thea couldn't help but notice the murderous glee coming from the one that swung the weapon.

"Then he'll know we're from…" She dared not say the word 'Coven' even in whisper, though Rafe seemed to catch on.

"All the more real our threat is then," he replied gruffly.

She opened her mouth to say something, but someone shoved her roughly to the side. She careened into another person, who shoved her back just as roughly. She used that momentum to duck through a group of scantily clad women surrounding a table of rolled parchment papers. When she looked back up, she had lost sight of Rafe.

Not good. Not good.

She stomped down her rising panic. Even though she wasn't tall enough to see over the sea of people, and Rafe was no longer his normal, towering height, that didn't mean she wouldn't find him.

She took a deep breath to steady her nerves, ignoring the women tittering to the side and giving her weird looks.

He'll know to meet me at the auction house. Just keep heading in the direction we were going.

So, she blended into the crowd like she would any other market, slipping in between the cracks and filling the spaces where people no longer stood before she was gone the next moment. Her dagger was a familiar weight under her palm.

Unidentifiable meat was cooking over a peat fire, filling the air with a zinging scent. She held her breath as she passed by the hut, and nearly collided with a slave trader tugging along a group of three beautiful sirens. He leered at her in a suggestive fashion, but she ignored him, too focused on the enchanted rope glowing and leading up to shining collars around the sirens' necks. The sirens had lithe bodies and milky blue complexions that glowed just as the rope did. Their long hair, coral pink, seafoam green, and sandy white, pooled around their arms and billowed around their feet. They appeared fresh off the boat, still wearing their seaweed and rope mesh skirts along with bras made of clustered shells and colored glass.

They were so beautiful it almost hurt to look at them, and it made Thea utterly miserable inside to realize she wasn't even surprised to see them in this dismal place. Their ultramarine eyes were such a deep blue she felt like she could fall right in, shimmering with either an iridescent film or unshed tears, she couldn't tell. When they opened their mouths, melodious notes escaped instead of actual words, and she had the feeling they were telling her to help them.

She moved on before the slave trader could grow suspicious, but she would never forget their silvery voices rising in volume as she walked away. She would never come back to this place. Forget what Rafe had said, there was no way she could survive coming back here a second time.

It was as she was gliding past a merchant offering samples of poison elixirs that she felt the need to stop. Call it intuition, she didn't know, but she sidled up to a table under one of the pitched tents. Spread out before her were amulets darkened with black magic, exotic gemstones the size of coins, dark violet pearls, several unicorn horns with crude carvings to make wands, ivory carvings of dragons, and there, on the end of the table, lay what she was looking for.

The vendor was preoccupied with another buyer at the moment, explaining away the trials and tribulations of obtaining the unicorn horns.

"The beast kept thrashin' even with three of us tyin' it down. Took us no time at all to saw it off though with an extra sedative spell, but those things are expensive. It's why I'm askin' so much."

It would be so easy to snatch the tethering stone off the table and slip back into the crowd. Thea worked her way closer to the edge, subtly eyeing the vendor. She'd have to forgo sinking her knife into his potbelly, but if he kept going on about that poor unicorn, she'd be hard-pressed to stop herself.

She bit her lip as she contemplated her next move while her eyes flashed from the stone to the vendor. She could try to blend into the crowd and then make a run for it if he spotted her. Rafe had told her before that other Summoners had done so as a distraction, even if it had been a last resort. She could do that…or she could take her chances and hope the merchant was greedy enough to add these to the auction house list if nothing sold, but then there was the possibility that someone could buy it, and they'd be back to square one.

"Hey, there pretty little thing."

Double-dip a candlestick!

Thea glanced up and—big mistake—locked eyes with the dullest hazel gaze she'd ever had the displeasure of meeting. Chills raced up her spine. Something moved inside those eyes. Something evil, and she could feel it curling around him like a second shadow.

He's dabbled in black magic before.

"Find yourself somethin' pretty?" He leaned heavily against the table, drawing his whiskered face closer. "I'm willing to bet my whole collection here you'd look captivatin' dripping in my jewels." His putrid breath rolled off his white-coated tongue, and Thea nearly gagged her disgust.

Just pretend he's one of the old geezers at the galas mom forced you to go to.

Seeing as he wouldn't be able to see the fake smile adorning her face, she let her eyes dance with practiced vivacity. She knew the cobalt stood out extraordinarily against the black of her face mask and hood. They'd been described by the business sharks her father often made connections with as "striking" and often compared to "a beautiful twilight just before dawn." The words had grossed her out as a pre-teen, but she had found power unlike anything else the way she could manipulate just by batting her eyelashes to men too old to be looking at her in that way. It was the only amusement she'd gotten from those stuffy affairs her mother had forced her to be a part of. Who knew the tricks she'd used to make the men's heads spin would come in handy so many years later and under such circumstances? The sharks, thankfully, were never brave enough to put their hands on her, but with this man, she couldn't be so sure. That was okay, though. She was just itching for a reason to slice a hand or two off.

She pointed to one of the gems randomly, never looking away from the disturbing images swirling in hazel cages. He blinked slowly, as if in a trance, and Thea knew she still had charm before he looked away first to see what she had pointed at. She looked down too. Tanzanite. Well, it wasn't her favorite stone, but whatever.

"Ah, these are found in the tallest of trees in the Jeweled Canopy. Had those Cyan Spider Monkeys spelled to fetch 'em for me before we stuffed 'em in those cages over there." He gestured to what she had no doubt were the rusty coops she had passed by earlier.

Goddess above, strike down this man before I do.

"Very fitting I say." The sleazy man winked and said, "Matches those pretty blue eyes of yours."

Her eyes flashed with false pleasure, stunning the man into a short silence before he was going off again about the other jewels on the table. She shifted her weight and leaned her gloved palms onto the table, ever so close to the stone.

It was as he was commenting on the process of polishing the opals that she felt a looming presence coming up behind her, and it was a presence she knew all too well.

Banish a banshee — what the?

She glanced over her shoulder and inwardly cursed her dumb luck. Torro McTaggart, one of the High Priests on the Council, was here at the Dark Market.

Her surprise must have betrayed her, but in this instance also might have saved her life. The shady merchant caught her widened eyes and turned to find the object of her focus shuffling just down the street from them, dressed in multiple layers of cloaks and walking with a determined stride instead of flowing with the crowd. One would have had to have been in his presence before in order to be able to determine who he was, but since most of these criminals had escaped judgment from the Council and therefore never went before the blue cloaks, they couldn't have guessed who Torro really was.

The man would have been in the clear if he hadn't sealed his magic's presence. One could tell without his power present that he was a formidable person, and when a formidable person sealed their magic, it brought on more attention rather than none.

Why is a member of the Council here? Are there other blue cloaks here? He's the only one standing out, but if there are others here, could they have just cloaked their magic instead of sealing it? Is he a distraction? For what?

He was getting closer. The peddler leaned over to her, yet she kept her eyes on Torro, joining the growing stares the man was receiving. "You thinkin' what I'm thinkin'?"

Probably not to the same extent, but she nodded regardless. He was drawing closer and closer still. Would he notice her? Had he already recognized her magic? He was only a few tents away now. It had grown steadily quieter, and more people were staring. Didn't he notice them? Of course, he did, he had to. What was his angle, though?

Thea turned her attention back to the table, dug out a Nightingale feather from her pouch, and hissed, "Blessed be, conceal my magic from even me," and held her breath while the feather went up in a small flame and dissolved in her hand. The man running the tent quirked an eyebrow at her but otherwise said nothing. She was counting on him thinking she was just another fugitive paranoid enough to hide her magic presence.

Torro brushed right behind her, his outer cloak grazing against her own in doing so. He stopped. Fear whispered up the skin of her arms, and the hairs on the back of her neck stood up. There was no way he could single her out. Out of the hundreds of Hunters, Cleansers, Record Keepers, Spellweavers, Summoners, seconds, and medical staff flowing in and out of the Council room, there was no way he could pick up and single out her presence.

He doesn't know it's me. He doesn't know it's me. He doesn't know it's me, she kept chanting to herself, even though she could see out of her peripheral that he had started to turn in her direction.

Screw the mission—run!

"Hey, you!" someone shouted, and before Thea could prepare herself to bolt, Torro was being shoved into her so hard it sent them both flying back. Someone caught her in a rough hold—the merchant—but her attention was ripped back to the High Priest and the flash of his blue hood that was revealed to everyone, and it was enough to send the entire market into chaos.

"It's a blue cloak!"

Chapter Thirteen

Sticks and Stones May Break My Bones but Your Words Have Shattered My Soul

The ground rushed up to meet her as she plummeted down to a lush, rainforest floor. Outreaching branches snagged her cloak and broadleaves smacked her in the face while her arms flailed uselessly about. She couldn't even scream.

Instincts came flooding back to her, and she dove a gloved hand into one pouch on her belt, then the one beside it, then from another one behind her. She squeezed her eyes shut, channeled all her energy into her thoughts, and huffed out, "Feather Fall!" before the wind could steal her breath again. Weightlessness was immediate. Branches still snagged her clothes and pushed and pulled her in different directions as she began her slow descent down. She gritted her teeth as rough bark scraped up against the side of her face when one branch sent her slowly spiraling into a tree. She shoved off from the trunk, but the momentum she created caused a new problem to present itself when the floating spell turned her upside down.

She kicked out her legs and waved her arms trying to right herself, but all her movement dislodged the crystal ball in her pocket and caused it to fall out.

"No!" She dove for it, but gravity affected her differently while spelled, and she watched in horror as her only means of communication slipped through her fingers and plummeted to the ground. It crackled loudly upon impact, echoing through the dense jungle with its static screams. She frantically paddled her arms through the air to further pull herself to the ground, but her attempts were in vain.

When her feet finally touched the ground, she sprinted over to the glass orb and went to grab it, only to lurch back when it zapped out an electric current and protested in a series of firecracker pops.

"*No, no, no,*" she whined, dropping to her knees and gathering her broken crystal ball.

Please, Goddess, let it still work, she prayed, even as she knew when she brought Rafe to the forefront of her mind that it was a useless endeavor.

A static whirring buzzed loudly, and the orb trembled in her palms from the effort, but Rafe's frenzied expression filled the glass's surface, nonetheless. Thea gasped in a mixture of elation and surprise.

"Rafe! Rafe, can you hear me?" she yelled, clutching the crystal ball tight in her hands. Tears surfaced as relief sang throughout her body, but it was short-lived when the Summoner tried to talk.

"T—uo—me?—re a—you?" His image wavered while he spoke, his words coming out chopped and unintelligible. Then the glass ball erupted in high-pitched squeals before the connection winked out, and the orb darkened.

"No!" she screamed. She desperately shook the orb and screwed her eyes shut. She pulled Rafe into the front of her mind and concentrated on bringing him back to the crystal ball. She pictured his imposing height, his long black hair and how it shone in the moonlight when they went on night runs, his aqua eyes always sure, his smile always confident.

"Bring him back, bring him back, bring him back," she sobbed aloud over and over again until she dared open watery eyes only to find the crystal ball unresponsive.

She cursed viciously and hurled it into the nearest tree where it shattered, and the last of its magic reserve puffed like sparkling smoke into the air. She screamed until her throat burned.

Thea knows everything!

If you're so stuck on being suicidal, then leave! Have fun dying!

Fine then! Join the stupid Coven and kill yourself! Have fun!

She clapped her hands over her ears and squeezed her eyes shut. Not now, not now. She couldn't deal with them now. She shook her head violently, and an uncontrollable sob escaped her.

Don't expect any support from us!

You're going to shame all of us! For what? So, you can go play pretend superhero! You're not going!

You're going to get yourself killed, and for what? You'll disgrace your whole family, and for what?

Don't expect your father and me to support you!

She curled in on herself while her fingers clawed at her ears and ripped loose curls from her hair bun and yanked at the strands. She could see it. Her mother's disgust. Her sister's smug smile. Her father's condescending looks and blatant disinterest in her existence.

Women were meant to be soft, Thea. You're going to ruin your image.

Let them fend for themselves.

You're never going to find a man who'll love you.

She snarled and pounded her fist into the ground, slamming her knuckles into dirt and rocks and roots and leaves and—and she screamed. Blood dripped from her clenched fist, but the pain went unnoticed.

Her family was wrong. They were all wrong. Someone did love her. He admired her weaknesses as well as her strengths, both mentally and physically. He loved her sense of justice. They had bonded over saving the defenseless and aiding the weak. They had each other's backs when standing up for those in need. They fought in battles of wits and weapons, ending their disputes in breathless laughter. They fought and bickered and teased but stood like an iron wall of defense against common foes. There was no one else she trusted outside of her pet more than him. She would give her life for him, and she knew he would give his life for her. He gave her strength when she needed it. He was her rock, her support. He never once made her feel inferior. He never once questioned her morals. There was more to her than just her looks, her last name. He could see that. He had always been able to see that.

She wished they had been able to see it too.

Many Years Ago

Her mother gave her a look of unbridled disgust and said loud enough for the rest of the family to hear, "Thea, what are you wearing?"

Thea matched her mother's stare with a look of contempt. "It's the dress *you* picked out for me, Mother."

Colleen Bauer gasped audibly, and one of her dainty hands flew to her mouth. "Dear Goddess above, this looks nothing like it did on the model!"

gearing toward something so much more rewarding and fulfilling was as nerve-racking as it was invigorating. Her family had never been close-knit, and the words "I love you" had never once been uttered to anyone. After all, her mother and father had never loved each other to begin with. They had only married under a business arrangement to give her father more wealth. Her mother had been the heiress to a large furnishing distributor, and she'd been married off young. Thea wouldn't have to worry about that fate befalling her. Not anymore.

Not after tonight, she grinned to herself.

She toasted her champagne flute—even if it was only sparkling cider—in the air along with the rest of her family for the umpteenth time, schooling her features into a pleasant smile like she'd been instructed to do too many times to count. Her tight dress flickered like blue flames in the low lighting of the exclusive restaurant in the prestigious Adalith district. Her father had bought out the place for the night, and it was as much a way to flash his wealth around as anything else.

She ignored the bite from the fabric around her arms, pulled taut over muscle her seamstress hadn't accounted for, took a deep breath and—

"Thea, we really must discuss marriage at some point," her father declared suddenly, and all the air in her lungs *whooshed* out of her. She was grateful she hadn't taken a sip of her drink, or she would have spit it out all over her outfit and give her mother another reason to find fault in her.

"Wha—excuse me?" She glanced between her father, furiously chugging down his champagne, and her mother, who eyed her disapprovingly.

"Oh, come now, Thea." Colleen rolled her eyes. "You must have known that eventually your father and I would line you up some suitors. You're plenty old enough."

Thea could only gape at the woman. "I'm thirteen. I'm not getting married anytime soon," she said, tone obvious.

"Of course you are," her father argued but quickly amended his statement with, "after a few years of courting, that is." His cobalt eyes, so much like her own, glanced nervously between her and her mother.

"Don't worry, sis," Arabella piped up sweetly from her chair sandwiched between Thea and their mother. "No one's going to marry a man in a dress anyway."

Thea steeled herself against the violent urges she felt for her sister just then. She was sick of being her little sister's punching bag and snapped, "Is that why you keep insisting on a cat? Because you know you'll be alone forever?"

That trademark Bauer sniff. "You're just mad Mama and Papa have to put you on the market so early because it's going to take you forever to find a man more muscular than you."

"Enough, you two," their mother groaned, massaging her temples as she did so. She turned her stern gaze back to Thea and continued from earlier. "We have several suitors that would all very much like to—"

"I'm not getting married," Thea repeated, setting her shoulders back and straightening her spine. She was not rolling over this time. She refused to be groomed for a loveless marriage like the one her mother and father were stuck in, and if they thought for a moment that she was the awful, high strung, loose cannon, problem child *now* than they were in for a rude awakening when she told them the news. She was going to show them just how awful she could be.

Colleen was losing all patience at this point if the ticking vein at her temple and clenched jaw were anything to go by. Quietly and with more patience than Thea thought possible, she tried again. "Thea—"

for her to breathe more comfortably. She pulled her curls out from their now ruined bun and hissed in pain the movement caused her. The tresses immediately clung to her sweaty neck. The sweltering heat was back and near dizzying, but it only lasted long enough for her to re-gather her locks and sweep them back up into a tight up-do. She pulled her face mask down to cover her neck from bug bites and peeled off her gloves, stuffing them into one of her empty dust pouches.

The pain in her chest twinged with each motion, and she knew that even though the humidity and heat were near unbearable, she was going to have to keep her corset on to act as a brace, but to do so she would have to tighten the strings. It would restrict her movement in the jungle, but at least she still had her dagger and amulet around her neck for protection. Though it would have given her away as a Coven member if anyone were to have seen it while she walked through the Dark Market, her amulet provided protection that was too valuable to remove.

She dipped her hand into her less used pouch and brought out Tinker Bell's Spirit with a snap of her fingers and murmured so she wouldn't strain her already hoarse voice. "Tighten the strings on my corset."

The tinkling light flittered over her shoulder, and Thea sucked in her breath and hollowed her stomach right as the corset cinched around her body. She bit her lip hard to keep the pained groan inside and spit the taste of copper that filled her mouth onto the leaf-carpeted, jungle floor. Her breathing came easier, even if it was in shorter breaths. She didn't have any more blue dust to accompany her gold dust for a healing spell, so back to the basics she would have to endure. She suddenly found herself admiring Blythe all the more for having lived in a desert without the use of magic. She would have to ask the woman later if—

Secrets of the Sanctuary

A loud, high pitched whistling sound was the only warning she got before sharp pain impacted the crown of her head.

"Ow!" she cried, grasping her head and glaring up at the treetops. Nothing moved in the swaying branches that sheltered the forest floor from the sun, creating a live ceiling to block out the rays. She gently touched the tender spot and swept her eyes along the ground for the object responsible for the stinging on her scalp. Something shiny and purple glinted, half burrowed under decaying leaves and moist dirt. She hesitantly scooped it up and studied the rough stone.

Amethyst?

she had before it rained. Each movement took extra effort as she pivoted her hips and hiked her legs up and over fallen obstacles. She couldn't tell what was sweat and what was rainwater anymore. Heat smothered her skin under her clothes. If she could find a semi-private place to strip out of her pants and slice off the thermal layering, she'd gladly do so. However, she couldn't do that in a rainforest where who knows what lurked around the next tree. She couldn't afford to be caught with her pants down.

She lifted her stick to brush past another broadleaf but halted the action when she saw water pooling in the center. Inspecting it quickly, she crouched down, tipped the leaf over her mouth, and downed the contents. She sighed at the cool feeling that traveled all the way down into her stomach and started searching for more. It was probably the safest water to drink in the rainforest considering it had just come from the sky. Any standing water she would have found before the rain would have been a no-go. She didn't hesitate to pour a few of the shallow puddles over her head to cool her heated scalp.

It was as she was searching for more water that she stumbled across a large clearing and nearly dropped the stick in surprise.

Poachers, she hissed internally.

She slipped into the shade of another wide tree and surveyed the large campsite set up, dotting the clearing with yellow tents. She nibbled on her lip nervously as she mentally chastised herself. She should have been paying more attention to her surroundings. She could tell the surrounding trees were much quieter now as she strained her ears. That was always a dead giveaway that something dangerous was nearby.

The campsite was overly quiet, to the point Thea wagered a guess no one was there, or that it could even be abandoned. She doubted that, though. The tents looked fairly new, and the familiar feeling of anger bubbled up darkly inside her. She forced herself to take a deep breath and calm the rage, but that was easier said than done. All it took to fire her back up was remembering the bloody pelts, the stolen embryos, or the torture the unicorns had to endure while their horns were being brutally sawed off.

Cool blue-green eyes flashed through the mental slideshow next. She remembered staring into the steel traps protecting his worn heart, projecting a flat stare that twisted something inside of her painfully. Just like that, the fire was extinguished under a wall of ice, and she felt her mind clear from the festering inferno anger always ignited within her. She released a shaky breath she hadn't realized she'd been holding.

Think, she chided. Assessing the clearing quickly, she came up with three options that she could choose from. One, preferably her favorite, was to rush the campsite and destroy everything inside, slicing off another hand or two if anyone was watching over the tents. Two, she could ignore the campsite completely, because as much as it pained her to admit it, she needed to get back home and fix the problems that were currently underway. As vile as poachers were, they were not altogether stupid. They probably set up near water, and if she rounded the site and found one of the two rivers that flowed through the Jeweled Canopy she could follow it upstream and find herself back in the city by nightfall tomorrow. Or, there was the third option, which would be—she glanced down and spotted a heavy stone, half-covered in bright green moss.

Looks like she'd go for the third option: stealth and destroy. She picked up the rock, tossing it in the air and catching it to gauge its weight before she turned to scan the campsite for a perfect target. One of the closer tents would do, though it was still quite a distance into the clearing. She swung her arm back and hurled the stone, her chest screaming at the

Still, privacy spells were only used to keep others from hearing what the castor was up to, but it would not keep them from entering the spelled area. If Thea didn't want to be caught by returning poachers, she needed to hurry up and finish what she set out to do.

She got to work on one tent before moving on to the next, destroying everything kept inside before she deemed her destruction complete. She stomped the metal cages in with ease, snapped the net poles in half, and then sliced through the net's webbing until it was irreparable.

She hauled out the overflowing buckets of unpolished stones and lined them all up side by side behind the tents. Only after the last one was deposited next to the others did she proceed to kick all the buckets down the slope and into the thorny underbrush. She dug out the two stones in her pocket and chucked them into the bushes as well. She didn't need nor want blood jewels to fund her living.

She entered the biggest tent next, centered in the middle of the clearing. It was supported by two thick wooden beams, and Thea grimaced at the thought of one of those landing on her. Inside were stackable wood filing cabinets and a makeshift desk made from crates pushed together. A rather comfy-looking mattress was splayed out in the farthest corner, so the tent obviously belonged to the leader of the poachers.

She set to work right away, kicking over the filing cabinets and watching them detach from each other and tumble to the ground. Papers spilled out and scattered over the dirt floor. She reached inside and dipped her fingers into her gold dust pouch once again, brought out Tinker Bell's Spirit, and snapped her fingers.

When golden powder, if not used with any other dust, was dipped onto the user's fingertips and snapped, it created Tinker Bell's Spirit. Golden powder, or gold dust, was made from ground-up pixie wings. The short spell was capable of doing any small, simple task. Not to be confused with Will Powder. Will Powder was made from crushed pixie bones and gave a "will" to inanimate objects for a short period of time. Pixies believed in living on after death, and since they understood that their numbers were too enormous to bury all of the fallen, they let magic wielders use their bodies to create temporary spells.

"Burn all the documents," she commanded, and the tinkling light flitted around her shoulders before it hovered over the papers. Flames erupted from the bright little ball of energy and burned the parchment littering the ground and piled haphazardly on the desk into messy clumps of ash.

She was almost finished with her work when she felt it: a deep, resonating *boom* that echoed throughout the rainforest and rumbled the ground under her feet. Her breath caught in her throat, and her blood ran cold. She didn't have time to wonder about the noise, because whatever had made it was moving closer. The ground shook until Thea was forced to anchor her feet or risk getting thrown off balance. She hastened over to the entrance of the tent and nearly stumbled when the reverberations grew powerful enough to jar her legs.

Hesitantly, she peeled back one of the tent flaps just enough to peek out into the clearing, and she could feel all the blood slowly drain from her face at what she saw. Standing out in the middle of the campsite was a giant.

And he was wielding a tree.

Chapter Fifteen

Eyes That Reflect Your Greatest Desire

There were moments in Thea's life where she wondered if things would be different had she chosen another pathway, or if she would have just ended up exactly where she was now. This was one of those moments.

She dove to the other side of the tent, rolling away just as a massive crash blasted somewhere outside. Plumes of dust wafted into the tent from the ferocity of the crash. The ground shook, and her knees almost gave out from under her. She fumbled for her dagger and stabbed it through the material of the tent, slicing it open before plunging into the underbrush just outside. She gritted her teeth from the sudden assault to her face from stinging twigs and sharp thorns, and she could hear the tearing of her tunic as she ripped out of the nasty hold one of the bushes had on her arm.

She scrambled behind a thick tree and clamped both hands over her mouth. Her busted knuckles had started bleeding again, and her hair had fallen from its up-do once more, strands ripped out from grabby branches. Sweat trickled down her temple and grabbed the loose hairs, plastering them to her skin.

Even over the sound of blood pumping in her ears, she could tell how quiet the rainforest had become. Birds no longer called, the dull roar of cicadas and other insects hushed, and the random croons of ape-like creatures grew silent. The giant had stopped destroying the campsite in its search for her, and without its movements, she couldn't track where it stood or gauge how close it was. She tried to quell her racing heart and the panic that rose up inside her.

Stay still. Don't move. Stay still. Don't move, she chanted to herself. The adrenalin spikes throughout the day were draining what little energy she had left, and her fingers shook against her lips, trembling with the effort to keep her frightened sounds at bay.

There was a great tearing noise under her, the sound of roots ripping, and before she could react, the tree she hid in front of was jerked out from behind her. She toppled backward, landing flat on her back, and for the second time that day had the air knocked out of her lungs. The scene above her felt too surreal, even after witnessing the events of the past few days. The giant loomed over her, holding the tree she had just been using as cover in the air as if it weighed nothing, and bits of the soil that clung to the torn roots rained down onto the ground below.

The giant tossed it away from its enormous body, and the large trunk slammed into the neighboring trees around it. The trunk exploded upon impact with a deafening *crack,* sending chunks of bark flying up into the air.

A massive hand clamped around her prone body, jolting her back from her stunned stupor. She shouted furiously, jerking in its grasp, kicking and flailing until her enraged scream was cut off as the enormous being squeezed its thick fingers around her body. Her lungs burned from the starvation of air, and her limbs felt like dead weight. Her vision blurred, sharpened, and blurred again. Her head swam, but even dizzy she was able to make out the two impossibly green eyes that glared holes through her.

"State your business," the deep voice commanded, and Thea felt the vibrations travel down the beast's arm and

He was paler than most beings she'd come across with raven hair messily parted in the middle and onyx eyes that widened when they spotted her. "Guys, I found her!" he shouted, and everything after that became a blur of new faces and creatures crowding her and flashing gold insignias. A harpy's squawking cries could be heard from above, and Thea's blurred vision caught sight of a wingspan the size of a person gliding the creature in a protective circle over the group who continued to poke and prod her body. Then someone was grabbing her face, and she gasped when eyes she'd know anywhere sought hers.

"Rafe?" she asked breathlessly with a hand that reached out to touch rough stubble that hadn't been there that morning.

"No time to explain, T, we have to leave," the Rafe-look-alike told her as he hoisted her up. Her eyes widened at the old nickname, further confusing her as to whom this mystery person really was. She briefly noticed her saviors working on a teleportation spell, but she was more intrigued by the dark purple bags under the maybe Rafe's eyes, and the way his hair wasn't shiny like the Summoner's she knew, but lifeless and tangled.

Someone grabbed her hand. A man with blonde hair piled messily on top of his head, who smiled reassuringly at her. He had goggle-like glasses and green eyes that looked dull compared to the large ones she'd seen mere inches from her face earlier. Her head swung heavily around to find that the giant was no longer pinned by the creatures, but instead watching warily from a safe distance, half-hidden behind the forest's trees and nearly blending in with its surroundings.

She heard someone tell her to close her eyes, and when she did everything went black.

Falling, falling, falling.

Thea jerked awake in a cushiony bed, clutching a thick comforter to her heaving chest as her heart thundered frantically away inside. A plain ceiling stared back at her, one with familiar dips in the plaster and a weird stain she'd never gotten an answer about. She was in Rafe's guest bedroom.

Slowly, she sat up in bed, still clutching the quilted comforter to her chest while she took in the room. Soft white candles glowed from the bedside table, and sat between them was a small incense dish where a tiny ashen cone burned away. The thin strip of smoke danced in the draft coming from the window. The frosted pane of glass was mostly blocked by heavy, thick, burnt-orange drapes, but they were pulled back enough to let a small shaft of light filter in. It made the smoke in the room visible, clinging to the air like ghostly waves. The scent of jasmine finally registered as her breathing slowed.

Thea pulled back the blanket enough to see what she was wearing—a powder blue nightgown that Namara gifted her with many years ago—before a freezing draft of wintery air forced her to cover herself once again. She closed her eyes, mentally checking herself over as she tested the tenderness in the middle of her chest, her side, and then her knuckles. The small cuts and bruises on her hands had mended, but it was still uncomfortable to breathe deeply. She never before thought her lungs could feel overused.

She ran her fingers through her curls, and though she found plenty of tangles that were going to be painful trying to brush through, the strands felt clean. Her body did as well, and her face felt clear of oil. Her teeth even felt like they'd been brushed recently.

Secrets of the Sanctuary

Quiet footfalls could be heard approaching from down
the hall, and even though she knew she should be safe in
Rafe's home, it didn't stop her heart from picking back up and
slamming against her chest. Her breath escaped her in a panic
when her hand found the knife strap around her thigh missing.
The doorknob jiggled, and Thea eyed the candles as something
to throw at whatever was coming through that door—only to
stop when, not a monster, but a dark-haired woman opened
the door and strode in. She halted abruptly when her eyes
connected with Thea's, and Thea was struck by the oddity of
the multiple colors she saw in the noirette's gaze.

"Oh. You're awake…" the stranger stated awkwardly.
Thea nodded just as gracelessly, eyeing over the new-comer.
Subsequently, she realized the person bore a gold insignia.

Thea was on edge immediately. The Summoner wasn't
any of the Council's second chosens, at least that much she
knew, but it still unnerved her that an unknown Coven
member was in Rafe's house—waltzing into her room on top of
it all.

The woman wore only a faded plum corset with
matching shoulder pads and black leather pants with straps
that crisscrossed over her hips. Her bare toes scrunched into
the carpet repeatedly as the silence stretched between them,
the purple paint of her toenails catching the light every time.
Her skin was pale enough to rival Mokana's. Obsidian hair fell
over her shoulders like an oil spill with dark bangs framing
darker eyes. Except, one eye was not just one color. The top
part of her right iris was a startling bright, cornflower blue.

It was hard not to stare. She was stunning, and Thea
normally wouldn't feel threatened over the beauty of another
woman—even if such beauty was the embodiment of what she
had been supposed to strive for a long time ago. No, Thea
didn't fault other women on their good looks, but she hated

admitting that the woman could be so pretty while walking around *this* particular house.

"I'll go get Rafe," she said suddenly before turning and fleeing the room.

Thea was again left alone with a heart that wouldn't slow. The image of that man in the rainforest flashed through her mind. Had that really been Rafe? Had that really been the Summoner she knew and…

Loved?

Her heart ached, and it was sudden enough to steal her breath away. For some reason, she didn't hate the sensation. She shook herself. This was not the time to be thinking about stuff like that. She had to get dressed before said man barreled into her room. No one ever knocked.

She heaved her legs over the side of the bed and glanced around for a change of clothes. She had put away all her things before she'd left to go to the Grim Bean the other day. The clothes she'd worn were probably in the trash. The last thing she wanted to do was pull back on her scratchy, shredded, damp leathers and dirty corset. Her boots were most likely ruined as well but, in her field of work, she had to replace shoes often. She still had her steel-toed high-tops somewhere. She strode across the room to the far wall where the guest dresser was, and she was just opening the bottom drawer when the door to the room exploded into the wall beside her.

That was how Rafe found her. Arm reached out, slightly bent at the waist, dressed only in a nightgown, frozen in place from the sudden commotion. The man looked a little worse for wear, but his hair was damp and shiny from a fresh shower. The scent of aftershave came wafting in, mingling with the lavender. There were dark circles visible under his wide eyes, but they weren't prominent. His mouth bobbed open in his shock.

Then he was tripping over himself as he exited, taking the door with him and leaving behind the massive dent in the wall from when he'd thrown it open. She would no doubt lecture him on that later.

"She didn't tell me you were in the middle of dressing." She heard his awkward, muffled voice through the door.

"Not really in the *middle* of dressing, thankfully. I was just about to. Who is she, by the way?" She couldn't help but ask, not at all liking the green little monster residing within her. She hoped it hadn't surfaced in her voice.

"Who, Lilith?" a pause, then, "She's from my squad."

Oh, really?

"That's nice," she muttered stiffly, yanking off her nightgown and tossing it in the hamper with a huff. Why did she care about some woman from Rafe's squad? She didn't care. If Rafe wanted to casually invite over his friends while she was knocked out, healing from injuries she sustained while almost dying, what did it matter to her?

"She's also married to my older brother. You remember Richter?"

Oh. Thea wanted to thank the Summoner in the same breath she wanted to smack him in. Did he know she was being jealous? Was he teasing her? Or, was he was just trying to fill the silence? The man would rather take on a hoard of blood mages than deal with an awkward situation. He always visually cringed when he had to witness someone else make a fool of themselves.

Also not one for long silent pauses, she asked, "Is that the brother with the brown eyes or the ones like yours?" Pulling a thick tunic over her head and reaching for a new corset, she suddenly remembered the whole reason they'd gone gallivanting off to the Dark Market in the first place. "Where're my old clothes? Where's—" she flung the outfit to the floor and hurriedly started searching around the room for her dirty corset and pouches. "Rafe, where's—"

"I have it, don't worry."

She paused, refusing to let her body sag in relief until she knew for sure. "You have…everything?"

"Yes. I have everything that was in your pouches."

Silence followed the admission, and Thea could breathe easy. Even the slight soreness in her chest didn't bother her as much now with the sense of absolute relief coursing through her. It hadn't all been for nothing. They wouldn't have to start all over again. She quickly got back to dressing herself and only winced when she had to tighten the strings on her corset.

"And I'd like to think my eyes are unique," Rafe grumbled through the door a few moments later.

Thea snorted. "Half your family has eyes like yours. Hellfire, even Mokana has eyes like yours. I always found it ironic."

Another pause, shorter this time. "No, she doesn't. Her eyes are a lot bluer than mine."

She rolled her eyes. "You can open the door now." She needed to pull on her boots, but since all her belongings had been stored elsewhere, she was done as far as this room was concerned.

She was in the process of blowing out the candles and snuffing out the incense when she heard the door open. That split second afterward was all she had before hands landed on her shoulder and spun her around. The ache in her chest protested, but she didn't have time to complain when strong arms enveloped her and brought her in for a suffocating kiss.

Thea's eyes widened and a muffled *eep* escaped her. Her brain short-circuited. Her arms flailed around until they landed on his wide shoulders. He pulled back quickly, familiar blue-green eyes watching her like a hawk. Gauging, assessing.

She hesitated for the briefest of moments, a million things rushing through her head. That she wasn't good enough, that he deserved better, that she would only disappoint him. But she knew Rafe. She knew he was a man that thought of every possibility, every course of action before he went through with a decision. She knew he had to have thought about this for more than just today.

But, beyond all that, she *was* good enough. She *did* deserve happiness.

She gave him a hasty nod and gingerly wrapped her arms around his neck. Suddenly, all she could do was feel. The softness of his lips against hers, the heat in her cheeks, how her head began to swim as her eyelids grew heavy, forcing them shut. Rafe's lips were warm, and the heat of his hands as they pulled her closer burned her skin even through her clothes. Her heart raced in her chest, and the ache she felt there earlier grew. She didn't care. Air had become trivial in this moment, and if things could stay this way forever, she'd gladly never take another breath again.

When he pulled back, they both were left panting. Thea's arms remained around his neck, idly twirling his dark, damp locks around her fingers. Pressed as close as they were, she could feel his racing heart match hers.

"I thought I lost you," he said, moving his hands to cup her face. She could feel the slight tremors in his fingers, could see the emotions swirling in his blue-green gaze.

She swallowed around a lump that formed in her throat. "I thought I was going to lose me, too." For a completely different reason, though. She wanted to tell him about her break down in the rainforest, wanted to tell him about how she conquered her past, if only for now.

Instead, she kissed him again.

Chapter Sixteen

I'm Going to Pretend that I'll Remember all of Your Names

"The Jeweled Canopy is spelled."

Thea blinked at the news that settled around the packed living room like a dense fog. She couldn't tell why it was so tense, or why everyone seemed to have their eyes glued to her. Sure, she figured it might have had to do with her just waking up from being rescued in a jungle, but that didn't account for the way everyone in the room acted like they were holding their collective breaths as if waiting for her to strike. They were overreacting, in her opinion.

She aimed her gaze at the one who just spoke, the dark-haired female Summoner from earlier, Lilith. A massive white snake was woven around her neck like a scarf, and it raised its flared head to meet her gaze with swirling bronze eyes.

"That's…great. That still doesn't answer my question as to how you guys assembled a team and got to me so quickly."

Rafe cringed beside her, and Namara somehow looked like she was going to be sick.

"What? What's wrong?"

Rafe answered her, squeezing her hand slightly in assurance. When they'd left the room together, he hadn't been able to separate himself from her completely. "We didn't get to you that quickly, T."

Thea was still confused, quirking an eyebrow at him. "You got there pretty quick considering you didn't even know where I ended up."

"That's where my expertise helped out," Lilith chimed in from her spot by the hearth. The glow of the fire was throwing shapes across the harsh angles of her porcelain face.

"What do you mean by that?" Thea turned in her spot to face the other woman, but her gaze was pulled away when Rafe groaned as if a painful headache had suddenly taken hold of him. He sighed heavily and ran the hand not linked with hers through his damp hair, massaging his temples. "Can someone tell me what's going on before this big lug passes out?"

Rafe tossed her a glare, but it lacked its usual heat. He sighed again, and it was a resigned sound. "Thea…you were in the rainforest for a whole week."

Thea stared at the Summoner, holding his unwavering gaze until the overwhelming silence of the room brought her out of whatever stupor had gotten ahold of her. For a long moment, she didn't say anything. She flicked her gaze to each individual in the room, noting that they didn't negate what Rafe had said, and the way they were acting—as if holding their breath—finally made sense.

She gingerly rose to her feet and untangled her hand from his. "This isn't some kind of joke, is it?" she asked quietly, moving her arm back when he tried to reach for her again. "I must have been more delirious than I thought if I hadn't seen the sun ever go down in the sky."

"Do I ever joke around when it comes to situations like this?" Rafe asked just as quietly, rising to his feet as well when it was clear he wasn't going to get her to sit back down with him.

Thea's eyes hardened on the Summoner. "I don't know, Rafe, you could be laying one on me right now." Thea felt cornered, and not only cornered but defenseless. Not that she thought she'd ever use a weapon against a fellow Coven member—much less Rafe—but the thought of having so many beings in a room who she felt were trying to pull the wool over her eyes without the familiar weight of her dagger at her thigh was making her want to suddenly lash out, fight dirty.

"All right, you two," Lilith interrupted, snake gone from around her neck as she moved between the two with hands raised to separate them. She threw Thea a hard look that made the Spellweaver want to bare her teeth and growl at the woman. "That was the point I was trying to get at when I told you the rainforest was spelled. You didn't notice, but you were gone for several days, and this man right here stayed up for three nights straight before he finally crashed. I had to forcefully shove food down his throat just so he'd eat."

As much as Thea wanted to argue that it should have been impossible for a full week to have passed, she couldn't escape the images of the man in the jungle that looked and sounded just like Rafe—and now the stubble that had grown on his face, the dark bruises under exhausted eyes, and limp, greasy hair clicked inside her head. The ache in her chest returned, not liking the image of Rafe starving himself as he tried searching for her day and night.

Giving Lilith a small nod that she was now listening, she sat down on the sofa, hearing the springs protest as quiet settled around the room. Lilith moved back to where she had previously stood off to the side of the fireplace. The other beings in the room seemed less tense. The Summoner continued on with her knowledge of Thea's latest haywire expedition, calling back her snake that had taken shelter on the dark leather of the cherry wood chaise behind her.

"No one knows why or for how long the forest has been spelled, but some have speculated since the very beginning of time. There is not much known about the Jeweled Canopy, in particular, especially the magic that thrives there. Old sea shanties sang about sailors washing ashore off the Black Veiled Sea and encountering *'gods in man's form'* and *'trees that glittered more than the king's crown,'"* she quoted. Her sharp, dual-colored eyes skittered over Thea but didn't linger, and for that the Spellweaver was grateful. "Those songs predate the Elvan Era."

"That still doesn't explain the time difference," Lilith's twin brother and the first Summoner Thea confronted in the rainforest, murmured from beside her. "Or the fact that the sun never went down." His naturally neutral expression was less severe than his sister's, though if he were to grow his hair out to the same length, they would have been identical — save for Lilith's heterochromia iridum.

Leto Remes, as he had called himself, didn't wear much either in the warmth of Rafe's duplex. A fitted, black leather vest with more pockets than a corset and tan trousers graced his pale skin. He was also barefoot, and his toes were also painted, except he had completed his dark look with black polish instead of purple. He was casually running his fingers through his large chimera's tawny mane, snatching back his fingers and glaring at the goat part of the creature when it tried to nip at him.

Lilith shrugged, and the snake around her neck moved around to get comfortable. Its muscles flexed and undulated under the smooth scales, and it sent shivers up Thea's spine. "It could be that such an enormous mass of magic and energy warps time itself. There could very well be a very long, detailed theory that explains the makeup of the Jeweled Canopy…or it could be a 'just because' scenario. Alchemists and sorcerers don't have much to go on, and their thesis reports are nothing more than hypotheses." She shrugged again, and the snake hissed in irritation.

"Well, whatever it is, it's wicked cool," another Summoner, Helena Thomas, excitedly piped up with gleaming chocolate eyes. She was sitting on top of her manticore, the creature lazing across the floor. Its bat-like wings were gone, having melted back into its fur and disappeared. The spiraling horns remained, which Helena grasped and yanked on like a rowdy toddler. All the while, the expressionless face of the beast looked unamused but accepting. The woman turned her high-spirited gaze on Thea, and it was then that the Spellweaver realized the woman had twin scars just above both unruly eyebrows. "Dude and you fought off a giant all by yourself!"

She grimaced at the reminder. "I wasn't exactly winning back there." Helena waved off that concern as if it were unimportant. She could tell Helena was a carefree sort of person, but with an impish grin always in supply. She had heard stories of the Summoner, of all of them actually, though she'd never seen them before today. Helena's short russet locks were pulled back into two high pigtails, and she was dressed simply in a green, drawstring tunic with a large leather belt synching her waist and tan trousers.

"I believe that was only because you were ill-equipped," weighed in the last new-comer in the room, Ellison Durand. He was the blond man with the kind smile and a warm, big brother gaze Thea barely remembered from the jungle. His eyes weren't the dull green Thea had originally thought they were but a soft hazel. His goggle glasses that had been strapped around his head were gone, replaced with frameless, oval lenses. His hair was still just as messily piled atop his head as she remembered, and his nonchalant disposition extended to his attire. His leather vest was loose over a baggy tunic, and his black trousers were harem styled and hung off his waist to expose prominent hipbones. The harpy she did remember, though, and how it had circled above them in the jungle. It was crouched with its face buried into its knees and napping upright similar to how a bird would be by the fire, unperturbed by the discussions going on around the room.

"It certainly didn't help that you had just suffered an anxiety attack," Lilith commented.

Thea froze and became keenly aware that all eyes in the room had suddenly swung in her direction once again. She hadn't told anyone about her episode in the jungle—not even Rafe. She had distinctly left that part out when she retold her side of the story.

She slowly rose from the couch again. "How did you know I had an anxiety attack?" Her eyes narrowed on the Summoner, momentarily distracted by the white cobra slithering around Lilith's pale neck, and as if feeling her scrutiny, raised its splayed head to meet her stare. She wondered if this creature had anything to do with the fact that her little secret hadn't been a secret after all. She didn't know exactly what the creature was, as there were many demons that could shape-shift. Did it have the ability to read minds? Or sense certain fears? Lilith had mentioned she had been the reason they'd located her but had it really been her who found Thea or had it been the pet hanging off her neck?

Lilith looked taken off guard, and her multi-colored gaze flickered between both Thea and Rafe before settling on her squad member. "You didn't tell her?"

Rafe frowned. "I wasn't planning on it. Thanks for opening your big mouth."

Lilith's nostrils flared, and the snake around her neck hissed. It quickly slithered off its owner's neck to find solace onto Leto's outstretched arm.

Thea swung her gaze between both Summoners, growing more aggravated with them for withholding something from her. "Will someone tell me what you guys are talking about?"

She was ignored.

"I didn't realize it was a secret," Lilith continued as if Thea hadn't spoken.

Oh, I did not just get swept under the magic rug, she fumed. "Someone tell me what's going on *now!*" She felt the dam give way, disregarding the startled hiss from both the snake and Mokana, who'd been silent from the start. She felt Namara's damp fingers twine with hers but snatched her hand away. She was not in the mood to be placated. She threw her furious expression on Rafe, who finally, *finally*, looked at her. "What haven't you told me?" she gritted out. Her nails bit into the calluses of her palms, and the room felt swelteringly hot. Rafe had never, ever, withheld information from her, even to spare her feelings. Why was now any different?

"How does she know? How do you know?" She didn't care about the fact that he did know. She didn't care if they all knew. She didn't care if the whole world knew. She could say without any hesitation she wouldn't even have cared if her family knew that their cruelty had finally broken her down years later. What she wanted to know was *how*.

She pointed her silent query at Lilith when she got nothing out of Rafe, and the female Summoner sighed. Despite her eyes being dark, they were exceptionally clear. Honest. Glass lakes under a starless sky reflecting midnight mountains.

"My pet is an alp. Alps come to their victims in the night, induce nightmares, and slowly drain their prey of their life force. It's like a vampire and an incubus had a baby," she ignored the offended hiss from said alp. "This is something all alps do. However, when I pulled him through the portal and introduced him to the intelligence spell, he has since been able to expand on his...abilities."

Thea nodded, resisting the urge to tap her foot.

"Alphred can manipulate people's subconscious, especially when they are...daydreaming. All he needs is to be near the person or near something of theirs." She gestured around the duplex where many of Thea's things had found a home amongst Rafe's possessions. "He can find a person's general location the longer the anxiety attack or 'daymare' is going on."

Thea felt a ball of ice drop in the pit of her stomach. "So, you had your pet induce an anxiety attack on me in order to find me?"

Lilith simply nodded, but Thea wasn't looking at her anymore as she sunk back into the couch cushions. She could feel everyone watching her, waiting with breaths collectively held for her reaction. Did they think she was about to fly off in a fit of rage? Or, that she was going to suddenly burst into tears? She could almost laugh at the tense atmosphere, and, in fact, that's exactly what she did. A bubble of laughter escaped her. The unexpected noise froze everyone in the room, and Thea laughed again. She didn't miss the bewildered looks tossed around as she dry washed her face.

"The...daymare that you forced me to go through was something that was very real. Something that I've been keeping bottled up inside and refusing to confront for the better half of a decade." She flicked her weary gaze at Rafe, Mokana, and Namara and could tell they knew exactly what she was talking about from the sympathetic and guilt-laced looks she received. "I know it wasn't your intention, but you made me face my demons, and I think it'll be easier facing them from now on. So, thank you."

Lilith blinked in stunned silence. "Uh…"

Helena snickered. "So not the reaction we were expecting, dude."

Thea shrugged, her small smile morphing into a smirk. "You had to do whatever it took to find me. For that I'm grateful. I ran away back then, but yesterday—er, whatever— when I relived that experience, I realized just how much I proved them wrong." She noticed the blank expressions on the group of Summoners and realization clicked. "You have no idea what I'm talking about, do you?"

Lilith shook her head, Leto perfectly in sync with his sister, Ellison looked sheepish, and Helena snickered once again.

"I can't see the visions Alphred places on people," Lilith grimaced apologetically. "I just know the gist of what happened."

Namara jumped up, sending water droplets flicking onto the coffee table. "I know what you're talking about," she assured, "and I'm proud of you."

"Yeah!" Mokana joined in. "Of course, you proved them wrong. You graduated top of your class at both the academy and the secondary academy—hellfire, you took on a hellhound and a soul eater!"

Surprise registered amongst the group of Coven members, and Thea threw an exasperated look at the rusalka. "Did not. That was a group effort, and I did more of the running away than anything else."

Mokana only grinned. "You survived, and that's a lot more than most people have done when encountering the two.

Besides, I distinctly remember you kicking that ugly thing in the jaw."

Thea winced at the reminder. "Yeah, and I paid for that, too. If I knew this past week was going to kick my butt this hard, I would have prepped some serious defensive spells."

Helena cocked her head to the side like a curious puppy, auburn bangs flopping over one eye. "Don't you mean last week? This week you were out cold. We thought you'd never wake up!"

"What?" Thea shrieked, whirling around to pin Rafe with an incredulous look, only to find the Summoner sighing into his hands.

"Does no one know what a 'sensitive subject' is?" he asked to no one in particular, scrubbing his face with his hands as he tossed a weak glare at the smaller female Summoner.

"Oops." Helena gave an apologetic look. "Sorry, dude."

"Don't be sorry," Thea snapped, still frowning at Rafe. "Were you not planning on telling me about that, too? Why was I out for a week when a Coven doctor could have cured me?"

"I was going to tell you," he groaned. "I reported to the Coven what happened at the Dark Market. They asked where you were and I..." he trailed off, guilt morphing his features and lacing his next words. "I told them you were hurt and healing up in bed, and that you didn't want to run up a bill. I didn't want them knowing you were missing. I didn't know where you were until the next day when the call came in, and even then I couldn't pinpoint your location until I had Lilith induce a nightmare—daymare—whatever. I didn't want someone I couldn't trust finding you and the..." he let his words die off again, but Thea heard the unspoken words just as clearly as if he'd said them to her. He didn't want a Coven member happening across her—which might not have even happened since she had been in the Jeweled Canopy—and finding a tethering stone in her possession.

Thea glanced over her shoulder at the group of Summoners. "Do they know?" she asked quietly.

Lilith answered. "No, but we trust Rafe. He's never led us astray, and if he's willing to risk so much for something so important…then we don't need to know the details. But don't think you don't owe me a huge favor after this," she directed at the man.

Rafe smiled but it didn't reach his eyes. "I know. I owe all of you."

"You might not like what I—" she went on to say, but the twinkling of her crystal ball alerted her of an incoming call. "Blast it all with hellfire, we just got back from a mission. Lilith Remes speaking," she answered the orb, dual-colored eyes narrowing at the speaker until the glass darkened. She spared her brother a glance. "Feral lamia in the Adalith district. You ready?"

"Always," her brother supplied, already pulling on his shoes and grabbing his heavy cloak. He pulled out the ingredients for a teleportation spell while his sister was gathering her belongings together. They were quick, efficient, and within seconds they were both gone along with the alp snake and chimera.

"We'll be heading out, too," Ellison stated with a kind smile aimed at the Spellweaver. "I hope you get to feeling better, Thea. We're not as good as Dr. Snow, but under the circumstances, we tried our best."

"Yeah, man, you had a wicked cough at the beginning," Helena added, jumping off her manticore and dumping out all the ingredients out of her leather belt pouches.

Not only did the materials for the spell spill out onto the floor, but so did her talismans, her amulet, some feathers, runes, and—of course—a shimmering wand went rolling across the hardwood. Thea couldn't picture the redhead wielding anything else.

"When will you stop being so careless with your things?" Ellison asked in exasperation, but his voice never rose higher than the soft pitch he said everything in, like a mother to a small child. He ran his hands through his messy blond hairdo, pulling it out of its clip and re-piling it on top of his head.

Helena, very much like a small child to its nagging mother, stuck out her tongue. "Would you quit your worrying? My wand hasn't cracked in ages, and the rest of this stuff don't break. Let's go see your cousin, the other blonde Ell. Bet she'll give us something cool to do."

Ellison huffed, his bottom lip sticking out a bit as he mumbled, "I'm allergic to her cat, though."

"Oh, suck it up, man. Pristine is my favorite cat ever..." She glanced worriedly at her dead-eyed companion and dropped to her knees to smush the too pale cheeks of the manticore. "Except you, snookums! You're the best kitty in the whole wide world, yes, you are!"

Thea watched incredulously as the beast's corpse mouth quirked up into a smile. She glanced at Rafe to see if the man was seeing what she was seeing, but he only rolled his eyes skyward as Helena continued baby-talking her pet.

Ellison whistled for his harpy, who opened slitted teal eyes and leaped up over to him, using her giant wings to propel her farther. "Would you be a dear and help me with the spell? Someone's preoccupied."

"Of course," the harpy replied with a gritty voice that rivaled a chain smoker's.

When they were finally gone, Thea breathed in a sigh of relief. It wasn't that she didn't like the Summoners, but the meeting with them had left her a little drained. Wet arms surrounded her around her shoulders, and she turned in the embrace to give her pet a proper hug. Their reunion had been kept short when she'd walked into the living room earlier, and she could tell Namara had been nearing the end of her patience when the squad members started leaving.

"I'm so glad you're okay. They wouldn't let me sleep next to you," her kelpie pouted.

Thea rolled her eyes playfully. "Probably because you're actually back to your waterlogged self, and you'd drown me in our sleep."

Namara scoffed. "You know what? I liked you better when you were out cold." She dropped her arms, a smirk betraying her words.

"I don't!" Mokana interjected, bouncing off the couch and throwing her arms around the Spellweaver. "Now Rafe can stop moping around the house."

"I do not mope," said Summoner griped, crossing his arms stiffly over his chest.

"Not anymore," Mokana giggled.

Thea flopped down into the cushions beside the man, circling her arms around his neck and grinning when he refused to look at her. "Aw, Rafe," she cooed, grin widening when he stiffened beside her. "Did you miss me?" she teased, hoping her light-hearted banter would disperse the ghosts she saw in his eyes. It worked when amusement flickered there in those blue-green depths.

He glanced at her, gaze lingering on her lips long enough for her to feel her face start to warm. He turned away with a "Nope," popping the 'p' of the word.

Thea sighed dramatically and hauled herself off the couch. "Guess you won't miss me then while I'm off making my report?"

Rafe looked up, surprised by her words. "You're going to the Coven?"

"I have to state my side of the story, and I'll need your recount of the situation." She plucked her Coven grade cloak off the hall tree and wrapped it around her shoulders.

Rafe groaned again before he, too, stood up from the couch and walked over to the coat rack and slipped on his own cloak. "I wrote in my report that, while I was away on an official raid, you stayed behind to check up on your injured pet. Later, you crossed paths with Leslie up to no good. In an attempt to evade arrest, he offered up a portal keeper. The following day we went undercover to the Grim Bean and met Sheldon, who allowed us through after mentioning Leslie. I left out seeing Torro there. I knew that somehow reporting that would land me in more trouble than the High Priest."

Thea nodded. "Smart move…" She bit her lip as guilt nagged her. "Double-dip a candlestick. I told Leslie I would leave him out of this."

Rafe shrugged. "You promised him. I was the one that reported him."

"Yeah, but I can't leave that bit of information out now. It'll look like I'm protecting a criminal." Thea rolled her eyes skyward. "Whatever, I'm sure they'll detain him for questioning and let him go. They always do. Anything else I should know about?"

"Mass hysteria flooded the market. We were separated, you were trampled by the crowd and injured severely, and I recovered your body at your duplex after you managed to get to the portal. You didn't want to run up a bill with Dr. Snow, so I kept you under surveillance at my house."

Thea nodded again curtly. "Good to go. I'll head out now. I'll see you later. I assume I'll know where you'll be?"

"Yeah, I'll head there right now. Oh," Rafe glanced over at his pet. "Mokana, can you grab Thea's dust belt out of my room?"

"Sure." She flitted out of the living area and down the hallway, and Namara looked torn.

"Are you going to suggest we stay here and out of that…monster's way?" she asked, though Namara already knew the answer, and she didn't like it. Thea couldn't tell if the kelpie was talking about Cressida or the fallen demon prince with the monster comment, but she nodded regardless.

"It's safer this way. Who knows how the magic used could affect you and Moka."

Speaking of the rusalka, Mokana came back into the room with Thea's knife strap and dagger, her belt, pouches and—

"My sickle!" she cried excitedly, snatching the object out of the creature's hands. "How…?"

"A couple Summoners chased a demon out into those woods a few days ago," Rafe supplied, helping her slip on her belt and the sickle straps over her shoulders before securing the weapon to her back. "Captured the thing and found your weapon in the wreckage. They turned it into the Coven, and Ell notified me." He reached around her and dug in her side pouch, retrieving the tethering stone. "I'll hand this over while you're reporting in. Things will be underway by the time you get there."

Thea breathed a sigh of relief at the feeling of the familiar weight on her back. She felt ready to take on the world. What were a throneless one and powerful sorceress to her now? A smile stretched over her lips.

Rafe grinned back at her. "Ready?"

She nodded.

"Ladies first, then." He swept his arms out for her, offering her the door first.

With a goodbye tossed over her shoulder at the creatures, she turned the knob and stepped outside—right into a wall of snow.

She jerked back, sputtering and sending chunks of ice scattering as she hastily spat out the frozen water that covered her entire face and upper body. Her boots caught the semi-melted, slippery substance, and she felt herself lose her balance. She landed on her bottom, hard, and the air in her lungs exploded out of her. She was dimly aware of Mokana and Namara losing their minds in the background with laughter.

"Oh, right. Thea, you missed the blizzard."

She glared over her shoulder.

"Rafe!"

Chapter Seventeen

Pristine and Not-So Pristine

Thea hurriedly stepped out of the spelled pad of the arrival gate within Coven Headquarters. After the little stunt Rafe had pulled on her, she had demanded he send her to HQ with a teleportation spell. Immediately afterward, two more people—Hunters, by the look of their bronze insignias—appeared out of thin air. They scurried off with their pets without so much as a look in Thea's direction, and the Spellweaver noticed they were not the only ones in a rush. All around her people were running to and fro, carrying scrolls and thick texts in their arms. Summoners were barking orders. Demonic pets were trying to keep up with their frazzled owners. She noticed the notorious Riker looking grim as always and made a mental note to steer clear of that particular Coven member today. HQ was never this busy, or frantic for the matter.

She spied Ell at the center desk, fumbling back and forth with a giant stack of papers in one arm hugged close to her chest. The other hand scrambled across her workstation in search of something, and Thea made her way across the massive circular room, skipping over the marbled phoenix emblem that could only be fully seen by aerial view, to stand in front of the desk. She peered over to see what the distressed blonde was looking for but was startled to find a pure white cat with mesmerizing blue eyes perched daintily on one of the filing cabinets, idly licking one of its paws.

"Ell?"

Olive eyes popped up, wide and rimmed with lines of exhaustion. Heavy bags marred her usual soft expression, and her hair was far too greasy to have been recently washed. The woman looked like she hadn't slept in a week.

"Oh, hi, Thea." Her voice was less chipper than normal, and then she went back to looking for whatever she was trying to find, dismissing the Spellweaver. She began mumbling as she flipped scrolls over and shoved stacks of statements out of the way. "Where is that report? Debriefing details…mission reimbursement, no…no, that's not it."

"What's going on?" Thea lowered her voice, even though she doubted anyone else would be able to hear her with all the hustling and bustling from the other Coven members.

"Oh!" The woman peered up at Thea again, as if finally clearing the haze from her brain. "That's right, you've been gone for a couple weeks! Oh, Thea, the Coven's in shambles. So much has happened. The Council—ah!" She snatched a piece of paper left under a stack of reports and scrolls, stained with coffee droplets and smudged from the leftover breakfast pastries abandoned on the desktop, with a triumphant smile. "Sorry, got to go! Just write a report and leave it with Pristine!"

"Um, who…?" Thea watched the receptionist trip over herself trying to get down one of the hallways that branched off the room, probably into a debriefing office if the mass of reports in Ell's arms were anything to go by.

She reached down and grabbed a blank report form off the desk and grimaced at the couple of smudge stains on one of the corners. She quickly listed the events leading back to Leslie and her strange encounter with him, although she had to fabricate a few things just like Rafe had told her to.

When her report was complete, she looked around at the other members rushing around and snapping orders left and right. No one looked like a Pristine. A flicker of movement caught her attention, and when she looked down onto the desk, she was again struck with deep blue eyes from a bright white cat. The animal's eyes reminded her of the sirens' at the Dark Market.

"Can you make sure Ell gets this," she spotted the blue collar around the cat's neck where a gold nameplate hung from it. "Pristine?" Goddess, she was such a dunce. She didn't know if the cat could even understand her, but after the incidents of the past week—er, three weeks, she wasn't going to be surprised if it did. "I assume the Council is too busy to see me at the moment? I'll have a new crystal ball hopefully by the end of tomorrow should they wish to summon me." She was hoping they wouldn't, but luck hadn't been on her side lately.

The cat opened its mouth, jaw unmoving as it stated, "Of course, Spellweaver Bauer," like the soft voice had been projected out of the small creature.

Ah, a familiar.

Familiars were the soulmate, or 'other half,' of a person. Everyone had one, yet not everyone was willing to go through what it took to get one. It was rare to come across a person with a familiar because those that had one had to risk their very being to find their soulmate.

Ell had to have entered the spirit world. To do so meant she had astral projected her soul into another plane of existence while her body had remained behind. Coven members, a long time ago, had had the choice to choose between a familiar and a demon pet. Despite the benefits of a soulmate, a lot of members chose to simply pluck a creature out of Hell rather than risk losing themselves forever in the spirit realm. Over time, the Council decided to simply eliminate the choice of a familiar. If a member of the Coven wanted to forge into the spirit world, their family could not come after the Coven should the person not make it back to their body.

A familiar bonded with its other half on a level that could not compare between humans, or even a Coven member and their demonic pet. There was a spiritual connection that went unparalleled, and what one lacked the other made up for. They taught those practicing magics the right tools to use, what spells to cast in certain situations, and knew things most texts had yet to record. Thea's respect for the timid receptionist soared.

She quickly nodded her goodbyes and scurried over to the far back wall where the communal crystal balls were lined up, dodging and weaving through the crowd of scrambling members ranked from Cleanser all the way to second chosen and everyone in between.

Beside the communal crystal balls were a series of arched doorways, differentiated by the runes marked into the wood that dissected the massively large basement of HQ. The sub rooms made up the huge underground library. One contained carefully cataloged reports that were stored after a case was closed, another was information on every living thing on Raen, and the last were classic and historical reads that pertained in some way to the Coven. Sometimes texts or scrolls would get mixed up, and Thea had personally witnessed Ell reorganizing shelves for the better half of a day.

People kept running in and out of the first two, hardly giving the doors a chance to shut before it was being ripped open again. She eyed the members around her to see if anyone noticed her presence before sliding in a couple of copper coins into one of the dispensers. The darkened orb lit up with the intent of being used. She placed her fingers on the cool glass and brought Rafe to the forefront of her mind. She felt the tiny shockwaves of the crystal ball connecting with her magic before the Summoner picked up, eyes wider than normal.

"Second Rank Rafe Mac—Thea?" He squinted into the orb. "Oh, thank the goddess it's you."

Thea crowded her body around the orb and dropped her voice. "Why? What's going on?"

"Nothing," he dismissed quickly but kept glancing behind him. "I'm at the sanctuary." The meaning of the statement wasn't lost on her.

She nibbled on her lip before nodding once. "Okay, I'll be by to check in shortly." Conversations on the communal crystal balls could be traced and recorded easily by a second chosen or blue cloak, and she wasn't going to take any chances after her long absence. It wasn't why she contacted Rafe anyway. "Before I do, tell me what's going on with the Coven. It's a madhouse here. Ell's got a talking cat now? Everyone's running around like alectryons with their heads cut off."

"Thea, I wish I had time to tell you the full story, but I have to go like," he glanced behind him again, "*now*. Long story short, Hunter Peterson and Spellweaver Zvěrokruh confronted the Coven after exploring the academy's underbelly and finding a lot of…questionable things. I haven't had time to read the report myself, but it turns out the Council had two corrupt members—Isolde and Dmitri—and a fight broke out between everyone. The Hunter unleashed some sort of unimaginable power that's gotten everyone shaken up. The Council room is still in the midst of being cleaned up and restored, and the second chosens of both blue cloaks are being interrogated. If they're cleared, their ceremony will be held immediately after their trial."

Thea nodded along dumbly. "And this is the short version?"

"Trust me, I am cutting out a lot of the filler, like Ell's familiar. Anyway, shortly after the hellhounds—don't give me that look, yes, hellhounds—were brought in and contained, mass reports started pouring in of multiple other demon sightings."

"And you couldn't think to tell me this beforehand!" she spat angrily. She knew there had been at least a soul eater on the loose with the possibilities of other ferals lurking throughout the city, but to hear it confirmed that there were many demons escaping Hell, it sent a chill down her spine. No wonder everyone was in a state of panic right now.

"I'm sorry," he growled into the orb, "but your wellbeing was my number one priority at the moment."

She pressed her lips together, deflated. "Still, you could have told me afterward."

"Excuse me for being exhausted. I haven't gotten much sleep since you got hurt. Now, hurry up and get over here. The sorceress is getting reckless. She's looking bad, T." He hung up, leaving her to stare dumbfounded at the empty glass sphere. She retracted her fingers and stepped back, but his words were still ringing through her mind.

Your wellbeing was my number one priority. I haven't gotten much sleep since you got hurt.

She found herself smiling. The noise from the hall came back to her, and she jerked her head around to see if anyone had caught her in the act. She'd allow herself to think more on his words later, but she had more pressing issues to worry about right now. The last thing he said especially concerned her.

Chapter Eighteen

When You Think Everything is Okay

The wind outside was still bitter, slicing through Thea's body like a knife. Snow no longer fell from the dark gray skies now that the blizzard had gone and hit the city, though it left its devastating effects on the townspeople of Tolvade. It couldn't have come at a worse time, either, and she had a sickening feeling many people were going to venture out despite the dangers to find food and materials rather than wait for the Cleansers.

In emergency situations, Cleansers brought more to the table than simply cleansing, purifying ritual sites, and clearing debris from the roads. They were dispersed between the medical wing of the Coven and helping the Hunters, where even members with only basic knowledge of magic could put their other skills to work by bringing aid and relief to the citizens hiding out in their homes.

Using the arrival and departure gates within HQ, a Coven member could teleport to anywhere in Tolvade. The only exceptions were inside beings' homes, and their only downfall was that there was a delay when overused. Not only was there a physical line but when too many members used the departure pads, the magic caused a sort of limbo traffic jam. Teleporting went from seconds to sometimes half an hour at worst. It was why Thea had chosen to face the elements outside, and it looked like she was practically the only one.

Secrets of the Sanctuary

A city-wide ordinance must have been sent out to everyone in Tolvade, ordering people to stay in their homes. If the Coven was busy finding and containing demons, Cleansers probably had assignments up to their eyeballs, and the snow on the ground was most likely on the bottom of their priority list. The city felt abandoned. The town's market was bereft, and not a soul was around. All the wares had been boxed up and crated off back to the neighboring districts before the storm had struck, and the food stalls had stocked all their perishables into the Coven's emergency rations warehouse that sat behind HQ. Whatever was donated was written off the businesses' taxes.

She felt the same wave of unease trudging through the snow-packed streets as she had back in Siobhan's forest. The only lights lit were the ones lining the roads, though even then the world seemed cast in deep shadows. Townhomes and apartments were dark, with shops closed up and stables locked. She wasn't surprised to find Tasgall's shut down—it was every year. She wondered how the fiery redhead was doing, and she hoped Torro hadn't been too busy running around the Dark Market to not keep his only daughter safe.

She paused when she heard voices echo over the near vacant city square. Tiny figures that dotted the gloomy horizon were huddled together, and Thea could tell from their strict rigidity that they were Coven members under a Summoner's orders. She blended into the shadows of a crystal ball shop and watched the group rush off in the opposite direction of where she stood. She hoped that, whoever they were, they made it back to whatever home they had.

The wind picked up, howling through the empty streets and down the back alleyways in search of its next victim while it sang its eerie song for the few who listened. She clutched the cloak around her body tighter when it whipped through her clothes. It wasn't lost on her that only yesterday—what she considered yesterday, anyway—she was traipsing through the Jeweled Canopy and sweating worse than a guilty culprit before the Council. Now she was having the exact opposite problem.

Toward the outskirts of the city, the snow blanketing the ground was worse. Her breathing grew labored under the added effort it took to hike through the extra snow, and the wind was even more vicious now that the brick and mortar of the city had been exchanged for thin, snow-capped trees and scattered boulders as the only means of shelter.

Her heavy, steel-toed boots were not the best option to wear for these situations, and even under her thermal socks, her toes were burning from the cold, along with her lungs, her nose, cheeks, and fingers. She wished she'd brought a warming spell along with her because the gloves and facemask she wore were not cutting it in this weather.

One foot in front of the other, she trudged on until a specific landmark caused her to pause. A large evergreen split in two and charred from a past lightning strike marked the start of the Vemeese Lake just up ahead. Only a few weeks ago Namara had hidden out in that very lake when Thea had first ventured to Srbeveara, but now it was frozen over and lightly dusted with snow.

That familiar feeling walking around the woodland nymph's home registered with her once more. The forest was already deathly quiet, but now an aura of emptiness settled around her like a second skin. Apprehension curled in her stomach, clawing its way up until it wrapped its cold fingers around her heart and squeezed. She could tell something was not right as she neared the sanctuary, so she forced her numb legs to move quicker. This place no longer felt familiar to her anymore. She hadn't even reached the clearing where Srbeveara stood when she saw it.

The once glowing, pulsating dome barrier that encompassed the mythical haven was just…gone.

The shelter that had once appeared as a cozy and inviting dwelling to those who sought asylum now stood coldly against a backdrop of frozen, naked trees as their branches twisted in the wind's icy grip. Thea had been wary before due to the heavy rumors about the sanctuary that swirled around HQ, and it turned out there had been some merit behind the long-winded warnings she'd gotten before taking the mission. Now, however, she was truly leery of what lurked inside.

Gloved fingers hesitated at the huge wooden doors. Rafe had said it was bad. How bad? What had happened in the time she had been gone? The shelter felt hollow and empty as if she'd been away for years instead of two weeks. Had Cressida's power waned this much? Or were her black magic urges starting to overtake her?

She squared her shoulders and took a steadying breath. The only way she'd know was if she went in and found out. She was prepared for the heft the doors usually carried, but with the slightest touch, they rocked backward as if light as feathers. A chill danced its way up her spine, and she didn't know if it was entirely the cold's fault. The magic in the building felt sapped dry. She stepped inside and heard the sounds of her boots echoing off the concrete like claps of thunder. The mysterious singing woman that could never be found but always heard was gone. The cascading stream of water was no more, and the only evidence there had been a waterfall to begin with was the stagnant water held within the circular ring of stones under it.

Her breaths were loud in the quiet stillness of everything, visible from the cold that seeped in from outside. She closed the doors behind her, and again they clicked shut with the barest of touches. She checked both Blythe's and Cressida's parlors before stalking forward. The only signs of life had been the abandoned teacups in Blythe's room, though she couldn't detect the distinct smell that came from the foreign tea, so she couldn't guess how long ago the woman had been there.

Inside the cave where Namara had been ordered to soak for a week, the still water reflected like glass in the low light. Had Namara witnessed any changes in Blythe or Cressida? How long had Srbeveara felt like this? Is this what Cressida was feeling now? Or, was she experiencing something worse than this?

A lump caught in Thea's throat. She didn't like the sorceress. She hadn't liked her from the start. She couldn't understand most of her reasons for the things she did, but she did understand desperation, fear, loneliness, finding someone, and wanting to hold onto them even though they were threatening to fall through the cracks.

She just wants to live. We all just want to live.

Thea didn't even know if the Cressida she had dealt with had even been the real Cressida. Black magic wasn't something that someone could escape once they dabbled in it. A small spell, a tiny incantation, reading aloud the wrong passage over the right tools. That was all it took to get beings hooked. It changed them from the inside out until, eventually, they were no longer the same.

How could Blythe, a bubbly, cheerful, and generally happy soul find love in someone who was always so cold? Yet, the woman looked upon the sorceress as if Cressida was her entire world, which made Thea wonder at the person the sorceress truly was, or at least who she used to be.

She picked up her pace down the narrow strip that circled around the healing waters, moving faster until she found herself sprinting down the pathway, bounding over the uneven ground. She skidded to a halt when she finally came across the opening of the once-secret passageway. The stones that had closed it off and hid the stairwell from view were now nothing more than a pile of rubble from the lack of magic circulating the building.

Distant screaming crawled its way up the steps and out of the darkness. The distraught wails awoke something in Thea, and she launched herself into the darkness without a moment's hesitation, taking the stairs two at a time with her hand flying down the rough wall and scraping her gloved palm in an attempt to keep her balance. There were no lit torches to guide her way, only the rhythmic distance of steps carrying her further down into the unseeing abyss, accompanied by the growing pressure that tried to force her back up them.

She finally saw light, the unnatural green that slithered up the stones at the bottom. The headiness from whatever magic was being performed was swamping the stairwell the closer to the ground she got, pressing on all parts of her body like an unwelcome embrace. She jumped down to the floor after the third to the last step and burst out of the stairwell, only to immediately drop to her knees under the magic that slammed into her body. She crumpled against the wall and gasped for air. Throbbing and heavy, with pressure clogging her ears with every tiny movement she made, her head snapped back. She hissed from the pain that skittered up the side of her skull when it connected with the stone wall behind her. With effort, she managed to turn her head enough to where she spotted Rafe on the opposite side of the chamber, similarly hunkered down and facing the same fate as her. He had his staff out, and Thea remembered him saying he had to neutralize the spell. His arms kept swaying though, and she could tell he was losing focus. How long had he been down here?

In the center of the room were Cressida, Blythe, and the throneless prince. Gaunt, hollowed cheeks and deep bags aged the sorceress's strong features dramatically. She stood before an open, thick tomb, where fat plum, crimson, and obsidian candles flickered with hostile green flames. Surrounding the book that was laid out on the ground, the candles took up nearly every available space in the small chamber.

Strange yellow dust was scattered across the cobblestone floor and clumped in random, messy piles. Cressida's palms were slit and dripping blood onto the splintered bone pieces littering the blank page of the open text, and the sable markings carved into the bones bled black, mixing with her blood and forming words Thea couldn't read from the angle she was sitting at.

"Onch'pis kerugh ais de enil!" Blythe was screaming in her native tongue. Her hair was a mess of ratty buns sloppily pulled up, makeup smeared over rapidly blinking eyelids while tears streamed down her sickly pale cheeks. She was banging against an invisible barrier encasing Cressida, Asmo, and the spell. *"Dederits'rik' se! Ais erzheno ch'im! Khndrym aim, pitk' i kengnik' home!"*

Cressida's eyes snapped open, and the green irises flashed with the same hostility from the unnatural flames that threw the room into a sinister glow. "I *can't* stop this, Blythe! Would you rather I die? Do you care that little for me? Do you not love me?" she yelled over the woman's broken sobs, and

Blythe jerked back as if physically stung. "If you love me let me do this!" Cressida bellowed, before screwing her eyes shut and grabbing the waiting, bloody hands of the throneless prince. Blood welled up from where their fingers interlaced and trickled down to their wrists. They both began chanting, and the fractured bone pieces ignited into a growing fire that swiftly burned lime in color.

"*Oherki, ais sorym aim k'iz!*" Blythe screamed so loudly her voice cracked, both fists banging against the barrier in her desperation. Thea felt tears prick the back of her eyes as she watched helplessly. Blythe flung an accusatory finger at Asmo, who had previously watched the two interact with old, amused eyes but was now ignoring the woman with ease. "*De divi, dyk' ch'ik' kerugh vstehil!*"

Her pleas, or demands—Thea wasn't sure—fell on deaf ears. The sorceress and the throneless demon were blatantly disregarding the screaming woman now. Their chanting grew in volume until it was not just Cressida's and Asmo's voices Thea heard. Thousands of whispers spiraled into the chamber until their voices were so loud Thea had to clamp her hands over her ears to muffle them. She pulled her hands away when she felt wetness trickle down her temple, bringing them in front of her eyes which widened at the sight of blood. It began leaking in earnest out of her ears, and then she felt the burning of her inner corneas as blood started to run down her cheeks like tears.

The magic in the room began to swell, building the pressure in her body until she felt like she was going to burst. Suddenly, a pillar of bright white light shot up from the pages of the book, disintegrating the bones. The pressure peaked until it imploded inside the chamber with a deafening boom. Thea felt rather than heard herself screaming until the blood loss took its toll, and she fell under the pull of unconsciousness…

Images floating in blackness were the next thing she remembered. That and pain, pulsing its way through her skull. She didn't know how long she was out, but when she regained consciousness, the pressure in the room had dissolved, the dripping wax candles had been snuffed out, the yellow dust covering the now singed cobblestones had mostly disappeared, and Cressida was lying lifeless in the middle of it all.

Blythe was full-on sobbing, and when Thea hastily wiped the blood from her eyes, she watched the woman crawl shakily over to the pale sorceress where she collapsed, shrieking something in her mother tongue. Her hair had been blown out of its messy up-do and her dress was filthy and torn in places.

Thea met Rafe's eyes across the chamber. He had slowly climbed to his feet, blood drying on his cheeks and saturating some of his hair until it clung to the side of his face and neck. She pushed herself up as well, gloved fingers biting into the rough stones behind her. Dizziness gripped her for a moment, and a moan slipped out. She fell back against the wall and winced when her head connected with the stones once again. Pinprick needles tattooed across the skin of her arms before numbing out. This feeling continued through her chest and down her legs. Her fingers and toes felt like they were burning, but it wasn't the same feeling as when they were thawing out from the cold. She had to remind herself to breathe slowly. In, out. In, out.

Soft coos reached her bloodied ears, broken by quiet sobs. Light blue skirts pooled around the prone sorceress while

Blythe's long, tangled, deep brown curtain of hair hid Cressida's face largely from view. The Ernimoen was gently rocking the woman in her arms, cracked voice hushed in the still room. Her tanned, calloused fingers traced loving circles across pale, hollow cheekbones.

"Om sir. Om gighits'ok keresela. Om hugon," Blythe whispered, the words tumbling from her mouth like a prayer. "Come back. Come back to me, *om keresela.*"

"Rafe," Thea called weakly, but her voice cracked and sent her into a rough coughing fit. The Summoner dazedly glanced in her direction. Thea wheezed out huskily, "She may need a healing spell."

May because she may be beyond help at this point. Thea bit her lip and tears threatened to spill. She didn't know if all these feelings were purely her own, but she felt a whirlwind of emotions battling for attention inside her soul.

Blythe made a weak noise, a gasp or a sob Thea couldn't tell, and lifted her hand where some of the strange yellow dust clung to her fingers. She only hesitated for a moment before closing her puffy, red eyes. She didn't even need to chant a spell before her fingers were illuminating a crystal blue color. Her eyes flew open, gasping softly at the sensation, and Thea knew she was experiencing the tips of her fingers tingle as if they were freezing and burning all at the same time. Blythe experimentally ran her glowing fingers up and down Cressida's body.

The once-powerful sorceress, now stripped of her magic, convulsed whole bodily. Her cheeks regained some of their fullness, but they were still gaunt enough to be underweight. The color returned to her, and though she was still pale, it was a healthier complexion. The one hand Thea could see healed right up until only the dried blood remained caked to her palm. Her hair regained some of the shimmer until it was no longer limp and dull, but the pure ginger color Thea remembered.

Cressida suddenly gasped for air like a woman starved and sprung upright. The sound she made afterward was scratchy and abrasive, and immediately she collapsed back to the ground in a fit of dry coughing while curling in on herself.

Blythe couldn't seem to help the radiant smile that brightened the room when Cressida calmed and blinked blearily up at her. She giggled breathlessly, and her tears dripped from her wet cheeks onto the woman below her. She pressed hurried and sloppy kisses all over Cressida's face, her giggles breaking through and mixing in with her wet sniffles.

Cressida clamped her eyes shut against the onslaught, and a drowsy smile surfaced. Lazy green eyes roved the newly made sorceress's fallen hair, and her cracked lips pulled down into a thoughtful expression.

"I've never seen you with your hair down before."

Blythe's smile fell, and the anxiety that had slowly been seeping out of the room snapped back to attention. Thea watched as the happiness slowly drained from her face, taken on by a stricken expression. She grabbed Cressida's face, panic imbued in her foreign words. *"Onch'o meson ais khusym? Oherki, dyk' ynik'!"*

Cressida's soft smile grew dazzlingly bright, and a girlish giggle escaped her, surprising everyone in the room. She reached up and twirled a bloody finger in the long brown locks, admiring the shine. "Blythe, darling, you know I can't understand you yet."

Then her body went limp.

Chapter Nineteen

But It's Not

A slow, booming clap resonated around the chamber, and all eyes swerved to the forgotten throneless one leaning gracefully against the wall. A smug smile quirked Asmo's striking features into the embodiment of pure arrogance.

"You humans are always so entertaining."

He stalked forward with a wide grin full of pointy onyx teeth, the new power evident in his fluid movements. He glided over the cobblestones, his revealing garments whispering against his hoary skin. He stopped in front of Cressida and Blythe. He slipped into a crouch and flipped a lock of ginger hair out of the way with a sharp, black talon, ignoring the way Blythe tensed up protectively.

He took in Cressida's furrowed brow, her sunken cheeks, dry lips, and pale skin with deep, assessing eyes. He drew those eyes toward the blue veins on her arms, the ripped emerald corset and dirty trousers that hung loose and lay wrinkled over thin legs. Grabbing one of her hands, he picked at the rusty, dried blood under her chipped fingernails before dropping it back to the ground.

He threw back his head and laughed.

His harsh, grating, maniacal laughter caused Blythe to flinch back and gather Cressida closer to her. A serious expression settled over her face, even as she licked her lips nervously. "You can fix her, right? You can help her?"

Asmo continued to laugh as if she had just told the funniest joke he'd ever heard. He staggered to his feet, shoulders shaking and chest heaving. Thea didn't know exactly if demons needed air like most beings did, but Asmo seemed breathless.

"Who would have thought that it would end up like this?" The laughter died abruptly, and the arrogance was back. His soulless eyes gleamed, and his smirk revealed sharp teeth once again. "Oh, that's right. I did."

"What are you talking about?" Blythe stated slowly. Her accent was becoming thicker, the words harsh with more emphasis on the vowels. She sniffed, laying Cressida gently down onto the cobblestones before standing on trembling legs.

Her dark, glassy eyes sought Thea's gaze, then Rafe's, as if they knew something she didn't. Thea had nothing to tell her. This plan was supposed to go off without a hitch. Asmo was supposed to be back in Hell already, doing whatever horrible things fallen demon princes did to regain their throne. Cressida was supposed to be okay—was supposed to be freed from both the disease and the black magic urges clinging to her bones. Blythe was supposed to be happy because *that's what Cressida said would happen.* The woman had seemed so sure, so invincible. It was unnatural seeing the woman on the ground.

Thea looked on helplessly. She had unintentionally put more faith in the sorceress than she'd meant to. She had risked everything on a gamble; her career, her morals, her life on more than one occasion. All to ensure Raen, and more so Aeristria, would be safe from the hell Cressida had dumped onto them all.

Her glare was directed at Asmo, but it fell to Cressida. Thea hated her in that moment, and it was easy in the face of Blythe sniveling and standing in a room with people who were practically strangers and a demon laughing at her pain. Thea hated her more in that moment for what she'd done to Blythe than she could ever hate her for what she had put the others through.

Asmo was still talking, chuckling between his words as if the situation was really that funny. Though, Thea supposed to something like him it would be highly amusing.

"Your…what did you call her?" The demon grinned devilishly before wondering aloud, "*Keresela*? Fitting, I suppose. Powerful felines, though certainly not the strongest of cat creatures. Your little kitten was indeed gifted with powerful magic, and that is what kept all those dark urges at bay." He shrugged flippantly, though his black eyes were practically gleaming at the horrified expression that was slowly morphing Blythe's features. "No magic…nothing to keep the urges from taking over."

"But she does not have any magic! Why should urges continue?" Blythe cried, words losing their fluidity, and she was looking so lost it hurt Thea to witness.

She stepped forward and reached for the woman's hands, noting how they shook. She leveled her best glare at the demon. It didn't matter that she was standing in the same room as the most powerful creature on Raen currently — Cressida had been far more intimidating than this cocky creature from Hell.

Then his words clicked.

"The urges remain, yet she has no magic to indulge them. Her body's going through withdrawals, isn't it?"

Asmo scoffed. "Could you stop trying to be the smartest person in the room? It's kind of annoying."

"And you knew this would happen all along?" Thea continued.

"Of course, I did." The throneless one rolled his eyes and flicked an invisible speck of dirt from the decorative skulls adorning his shoulders. "I may have never partaken in a ritual quite like this, but I've dealt with black magic for eons and lived for even longer. It didn't take me long to figure it out. I'm surprised you never did."

Blythe snarled, and Thea and Rafe both startled at the noise. Power surged in the air that forced Rafe up against the wall and Thea staggering away, out of breath all of a sudden. Even Asmo looked somewhat impressed, though the sinister grin never wavered off his otherworldly face.

"I hold power over you. I am your master. You are tethered to me, and I am telling you to fix her." Blythe flung her arm back at the prone woman passed out on the floor and hissed with finality, "Now."

The demon threw back his head and barked another jarring laugh. "You are centuries too young to be going rounds with me, little peacock griffon."

Blythe faltered at the nickname, and the magic in the air deflated.

"I believe we're done here." Asmo appeared thoughtful, nodded once, and then winked at Blythe.

Thea blinked, and he was gone. She whirled around, but the demon had disappeared, she assumed, back to wherever it was he needed to be in order to retake his throne. She glanced at Blythe to gauge her reaction, but the panic that had twisted the foreigner's face was easy to read and didn't need to be deciphered.

"Blythe—" she started to say but lurched backward when pain shot through her body. Her knees buckled out from under her weight and collapsed to the ground with a garbled shout as power exploded around the room.

Thea knocked over candles, suddenly lit with bright orange flames, in her haste to roll away and create distance. She barely heard Rafe make a pained noise caught between a growl and a groan. Her vision blurred, watery again, but she couldn't even lift a hand to her eyes to see if it was blood or tears.

She had managed to roll a few feet away before the magic rendered her paralyzed, but she could see enough out of the corner of her eye. A blurry shape she knew was Blythe was standing in the center of the chamber among all the candles that blazed with hot flames.

Suddenly, the magic was gone, and Thea gasped, relieving the burning in her lungs. She shot up into an upright position and hastily scrubbed the blood—as she found out—from her eyes. She could feel the effects of losing too much in the way her head swayed and felt like it was much heavier, but she forced herself to look up.

The candles' flames had extinguished, leaving soft smoke wafting into the air and filling the room with their faint smells, all indiscernible to Thea at the moment because of the blood drying in her nostrils and coating the back of her tongue. Blythe had dropped her raised arms and the panic was gone, replaced with shocked surprise. Before her, Asmo stood with an expression that mirrored Blythe's.

"I…" Blythe floundered for words, glancing helplessly between Thea, grimacing when she saw the state the Spellweaver was in, and Asmo. "I did it?"

The surprise melted right off the demon's face, replaced with dark mirth that radiated off of him. His black daggers for teeth flashed again, and a shiver skittered down Thea's spine. "Afraid not, little peacock griffon."

Blythe's face scrunched up in confusion, though Thea noticed the nickname still affected her when she swallowed thickly before she was able to find her words. "You're here, though," she replied quietly.

"Oh, yes. I heard you knocking on my metaphorical door, but to open it and pull me out requires more than what you're capable of. I just wanted to see that last little bit of hope in your eyes crumble at my feet."

He blipped out of existence once again, cackling as he left. His raucous laughter echoed off the stone walls of the chamber before it, too, was gone, leaving all three magic wielders nonplussed.

It was Rafe who stepped forward after a long moment of silence passed between them all. Blythe looked so lost staring down at Cressida as if all the answers to her problems lay in ashes at her feet.

"Blythe?" Thea called quietly, but the sorceress barely reacted.

"I have her magic. I have her magic so why…she pulled him out. If she pulled him out, then I should be able to pull him out. Why?" She slowly dropped to her knees, eyeing her splayed fingers in her bewilderment until her focus drifted off into some unseeing vision.

"We should probably move Cressida somewhere more comfortable," Rafe tried, crouching down to her level. He caught Blythe's clouded, walnut gaze and nodded, and Thea watched in amazement as Blythe began nodding along with him.

"*Eau*," she concurred softly and staggered to her feet. Thea caught her and steadied her, but Blythe brushed her hands away. "'M fine."

Rafe hoisted Cressida up into his arms, and Blythe fretted over her sleeping figure the entire way up the now torch-lit stairwell. The stones keeping the stairwell hidden from the healing cave were back in place, giving way when Blythe reached out and touched their rough surface.

Secrets of the Sanctuary

The waters in the giant pool lapped against the sides of the enclosure as if welcoming the new sorceress. Thea could hear the waterfall tumbling into the rocks just outside the cave.

"Bedroom is hidden," Blythe muttered loud enough to be heard, though Thea and Rafe still had to strain their ears to hear her as they neared the cascading water. She reached a hand out to the waterfall and, like Cressida had done before her, pulled the water aside as if it were a solid, material curtain. "It is up the stairs."

Wordlessly, they followed the somber sorceress up the wooden planked stairway. The singing anomaly Thea had noticed missing earlier was back, singing her strange songs into the sanctuary's main hall with a soothing lilt. The trio had just reached the top of the second floor when a heavy knock rattled the entrance doors. The three glanced at one another before Blythe let go a shaky sigh and descended the staircase, striding over to the doorway with her head held high.

As if just now remembering her hair was down, she quickly pulled it up and tied it into a bow-like knot using nothing but the strands of her thick hair. Once somewhat presentable, she reached for the doors and opened them with the ease she'd always seemed to have with them. Two beefy-looking Summoners stood shoulder to shoulder in the entryway, and Thea noticed Rafe straighten beside her.

"How can I help you?" was Blythe's hollow query.

"Summoner Dean Brickard here on official investigation. Step aside, ma'am. We've been ordered to sweep the premises," the taller of the two announced. He sported cinnamon hair whipped by the wind, and it looked like it had been carded through with heavy hands many times. A fresh, severe hook-shaped scar adorned his jaw and right cheek, roughly stitched up. When he tried to push his way through into Srbeveara, the weariness left Blythe's body and her spine snapped straight. She moved herself into Dean's path and leveled his partner with a cool gaze.

"And who would you be?" Her voice held enough authority that it could rival Cressida's on a good day. Both Summoners straightened, and Thea internally panicked. If Blythe—a foreigner, who's heritage didn't interact with magic—suddenly started wielding defensive spells, the Coven would come raining down on the sanctuary in droves for answers.

Rafe quickly deposited Cressida on the staircase, leaving Thea to straighten out the woman's body before she could slump over. She quickly propped her up against the railing and watched Rafe jog down the stairs to interrupt the introductions.

"Summoner Ivan Manning, nice to see you again. Dean, it's been a while." He smiled diplomatically as he brushed past Blythe and subtly herded her behind him. He would have lost a limb stepping in front of Cressida and taking charge of the conversation like that. However, in this instance, it was necessary, and Blythe didn't appear offended in the slightest.

He clapped a hand on the bigger man's shoulder while flashing his gold insignia. Their eyes blew comically wide as they took in the current state of their fellow Coven member before recognition slowly started to register.

"Summoner MacBain, what happened to you? What are you doing here?" Manning questioned with assessing grey eyes. His hair was trimmed close to his scalp, a sharp design shaved around his temples. The man's ears were bright red, despite the fur-lined hood of his cloak pulled tight over his head.

Blythe met his analytical gaze calmly when it landed on her, but it soon moved over Rafe's shoulder to find Thea on the stairs with an unconscious woman. It probably didn't help both Coven members' faces were covered in drying blood. Thea watched in bemusement as he nudged Dean with his elbow and gestured to look behind Rafe. The other Summoner narrowed his eyes at Cressida. Rafe raised his hands to halt the two before they could start firing off more questions.

"Spellweaver Bauer and I already have everything under control. I apologize for failing to report in. It was—a mess," he finished bluntly. The two glanced over Rafe's shoulder again.

"Have you apprehended the culprit then?" Dean eyed Cressida's slumped over form again, and because of that, he didn't notice Blythe stiffening behind Rafe. She clenched and unclenched her hands, and Thea held her breath, hoping she would rein in her emotions long enough to see the men leave.

"There is no need." He waved away their concern. "The spell backfired, and the sorceress has lost her magic. She is no longer a threat to Aeristria."

Manning narrowed his eyes in suspicion, but a sharp series of buzzes snapped both his and Dean's attention away, and he pulled out his crystal ball to a hooded figure who barked out a coded message and a location loud enough for Thea to hear from the second story.

The Summoner shared a grim look with his partner. "We got another call. Reaper two blocks from HQ. You guys got this?" he aimed at Rafe, who nodded. "Good. Don't forget to report in. We'll pass the word along back to the Coven."

They both rushed off after a hasty farewell, and Rafe quickly shut the door. He turned on Blythe, about to no doubt lecture her on the lengths he and Thea had just gone through for the now incapacitated Cressida, but the woman held up a roughened palm and spoke up before he could even open his mouth. "I don't know what Cressida promised you. She never once made me aware of what she was hiding down in that chamber. I doubt Cressida will even remember if she is ever able to wake up, but I will tell you this, Mr. MacBain: should you need anything in the future, I will aid you however I can. It is all I can promise you at this point." She turned away and ascended the stairs, her long blue dress trailing behind her much like the robes of the sovereign she just proved herself to be.

Cressida and Blythe's bedroom was indeed hidden. The first time Cressida had allowed Thea to conduct her investigation, the Spellweaver had merely passed a glance at the wooden informational bulletins propped up on the wide stone walls that divided the corridors. She'd only really read them after she'd been thoroughly soaked from the mermaid incident.

The middle bulletin hid a secret latch under the bottom edge that, when pulled, revealed the divider wall between corridors to be hollow. Inside was a long, skinny passageway that led to a door at the far end of it. Rafe had to shuffle in sideways with Cressida in his arms, and Blythe kept wincing apologetically every time she heard an especially loud scrape against the rough walls.

Her bedroom was massive. On either side were wrought-iron, decorative doors that Blythe said led to the two balconies Thea noticed on her first impression of Srbeveara. The floor was made up of smooth, flat square stones while the walls were wide, horizontal wooden planks that hadn't been completely sanded down. They still held traces of bark attached to them. The four posters of the enormous bed were carved opulently out of tree trunks. Sheer white curtains hung from the rafters and sparkled in the honeyed light that emanated off the sporadically placed salt crystals and small candles. An altar, to what Thea could only guess was the goddess, took up one of the corners of the room, abandoned.

"Take her to the bathroom," Blythe ordered, bringing Thea's attention back to the situation. The sorceress guided the way to the open-access washroom. Rafe followed her, Thea trailing behind him, and watched him place Cressida in the circular stone bathtub. Flowering vines grew along the cracks in the walls and dangled from the ceiling over the tub. It was all very whimsical, though neither Coven member was allowed to appreciate the quaintness before they were shooed out.

"I'll take care of her from here. You may want to do something in the chamber should more Coven members show up asking questions. If they wish to see the place where the spell was performed, they'll know that *thing* was summoned by the markings on the floor and ingredients used."

"Do you have more halite," Thea pointed to the rock salt glowing on the bedside table, "or can we use that?"

Blythe glimpsed over the pink crystal she'd been using as a lamp with a thoughtful expression. "The ones in this room are the only ones I have been able to get a hold of cheaply. Cressida wouldn't let me dig them out of the lake. Now it makes sense as to why it is so expensive. You are more than welcome to it. If you should require white salt, you may find it in my—how you say…parlor downstairs."

Thea glanced down at her empty pouch pockets and grimaced. "Yeah, I'm nearly empty on everything. Don't worry, we won't take much. Maybe some herbs too, if you wouldn't mind."

Blythe shook her head quickly as the skin on her cheeks reddened. "Not at all. I never use them anyway. I just like the way they look…" Her blush deepened.

Thea gave her a reassuring smile. "We won't be long."

Rafe hefted the heavy pink rock onto his shoulder, and Thea led the way back downstairs, contemplating the entire situation they had put themselves in. Had all of this been for nothing? Asmo hadn't helped them eradicate any of the feral demons—was that even something he could do? He knew from the start how all of this was going to play out, and Thea should have seen it coming. At least the demon would go back to Hell and stay there. They didn't have to worry about him wreaking havoc on the world now that he had gotten the equivalent to a growth spurt in power.

She stepped into Blythe's eclectic room long enough to grab a handful of salt, deposit it into one of her empty belt pouches, and plucked an empty wooden bowl and a clean towel from the woman's vanity desk. She checked the vials of herbs before she left, taking the lavender and crushed yarrow with her.

"Can you run up and down the stairs and gather the water?" She asked the Summoner as they stepped up to the waterfall.

"I don't see why not. It's been a long time since I've done a cleansing."

"Water retriever it is." She handed Rafe the wooden bowl and took the halite crystal from him before splashing through the water. He followed in after her, shaking droplets out of his eyes.

She made her way back down to the chamber first, Rafe having stopped to collect the healing water. The large salt rock glowed through the darkness more than the torches could ever hope to. When she reached the dungeon, she immediately started clearing the room of the candles.

With a quick incantation, she said, "I absolve you of the burden placed upon you. Be gone." The candles burned down into nothing but puddles of clear wax, devoid of their original colors. Pinches of salt were tossed onto the floor, over the wax puddles and ashes left in the center of the room. She placed the halite over the ashes, dusted it in the crushed yarrow, laid down the lavender stalks around it, opened her hands up to the goddess, and closed her eyes.

By magic, body of the goddess.

By water—she heard Rafe splash some down onto the floor—*her rushing blood.*

By air, the breath of the goddess.

By fire, her burning soul.

In the name of the goddess may this room be blessed and made pure.

Time seemed to suspend itself.

She repeated this chant inside her head over and over. The smell of the salt swamped the air, broken only by the lighter smells of lavender. The chamber grew humid, warmed by the glowing salt rock in the center. The only sounds were the splashes of water thrown down into the chamber and the constant up and down steps of Rafe coming and going. Then those sounds stopped, too.

Calloused, yet surprisingly soft hands gathered hers. The spell strengthened the longer they held onto one another. She could feel Rafe's energy through his fingertips, and she channeled that energy back into the room. The humidity and lingering negativity eventually evaporated, leaving Thea feeling light as a feather and able to breathe clearly for the first time since entering the room.

The smell of salt and lavender could not be detected any longer, thus marking the end of the cleansing spell. When Thea opened her eyes, the chamber walls and floor were scorch-mark free, dry as if Rafe hadn't spent the better half of the last hour pouring water into the room. The ashes had been washed away, the puddles of wax had dissolved, and the herbs on the now diminished halite crystal were shriveled and dry. She picked up the pink rock that now could fit in her palms, and the wooden bowl left on the floor.

"I'm going to check on Blythe and see if she needs anything else. I left a towel by the pool upstairs. Go ahead and wash the blood off you."

Rafe sniffed himself and grimaced. "Right. You should too after I'm done."

"Gladly."

Chapter Twenty

Protect the Queen

Blythe didn't need further assistance. Cressida was in bed with a black nightgown clinging to her body, her hair was brushed and her skin looking more rejuvenated, though the gauntness remained. White candles were lit on the bedside tables along with some incense. The altar looked as if it had even been dusted off and reorganized.

"The chamber's been cleared," Thea announced upon entering the room. Blythe looked up from the bed where Cressida lay as if coming out of a daze. She smiled in acknowledgment, though it didn't reach her eyes. Thea knew her smile wouldn't be genuine for a long time unless Cressida magically woke up one day completely cured.

But magic didn't work that way.

"I think Rafe and I should be going…" Thea stood there awkwardly for a moment. She really didn't know what else to say. She wasn't suave like her mother or sister could be. Hex it, Rafe was better at smoothing over awkward situations. Thea had always been so…blunt.

Blythe hadn't noticed the weird tension in the room, having slipped into another daze. She came out of it again, eyes clearing just enough to properly meet the Spellweaver's. "Yes," she concurred softly. "I suppose you are right."

Thea hedged closer to the door. She waited to see if Blythe would say anything else, but it was apparent that wasn't going to happen. Blythe had fallen into yet another unseeing abyss, standing by the bed with seemingly no intention of moving anytime soon. Thea bit her lip as she considered what to do. She glanced at the door then back at Blythe.

It had to have been a full minute before she caved. Blythe was just *standing* there. There was no way Thea could leave knowing she was in this kind of condition. Not after what the woman had been through. Thea didn't have the heart.

"Actually," she spoke up, gaining the sorceress's attention with a small jolt, "outside of rounding up feral demons, there's nothing I have to do." That was a lie. She had to report to the Coven, she had to go get Namara and Mokana, and there was the whole *rounding up feral demons* thing she *really* needed to be getting to. Blythe was a grown woman. Granted, she had just gone through something traumatic, but she could look after herself. Thea and Rafe needed to be leaving. Now.

Then Blythe smiled, and despite what Thea had thought earlier, it reached her eyes, and the fog in her gaze lifted.

"Well, there is really nothing else to be done…" as Blythe said this, she took in Thea's appearance once again with a much more critical eye. She ended up ushering Thea into her door-less bathroom, ignoring the fuss from the Spellweaver. Thea flushed scarlet and couldn't make eye contact with Blythe even as she tried to politely refuse over and over again. It just wouldn't be proper.

"Oh, please, Ms. Bauer, I am a happily oath-bound woman. I won't be looking. Here, if it makes you feel better —" Blythe waved a hand toward the entrance of the bathroom, and immediately a black opaque wall shot up, effectively creating a barrier between rooms. However, it only lasted the span of a few breaths before it started to buckle and bow. The pair hastily backed up just as it started to warp right before suddenly collapsing in on itself and crashing to the ground soundlessly, disappearing like smoke in the wind.

Both women frowned.

"Um, that was not supposed to happen," Blythe uttered to the side. "Let me try again. I read this in a book a long time ago." She threw up her hand again, but instead of the black opaque wall Thea was expecting, the chandelier hanging from the ceiling above them exploded. The two threw up their arms protectively as the shattered glass rained down on them. Thea looked at the sorceress with stunned, wide eyes.

Blythe smiled sheepishly. "I just…won't look."

The rest of the day after her shower was spent tending to Cressida and listening to Blythe reminiscing about her life with the once-great sorceress. Thea learned how long the two had lived at the sanctuary together, how Cressida hadn't always been so cold, and how the sorceress had wooed Blythe with small "miracles" that were really just cheap magic tricks that Blythe had found endless amazement in.

Thea listened in silence while Blythe swept sweaty bangs away from Cressida's clammy skin with the utmost care. Rafe had left them alone for the most part. Since Thea didn't have a crystal ball—which, she realized belatedly, she didn't have a lot of things after the hellish few weeks she had endured—she left him in charge of reporting in. However, because of the severity of the black magic spell, they required her personal account.

Between disaster reliefs, demon sightings, corruption on the Council, and questioning the second chosens of those corrupted members, the Coven wasn't taking any chances and began firing off question after question concerning the black magic ritual.

What was the spell's purpose? Who performed the spell? Have they performed black magic before? What was the status of Cressida? How could they be so sure she didn't possess magic anymore? What of the foreigner that ran the sanctuary with the sorceress? Did she have magic?

Rafe handled it all with a practiced smile and half-truths. He only faltered when their concerns turned to Thea and if this correlated with her recent investigation in the increase of magic-based creatures at the sanctuary. Had Thea suspected the sorceress of black magic before? Was Cressida gathering magic-based creatures to draw from their power? Was she also responsible for the release in the demons? Was she working with Isolde and Dmitri, or was this a completely separate incident?

Thea had managed to stall them with a static spell that interrupted the conversation on the crystal ball enough for the call to be dropped. The reprieve didn't last long, though, when another Coven member showed up at the sanctuary asking specifically for Thea. Her stalling hadn't given her as much time as she'd hoped.

Now, she was currently retelling the happenings from the very beginning to said Coven member, carefully leaving out the bits and pieces that could get her arrested on the spot and thrown in prison for the rest of her life.

"The sorceress was suffering from the disease known as Medusa's Kiss," she explained while pacing Cressida's parlor downstairs. "Evidence points to experience dabbling in black magic before, and the Ernimoen states that, because she is naturally magicless, she was not able to differentiate between what magics the sorceress was using. Though, she believes Cressida was searching for a cure for the disease."

"There is extensive documentation proving a cure for Medusa's Kiss does not exist." Second chosen Winona Cavett lounged back into the sofa. A pen and pad floated by her head, furiously scribbling down the exchange, only pausing when there was a lull in conversation.

"That is what I told the foreigner," Thea replied, eyeing the dark-haired Summoner. Her gaze was sharp and all-knowing, silvery like the few strands in her hair. It was no surprise that the ever paranoid Torro McTaggart had sent his own second chosen out for further questioning. Second chosens were highly skilled Summoners that were in line to replace a blue cloak once they retired, died, or were stripped of their position. "Second chosens" weren't an official rank and there was no difference between them and another Summoner in terms of authority, but they did stick by their assigned High Priest and often handled the blue cloak's dealings and whatever their Council member deemed necessary.

Earlier, Thea had just stepped out of the hidden passageway to gather more healing water for Cressida when Winona appeared on Srbeveara's doorstep. It was only after the second chosen had checked on Cressida herself, noted her babbling, nonsensical mutterings, tested her magic ability with a simple touch to Cressida's forehead, as well as checked out the dungeon where the ritual was done that she allowed Thea to lead her to Cressida's parlor.

"However," Thea continued, "even Ms. Castel seemed adamant that was not true. Cressida believed there was a way to cure Medusa's Kiss, it just did not exist by practical and moral magic." She stopped pacing by Cressida's desk and looked over the abandoned works, some signed, some waiting for a signature that might never come.

"And you would know this how?"

Secrets of the Sanctuary

The Spellweaver peered over her shoulder at the skeptical, analytical gaze. Very fitting of someone who would precede Torro one day.

She shrugged. "I am simply reciting Ms. Castel's beliefs. They were very…close."

Winona arched a dark, thickly sculpted eyebrow at that. "Close?"

Thea turned to face the second chosen, steamrolling right on over that question that had nothing to do with what they were discussing. "Ms. Castel also believed there was a cure for Medusa's Kiss, though it was based entirely on fables passed around her tribe in the Golden Sea desert. She stated she had tried unsuccessfully many times to venture back to her homeland in search of the sand wyverns." That little bit of information had been withheld from her and Rafe until today when it had been just the women up in the master bedroom. To say Thea had been surprised would have been the understatement of the year.

The curious light in Winona's silver eyes turned calculating. "She is convinced a cure lies with the Draconians? How so?"

"I was not able to reach a conclusion. The conversation began to upset her."

Silence stretched between the two women. Thea felt the familiar feeling of unease settle around her. It came with every encounter she had with any of the higher-ups involved in the Coven, especially after the Torro incident and the uncovering of corrupt blue cloaks. She couldn't look at the Council the same after everything she'd been through.

Winona's gaze was unwavering, but suddenly, she tilted her chin up and inquired, "Where's your pet?"

Surprised, Thea sputtered. "What?"

"Where is your pet?" she repeated slowly. "I don't see Rafe's rusalka demon around here either. Is there a reason for that?"

Her eyes widened and then narrowed. What a crafty little trap. "During my investigation, an eye-witness to the soul eater I wrote about in my report gave us an estimated location of the demon. I wrote in my report that the village on the outskirts of the Vemeese District had been attacked prior to Summoner MacBain and I's exploration. I notated how my kelpie was severely injured during the fight that broke out between the soul eater and the hellhound. Did you even read my report, Summoner Cavett?"

Winona's smile quirked up at the corner, and she idly rubbed a calloused thumb over her bottom lip. "I did. That doesn't explain where she is, though. What of Summoner MacBain's rusalka, then?"

"She's at home, healing. Mokana is looking after her," she retorted quickly and crossed her arms over her chest.

Is she just being thorough, or is she trying to trip me up? Could this be Torro's doing, or is she just going off down her own investigative path? If not for Torro, what's her angle?

"As opposed to looking after her master?"

Thea's jaw clenched. She took a calming breath and leaned back against Cressida's desk, hoping to look unperturbed by the Summoner's interrogation. "Yes. Where would your pet be?"

Winona crossed her legs, composed and relaxed against the soft cushions. Her smile morphed into one that eerily resembled the fallen demon prince's back in the chamber. "We're not here to talk about me, but, if you must know, he's outside. Now..." She let her sentence hang and locked eyes with Thea, swirling the proffered iced drink in her hand that Blythe had made for them earlier. "We listened to the call you placed to Summoner MacBain at HQ. It appeared he was here before the black magic spell was set off. Care to explain that one?"

Thea stilled.

This was it. This was what Winona had been waiting to reveal from the start. They had been down here for what felt like forever, dancing around each other in a dangerous tango. This could make or break her. Whatever she said could imprison not only her but Rafe as well, for a long time.

She thought back to the conversation she had with Rafe at Headquarters. She'd known the risks of her call being listened to when she'd placed it, but her need for information at the time had seemed worth it.

"Summoner MacBain seemed rather relieved that it was you calling him on the communal crystal ball. He remarked that he was at the sanctuary, and then you both go on to talk about the happenings with the Council. It's at the end of your conversation that has caught mine and Councilman McTaggart's attention, though. 'The sorceress is getting reckless. She's looking bad.' This is the same sorceress that performed a black magic spell so massive that those manning the viewing orb panicked and sent it straight to the Council."

Thea chewed on her lip and let her gaze rove over the second chosen for a few moments. A shadow of a triumphant smile was threatening to overtake Winona's features.

After a long, tense pause between the two, Thea let a puff of air escape her. "Okay," she conceded with a small nod. "I'll tell you everything you want to know if you can answer me one question."

Victory was an easy thing to read on the Summoner's face. "Of course, Spellweaver Bauer. I'm in no position to hide anything."

"Why was Councilman McTaggart at the Dark Market?"

Winona's smile vanished abruptly. Her eyes sharpened like knives, and she went to open her mouth like she was about to question how Thea could possibly know that but shut it so quickly her teeth clacked together. Another tense moment passed.

Her lips thinned and she stood, set down her drink gently, and dusted off her buttery brown leathers from the non-existent crumbs clinging to them. "I believe this concludes our discussion," she stated, and Thea's heart thundered in her chest as she watched Winona bring dust out from a zipped pocket of her black corset. The second chosen flung her hand up in the air and cast the notebook that been documenting the conversation on fire, sparking cerulean and magenta flames as the magic was consumed. She held her breath while Winona continued, "I'll report back to Headquarters that the sorceress is no longer a threat, and that you and Summoner MacBain are overseeing the crime scene to Councilman McTaggart." Her eyes sharpened, slicing into Thea the same way a blade would, and it left the lower-ranking member breathless. "I'll be in touch," she said the last part quietly, gathered her plum-colored cloak off the sofa's armrest, and saw herself out.

Thea let the air in her lungs escape her in a large *whoosh* when she heard the heavy doors click shut. Her whole body sagged against the desk until she could no longer support herself and collapsed down onto the floor. Her heart thumped so hard against her chest she feared she'd crack a rib, but all she could feel right now was the euphoria coursing through her veins. Her cheeks began to ache, and when she gingerly touched them, she found herself grinning like a madwoman.

She laughed airily, the sound uneven, bewildered, and just a touch insane. The absurdity of it all. Getting through the past few weeks of hell would forever go down in her book as the greatest accomplishment of her life, even if she were to later do the unthinkable and make High Priest status. Nothing could top this. As if the harrowing escape from death itself wasn't something to be celebrating about, she had also just ridden herself of all the people who could control her life as if she were nothing more than a puppet. Cressida and the Council. Her head fell back against the desk, laughter quietly bubbling out of her again.

I did it.

She sat there until her bottom started to protest the hard stone under her, and even then, she couldn't find the energy to hoist herself up. Eventually, she managed to get up off the floor, though she held onto the desk for a couple more moments while she tried to calm the shivers that quaked through her body. When she felt stable enough, she trudged back upstairs and entered through the secret doorway.

Peeking inside the room, she found Rafe watching over both sleeping women who were curled up with one another. Cressida was flushed red with a wet rag placed over her forehead. A bowl of water sat on one of the bedside tables next to a mortar and pestle with crushed herbs inside. Wisps of smoke clung to the air, carrying the scent of frankincense from the burning incense stick on the other bedside table.

"She finally fell asleep?" Thea asked quietly, motioning toward an exhausted Blythe.

Rafe nodded and pushed off the wall he'd been leaning against and let loose a huge yawn, stretching his arms high above his head as he did so.

She fought down her own yawn. Those things were contagious. "We should probably go. It's late."

Rafe snorted, dropping his arms. "It's early, more like it. The sun'll be rising in maybe half an hour."

"We spent all day here?" She rubbed the fatigue from her face and finally succumbed to the yawn tickling the back of her throat.

"Between the spell and the total catastrophe that came from it, cleansing the chamber, taking care of Cressida, and Winona's questioning, I'd say somewhere along the line we lost track of time. Torro's second was here for almost two hours."

She groaned at the mention of that horrible hidden minefield of a conversation. "I feel like I just got done playing chess with the being who invented the game."

"You're not in cuffs, though. Checkmate?" He grinned, holding the door open for her to walk back out of.

"I only asked her why a member of the Council was at the Dark Market." She snickered and stepped out onto the second floor. "You should have seen the look on her face. Goddess above, I'm still shaking." She laughed again and held up her hand to prove that she was, indeed, still trembling.

Rafe rolled his eyes skyward in exasperation as they reached the stairs. "I missed your reckless antics."

"Oi, if that ain't the cauldron calling the kettle black." Thea twirled around and stuck out her tongue, already having descended the stairs faster than her partner.

Rafe appeared offended and stopped on the last step of the staircase to hold a hand over his heart with an expression full of mock hurt. "I am not reckless."

"Please, this whole week—well," she paused and thought about her time jumping excursion in the jungle plus the time it took her to recover. It was going to take her forever to get over that, "I guess three weeks for you—just proves how reckless both of us are. Now, hurry up, I want to go home. I'm starving, and you know how I get when I'm hungry."

"Goddess forbid."

Thea shoved open the doors, properly re-spelled and unnecessarily heavy once again, and Rafe had to jog to catch up with her retreating form. Her half mask, which had been stuffed into one of the empty pouches on her belt, was pulled over her head and tugged over the bridge of her nose. She didn't even bother prying her hair out from under the fabric. It kept her neck and ears warm. Though the wind wasn't as vicious as it had been yesterday, the temperature wouldn't start to warm up for a couple more weeks. She couldn't wait for the snow to melt.

She could tell the sun would be peeking over the horizon shortly, turning the inky midnight sky into a deep blue twilight. Rafe came to stand beside her, gazing up at the speckled stars. They'd never seemed so brilliant until now. The quietness that fell between them was comfortable. Despite everything, they had come out of this alive.

"Your eyes match the dawn," he commented idly. His gaze never left the new morning sky.

She snorted, breaking the gentle atmosphere. She waited for him to continue the cheesy line she'd heard too many times before. *Your eyes are prettier*, or something equally as stupid.

"Well, I mean, sort of. At least with the dawn you get to see the stars," he added a moment later, waving a hand to the twilight.

Thea blinked. She looked at him and then to the sky, where she could just make out the brightest of stars still visible even as the sun's rays began appearing over the horizon, then back to him while her mouth gaped open like a fish. Her confusion must have been evident. Must have been written clear across her face when the silence stretched out between them, not so comfortable this time. Before he could fill the void by teasing her further, she broke out into unrestrained, unruly, and uproarious laughter. She laughed so hard and so loud for so long tears glittered in her eyes. Her sides began to ache, but she couldn't stop. She clutched Rafe's shoulder for support with one hand and held her stomach with the other when it started to really hurt. She laughed so hard she couldn't get enough air in her lungs to the point where she felt slightly dizzy, dissolving into hacking coughs.

When she was finally able to calm down enough to respond, she dove back into another fit of hysterics when she looked up and saw the bemusement on his face.

"Only you would say something like that," was her winded reply when she came down from the high of breathlessness. She started dabbing the unshed tears from her eyes as she looked up at him fondly.

"Ah, there they are." He flashed her a blinding smile as he bent down and cupped her face with warm hands. Those turquoise eyes she often got so lost in were now so close her heart nearly stopped. Then it started tripping over itself, going into overdrive.

"There what are?" she whispered, giddiness gone as she tried her best to keep up with the conversation, even while her heart thundered hard against her chest and the blood in her ears roared so loud it was difficult to hear.

His nose brushed against hers softly while his thumbs dipped under the material of her facemask and pulled it down. His lips were just a hair's breadth away from hers, and she could feel the warm puff of air across her fevered cheeks when he next spoke.

"The stars."

Epilogue

The protective barrier around Srbeveara was not the same light orange glow it normally was. Instead, it was a pale, baby blue that pulsed in lively succession rather than slowly and at random. It had only been a few days since Thea had last seen the place, though it felt much different compared to before. Lighter, airier.

She stood beside Rafe with Mokana and Namara in tow. The kelpie was sulking, and it had everything to do with the scroll rolled up in Thea's hands. The Coven's red wax seal with the phoenix emblem still clung to the parchment.

"You just standing there isn't going to make this situation go away." Rafe nudged her with his elbow.

"Shut up," she hissed. "I know that." She was mad. Had been since the scroll had been dropped into her lap the other day. She sighed heavily and stepped through the barrier. Instead of the little shockwave she expected, she felt a feeling of bliss wash over her.

"Huh, that's different," she muttered and didn't miss the hum of agreement from the other three. Lifting her knuckles up to the wood, she knocked loudly before pushing the doors open.

Still as heavy as they ever were.

The changes to the sanctuary's interior were not dramatic but noticeable. Cressida's old desk had been pushed into the foyer in front of the staircase and waterfall. A thick tomb was laid out over the walnut wood, along with a plethora of pens, papers, stamps, and a nearly empty inkwell. The waterfall was no longer a roaring cascade, but a slow trickle that allowed one to see the entrance to the cave.

A heavy hand clapped down on the back of Thea's head and shoved her forward with enough force to send her careening into the desk. Her hands immediately steadied the inkwell and papers from clattering to the floor out of pure instinct.

"Ow, what the—" She whirled around in time to see a broom go zipping between her and the rest of the group, flying straight through where she had just been standing. Namara and Mokana's eyes had gone wide, but Rafe's held more amusement than shock.

"Thea? Is that you? *Ú*, you brought everyone!" A chipper voice from above stopped her from smacking her *trusted* partner over the head. She glanced up at the top of the stairs to find Blythe standing with two buckets in each hand. Floating feather dusters hung in the air as if awaiting orders from their frazzled-looking master.

The sorceress dropped her buckets and waved them away in agitation. "Shoo, shoo! Go dust something!" She huffed and raced down the stairs to greet her guests. Her dress was the same baby blue as the barrier outside, patterned with gold and white splotch designs that bled into each other. Her hair was parted down the center and curled around her temples like ram's horns. Thea had seen the hairdo before and wondered if it was a favorite of the woman's.

"I am so happy to see familiar faces!" Blythe exclaimed and hastily wiped off her hands on her dress before grabbing a hold of Thea's. Her voice quieted as she whispered, "I can't thank you enough for helping out the other day. Please, please, come upstairs. Cressida's not awake, but you can see her if you like?"

Thea nodded along without a word, only sharing a look with the Summoner beside her before letting Blythe pull her up the stairs. "I see you've made a few changes," she stated passively.

"I don't see how Cressida managed to stay calm every day while doing this! I'm up to my elbows in cleaning products and cleansing tools if I'm not tending to the creatures wanting to book a room! *Ú,* and the papers! Paperwork for every little thing that needs to be signed or filed or mailed off or—this is a lot harder than I thought it would be." She groaned and rubbed the sweat from her forehead before unhitching the latch under the bulletin. The secret passageway opened up, causing both demonic pets to gasp in amazement. Rafe had the foresight to shed his thick winter cloak before entering this time and hung it up on the corner of the bulletin.

Inside the bedroom, Cressida was indeed asleep, though not peacefully. Thea sucked in a sharp, quiet breath at the condition the ex-sorceress was in. Tangled up in the sheets was a sickly, pale, shivering lump. Cressida lay in an awkward position, eyes screwed shut as pained moans left her dried, split lips. Sweat was dripping down her face and mixing with the woman's tears.

"Mama!" she cried out in a hoarse voice, startling Thea, who looked to Blythe for some sort of answer. Blythe's cheery demeanor had vanished into thin air. Her eyes were red and glassy, blinking in a futile attempt to stop the tears from falling.

"She's been having flashbacks," was all she said for a moment. Then, much more quietly, "It's been getting worse."

Thea regarded the scroll gripped tightly in her hand and sighed again, gaining the woman's attention. "Can I talk to you out in the hallway?" At Blythe's confused frown, she waved the scroll around in the air. "It concerns you…and maybe Cressida, too."

"*Mink' pitk' i*. Very well." She nodded and held open the door for the entourage to exit first. With one last quick look at the pained expression of her lover, Blythe shut the door behind her.

Cressida continued to gasp and writhe as fire blazed across her skin while ice burned her soul deep inside. Images flashed through her mind so fast they blurred together. Faces she knew, faces she didn't know. Scenes where she saw herself acting out but couldn't remember being a part of. She rolled over restlessly, before surging up in bed with eyes wide open. She whirled around, looking at the room she couldn't recognize.

"Mama?" she croaked. Pain erupted in her stomach, and she lurched forward, falling awkwardly in a crumpled heap with a sharp cry of pain. Quivers shuddered down her body. She gasped for air, even as she felt like she was breathing in a locked burning house with no escape, causing her breaths to come out in little, explosive huffs.

She couldn't have noticed the air twinkling by her bed in her condition, and the lack of reaction upon Asmo's sudden arrival seemed anticipated by the demon. He stood next to her, looking as gruesomely handsome as ever. A serious frown marred in his usual mischievous disposition, though Cressida took no notice that he was even there.

"I don't feel sorry for you," he said.

Cressida moaned in response.

"I really don't."

Silence, save for the choppy breaths coming from the tormented woman on the bed. Asmo sighed and rolled his eyes skyward. "Help me out here," he groaned up to the ceiling, though his old eyes were not glaring up at the plaster, but far beyond that. Silence replied back, but he didn't expect anything less. Never hurt to ask.

He reached out a hand, eyes roving over her convulsing form. "Think of this as me repaying a debt. I've managed to take back my throne because of you, but listen up, Cressi. I owe you nothing after this, and over time the pain will come back, but for now…" He snatched at the air just above her body. Cressida gasped sharply with eyes that bulged out, unseeing. Her body tensed up and held like that for a moment before she fell limp back onto the bed. A look of peace settled over her face, and her breathing evened out.

Asmo hummed, licking the tips of his claws as a thoughtful expression bled into the sharp contours of his face. "Hmm, that was more delicious than I thought. You might be seeing more of me yet, *om keresela.*"

The end. For now.